CYCLE

ABOUT THE AUTHOR

Geoffrey Lewis was born in Oxford, in 1947. Educated at the City's High School, and Hatfield University (then a polytechnic), he has since followed a varied career, including spells as a research chemist, security guard, and professional photographer. After many years in the motor trade, and eight years as captain of a canal-based passenger boat, he is now semi-retired, and concentrating upon his writing.

Photographer, bell-ringer, beer-drinker, and American car enthusiast, he lives in a narrowboat on the Grand Union Canal.

OTHER TITLES FROM GEOFFREY LEWIS:

FLASHBACK   The First David Russell Novel
STRANGERS   The Second David Russell Novel
WINTER'S TALE The Third David Russell Novel

CYCLE

Geoffrey Lewis

SGM
Publishing

ISBN 0-9545624-3-7

Printed in Great Britain

First published in Great Britain in 2005 by

SGM Publishing
Cosgrove Wharf, Lock Lane, Cosgrove, Northants MK19 7JR
info@sgmpublishing.co.uk

For Trevor, whose support and generosity
lifted me from a humdrum life

PART ONE

PHILIP

THE DEMON STIRS

JULY 1990

Chapter One

A bright, sunny Friday afternoon in early July – two bicycles, accelerated by the down-slope to something slightly above the legal speed limit, sped through the underpass. Overhead, the traffic roared by on the dual-carriageway which now bypassed the Southern edge of Grancester, a sprawling but minor metropolis nestling in the rolling countryside of Northamptonshire; beneath, the minor road, little used now, had once led to the County Town.

Beyond the bypass, the old road continued to the village of Bevington, a mile or more distant; but the two cycles, chromed wheel-spokes glittering in the sunshine, barely slackened speed to swing hard left, past rusting steel gates hanging drunkenly from broken hinges, and onto a rough track which led away Eastwards. The track gave access to an old abandoned sandstone quarry, long disused; once closer to the village than the old market town, it was still known to locals as Bevington Quarry. As the slope of the track gradually steepened, the cyclists slowed their pace: The leading boy, a tall blond twelve-year-old, slim but well-built, wore only smart dark-blue shorts and trainers with white socks, his slender torso sleek and tanned; his friend, following behind, as slim but shorter and dark-haired, in a red and white replica football strip. When the track grew too steep for comfort, they stopped pedalling, and stepped off their bikes:

'We'll leave the bikes here.' The second boy looked to his companion:

'Okay – you got the chain?'

'Yeah – I guess we'd better lock 'em up.'

They lay the two cycles together, and the taller boy wrapped the chain around the back wheels and frames, spinning the combination to a random number on the barrels. As they went on up the track, panting from the fast ride and the steepness of the slope, the blond lad spoke to his friend:

'It's a shame you've got to get home so soon.'

'Yeah, I know! I'm sorry, I'd forgotten that Dad's boss was coming to dinner today. And you know how he is – I'll be in dead trouble if I'm not there when they arrive!' The taller boy glanced round, a twinkle in his bright grey eyes:

'I reckon that's an excuse; *I* think you fancy Amy!'

'I do NOT!' Peter Moss, not quite twelve, aimed a playful blow at his best friend's head. Peter's father, Donald Moss, worked for a major local car dealership; Ken Frost, the dealer principal, was an old friend, and the two families met regularly for dinner together, alternating at each other's homes. It was always a family occasion, Peter and the two Frost girls, Amy and Victoria, included. Philip Dorman ducked, laughing, and his companion's fist sailed over his short-cropped hair. They ran the rest of the way up the now-easing slope to the top of the rise, where a ridge overlooked the flooded workings of the old quarry.

In front of the two boys, a vaguely diamond-shaped lake covered several acres; the bluff at the top of the old access track stood a little South of one of the narrower ends. To their right, old workings and spoil-heaps, now well overgrown, made a landscape of ridges and gullies, which continued around the far end of the lake; the Northern shore consisted of gradually-rising ground, mostly wooded.

Standing on the ridge above the water, Philip turned to his dark-haired companion:

'Let's go exploring!' Peter's dark brown eyes widened:

'We could already find our way around here in the dark!'

'Oh, come on! We'll go searching for the lost city of the Incas – over there, in the foothills of the Andes!' He grinned, pointing toward Southern area of uneven, scrub-covered ground.

'Yeah! Maybe there's a stash of hidden gold! Let's go!' Peter eagerly followed his enthusiastic friend around the shoreline to the South-East of the lake.

He watched Philip as he trudged along behind - taller, the older by a few months, his pal was the natural leader of the two, and his active imagination always came through with some exotic scenario for their shared games. Peter thought briefly of his up-coming birthday, a couple of weeks away – too old now for kiddies parties, his father had promised to take him and Philip out somewhere for the day; but he wouldn't say where! Boy, he was looking forward to it, wherever they went! He and Philip had been friends for about as long as he could remember, certainly since they first went to infants school; their shared affection now as close as brothers could ever be, he couldn't imagine a future without Philip around.

For his part, Philip felt the same about his friend – although, of course, neither would ever have admitted anything of the sort. Peter had come to be a kind of alter ego, always there, a sort of weird mirror which not only reflected the wilder workings of his own imagination, but gave much of itself into the bargain: Philip, too, would have been lost without his constant companion. Even at school, the two were recognised as a matched pair, the blond, grey-eyed ringleader of many of the funnier exploits in their class, and his dark-eyed, brown-haired lieutenant.

They roamed the wilderness of gullies and old spoil heaps for almost an hour. Then Peter, an eye on his watch, spoke up again:

'Listen, I'd better get going.' Philip checked the time himself:

'Yeah, I guess so. Come on.'

They made their way back to the ridge at the top of the track. Peter made to go down to the bikes, but turned when his friend didn't follow:

'You coming, too?'

'Nah – I think I'll stop here for a while. I needn't be home 'til seven, and it's too nice to be indoors yet. Can you chain my bike up again?'

'Sure. Shall we come here again tomorrow? Make up for the time we lost today?'

'Can do – if the weather's still good. I'll call for you –'round nine?'

'Yeah! See you then!'

'See you!'

Peter walked back down the track. He glanced back once, to see his friend sitting on the high point of the bluff, gazing out over the water. He unchained his bike – both boys knew the combination of the lock by heart – and re-locked Philip's electric-blue racer, and then set off free-wheeling down the slope, stopping at the exit onto the road to check the traffic, and then swinging back Northwards into the town.

* * *

Up on the bluff, Philip sat, letting his imagination run along the lines of their abandoned search for the lost city – he loved making up stories, and sometimes thought he might like to be a writer when he was older. The sunshine was warm on his bare shoulders – he loved to shrug off his shirt when the weather was like this, and feel the sun and air against his skin instead of clothes. In fact - he stood up quickly, gazed around at his deserted surroundings - it was still hot, and he fancied a swim…

Other kids sometimes came to the old quarry, he knew - but he and Peter were often alone there; and on hot days a quick dip in the lake was really fantastic, the water always with a delicious chill to it against your skin. Their parents wouldn't have approved, had they known - the lake was very deep, its hazards unknown but feared; and what they'd have thought of the two boys skinny-dipping was another question! Today, they'd seen no-one else since they'd arrived, and still there was no sign of life; at least, not the human sort…

Philip slipped off his shorts and underpants, a pair of the camouflage-pattern ones his mother had bought him as a joke, kicked off his trainers and socks, ran down the grassy slope and dived into the water. He drew breath sharply at the feel of cold water against his nakedness, then struck out away from the bank. He was a strong swimmer, capable and confident; he made a gentle circle, not going too far from the bank, then swam part of the way toward the wooded Northern shore.

Half an hour later, feeling comfortably tired, he returned to his starting point and stepped out onto the bank. Next to the pile of his discarded clothing, he sat on the grass and lay back to let the warm evening sun dry him. Time slipped by for a while; and then, he jerked out of a semi-doze as a familiar voice spoke from behind him:

'Hello, Dorman!' Philip turned, and saw an older boy standing there: Carl Evans was a sixth-former at his school, the prefect in charge of his class, but now he was dressed in jeans and a casual shirt:

'Evans! What are you doing here?' The older boy, like Philip and Peter, was a day-student, while many of their respective fellows were boarders. Philip grabbed his shorts, quickly pulled them on, not bothering with his underpants in his hurry to cover his embarrassment. Evans laughed:

'Same as you, by the look of it – trying to get away on my own for a while! You needn't worry about that, I've seen you in the showers often enough!' Philip gave him a grin but went on buckling his belt; the sixteen-year-old had the reputation of being easy-going and friendly with the youngsters, but this in itself meant that they regarded him with a vague air of suspicion alongside the respect that was due a prefect.

'Mind if I sit down?' Philip gestured his agreement, and the older boy sat beside him, a couple of feet away. Silence reigned for a while, then Carl asked:

'On your bike?'

'Yeah. You?'

'Yeah. You come here a lot?'

'Quite often – it's not far from where we live. Peter was here just now – did you see him?'

'No – must have missed him. I might have guessed you two would be together!'

'Yeah!' Philip grinned: 'He had to get home for visitors.'

'I live over the far side of town – I've only been here once or twice.'

'Do you fancy exploring a bit? I'll show you 'round.' Company, even that of an older boy, would help pass the time until he had to go home.

'You sure?'

'Yeah! Come on!'

He stood up; the older boy followed suit. The sixteen-year-old found the sight of the slender youngster's bare torso stirring his darker desires, already aroused by the brief, earlier glimpse of his nudity; to break his fascination, he tore his eyes away and looked around:

'It gets really steep in places, doesn't it?'

'Yes, it does!' Philip grinned.

'Let's cut ourselves a staff each.' He walked up to a nearby willow tree, which had a number of stout, young stems growing up from the broken-off stub of its trunk, and pulled a knife from its sheath on the back of his belt, where Philip hadn't noticed it before:

'Hey, that's nice – can I have a look?'

'Sure – be careful, I keep it really sharp!' Carl handed the knife over; Philip held it, turning it over in his hands, admiring the bright six-inch blade which looked every bit as sharp as he'd been warned it was. The leather-covered hilt felt good in his hand, the whole thing solid and well-balanced. He gave it back, and Carl selected two strong stems from the tree, lopped them off and stripped them down until the two boys each held a stout walking-staff. Then they set off, down the bluff towards the water and around the shore, into the gullies and mounds where Philip and Peter had been playing earlier.

The two boys spent half an hour exploring. By the time they returned to their starting point, they were getting on well together despite the difference in their ages, Philip even forgetting his doubts about his elder. They sat down again, companionably close this time, dropping their sticks at their sides:

'This is a great place, Philip! I must come here more often.'

'Yeah, you should. There's lots more I haven't shown you yet. Peter and I come here a lot.'

'You won't want me joining in, though, will you?' Philip looked around and grinned:

'That depends!'

'On what?'

'Whether you get bossy, like you are at school!'

'Bloody cheek! I'm not bossy!'

''Course you are! You're a prefect, it's your job!'

Carl swung a playful fist at the younger boy, who responded by throwing himself on his older companion and wrestling him to the ground. Taken by surprise, the sixteen-year-old found himself pinned down, Philip kneeling over his waist, leaning forward, his hands on the older boy's shoulders, grinning furiously. He grinned back, aware of being aroused at the feel of the twelve-year-old's lithe, supple body in his arms as they'd grappled; his feelings were confused, frightening - he felt a great excitement in the twelve-year-old's physical closeness, a desire to somehow possess and control the younger boy which left him trembling with the ache of it...

Philip went to get up, but was puzzled when Carl grabbed his hands to stop him as he rose. He knelt back down, suddenly troubled by the strange gleam in the other boy's brown eyes:

'Hey, come on! I beat you, fair and square - now let me up!'

Carl let go of Philip's hands. He grinned up at the younger boy as the twelve-year-old climbed to his feet, the wary look still in his eyes, then pushed himself up to stand close to him. He peeled off his own shirt, threw it to land on top of Philip's shoes and socks, the urge to repeat their physical contact, to feel the youngster's litheness in his arms again, the sleek warmth of his bare skin against his own, becoming strong enough to swamp all caution and commonsense:

'That wasn't *fair* - you jumped me when I wasn't ready!'

'Yeah - but you're bigger'n me, that makes up for it!'

'I bet I can beat you in a *fair* fight!' A slow grin spread across Philip's face, a twinkle coming into his grey eyes, his momentary doubts forgotten in the challenge:

'Bet you can't, even if you are older!'

'Come on, then!'

The two boys grappled again, staggering back and forth in each other's grip, laughing all the while. Any remaining nervousness Philip had felt quickly vanished as they wrestled; this time, the older boy's greater strength and weight told, and it was Philip who found himself on his back, held down, their previous positions reversed. For his part, Carl felt his deep, dark desires growing stronger than ever as the younger boy struggled in his arms, his slender, supple body squirming to get free, the hot animal smell of him rising to his nostrils. And when the twelve-year-old gave in and lay beneath him as he knelt in triumph, his slim chest heaving with each breath, his clear golden skin gleaming in the evening sunlight, they reached a level, a direction, beyond his control. Without thinking, he reached behind him and drew the knife from its sheath.

Philip, still laughing in his defeat, looked up in surprise when he saw the knife in Carl's hand:

'What are you playing at?'

'Perhaps I'm going kill you!' Carl was grinning down at him; he laid the knife-blade flat on the younger boy's bare chest, along his breast-bone, keeping hold of the hilt.

'Hey, stop fooling, that's not funny!' The troubling gleam was back in the older boy's eyes; Philip pushed against his chest, but couldn't shift his greater weight: 'Don't even joke about something like that, okay?' Carl raised the knife to the vertical, moving the point of the blade to a position directly above the twelve-year-old's heart.

Philip looked down at himself as he felt the point against his skin. He lay suddenly frozen, a real fear gripping him; he opened his mouth to speak, but only a gasp of stunned disbelief escaped him as he watched the blade thrust down into his chest. He had time for a moment of horrified realisation: *He's done it!* The quick flare of pain as the glittering steel pierced his heart faded as his consciousness spiralled down into darkness.

Chapter Two

Elwood Priors private boys' school stands in its own extensive grounds, on the North-Western edge of the market town of Grancester. The old manor house, which once housed the entire establishment, is now the administrative centre; the cavernous bedchambers of the upper floors are now the dormitories for the boarders who make up around two-thirds of the students. Modern, purpose-built extensions on three sides of the house provide the classrooms – the grounds are given over to sports fields, and an impressive new block houses a well-equipped gymnasium, a full-size swimming pool and changing rooms.

A fee-paying school, 'The Priors' draws its pupils from a wide area, but written into its charter is a provision that boys from the town are entitled to a degree of priority when places are allocated. And, benefiting from a bequest to the school from an old boy who had made a not-insubstantial fortune in the construction industry, two places are offered each year on a scholarship basis.

Carl Evans had been one boy to gain entry this way – a bright kid from the poorer Eastern suburbs of the now-sprawling town, he had been put forward by the head teacher of his primary school and accepted on the basis of his exceptional record there. He had acquitted himself well through the five years to his GCSE examinations, and was now nearing the end of his Lower Sixth year, aiming for a university place where his hope was to study civil engineering – the world of water supply, with its intricate combination of natural features like rivers and lakes with artificial structures like reservoirs and canals, and its whole purpose in providing drinkable water, irrigation, hydro-electricity and so on, held a deep fascination for him.

Apart from his academic abilities, which were perhaps not so remarkable in the surroundings of Elwood Priors, Carl was an unexceptional boy, not one to stand out from the crowd: Of a little less than average height, dark haired, brown eyed, neither strikingly handsome nor particularly ugly, generally quiet and withdrawn, he was accepted by his peers without being either especially popular or singled out for ridicule or bullying as a few were. He had his own friends, but generally did not mix well – not one to join in eagerly with whatever form of ribaldry currently attracted his contemporaries. Not keen on sports, his one real interest outside of school was classical music – he played the clarinet to a good standard, in the school orchestra, and had a large and varied collection of music on cassette at home.

Although regarded as a bit odd, he was at the same time given a level of respect by the other boys of his form – he had, in the fourth year, shown himself to be someone who should not be pushed too far when he had marched, unannounced, into the headmaster's office to complain about the excessive homework being set by the physics master, on days when no physics homework was scheduled. The result had been a gentle, private reprimand for the teacher, an overly-enthusiastic young man universally known as Boris, and a reduction in the workload, which had gone down very well with Carl's classmates, who had all felt the same but hadn't had the nerve to do anything about it.

But now, at the age of sixteen, Carl was a troubled youth. He was, perhaps, a bit of a late developer – puberty had only caught up with him at the end of his fourth year at The Priors, and he was still trapped in the confused, turbulent emotions of adolescence. He was in the throes of that ambivalent sexuality, that spell of repressed homosexuality that many boys pass through in their teenage years before their hormones settle down and life takes on its adult pattern. Throughout his sixth form year, Carl had found himself physically attracted to other boys, a fact that caused him deep concern; in school, he would find himself watching the eleven and twelve year old boys of the first and second years as they passed, chattering loudly, from class to class, or ran carefree in the playground during breaks, imagining the sleek young bodies concealed within their uniforms.

At the beginning of the year he had been made a prefect, and been given the duty of a form prefect. This meant that he undertook some of the delegated responsibilities of the staff, supervising his junior form at morning assembly in the hall, during lunch, and at the end of the day, making sure they left their form room tidy and on time. One day a week, after his form's games afternoon, he had also to supervise them in the changing rooms and showers of the sports hall. In moments of brutal honesty, Carl would acknowledge to himself that he enjoyed the opportunity to spend some time close to a group of younger boys, and especially to be with them as they changed their clothes, to see them partly or completely naked. There were those amongst the twenty-one boys in his form, 1A, who held a particular fascination for Carl, four or five youngsters who held a special appeal for him; principal among them being the two friends, Peter Moss and Philip Dorman. It gave him a special buzz to see the two of them together in the shower, larking around and laughing unselfconsciously, their lithe, slender bodies exhibiting an awkward but seductive grace.

He'd never *touched* any of the kids – his hidden urges were ill-defined, unfocussed, despite their growing power over him. To those around him, Carl appeared much the same as always, given that teenagers are expected to be a bit difficult at times. And he had the kind of mind that could compartmentalise his thoughts and feelings, keeping shut away anything that was irrelevant to the moment.

That Friday, approaching the end of the Summer term, he'd cycled home across the town as always, to an empty house. His mother was on late shift at the supermarket, and wouldn't be home until after eight, when she finished – his father had left when Carl was eight, and they only saw him very occasionally. He changed out of his uniform, into t-shirt and jeans. Now that the end-of-year exams were over, he had no homework that weekend – and it was a warm, pleasant evening, too nice to stay indoors; he'd go out somewhere on his bike. He reached into the back of a drawer, took out his knife in its sheath and attached it to the back of his belt. He'd never been too sure quite why he'd even bought it; he'd come across it in a second-hand shop the year before, and picked it up on impulse, paying a few pounds for it. Since then he'd honed the blade to a razor-sharp edge; he rarely got it out, but every now and then would wear it on his belt, just for the hell of it.

Downstairs, he got his bike out again, and stood thinking of where to go; he usually rode out of the town into the countryside when he went out alone, but he fancied a change. Making up his mind, he set off, this time heading back through the suburbs towards the South side of the town and the old abandoned quarry that lay just beyond the bypass. He'd been there once or twice before, and had always meant to go and explore it fully one day…

Chapter Three

In the grip of an excitement that was close to orgasmic, Carl let go of the knife and sat back on his heels. He was aware of the massive erection pushing at his trousers - but already his confused, sexual high was beginning to subside, the wild impulse which had driven him to stab the younger boy fading. Brutal reality began to intrude upon his consciousness; the sheer enormity of what he'd just done hit him like a punch in the stomach. He leapt to his feet, backing away a few stumbling steps until he came up against the whippy stems sprouting from the collapsed stump of Old Man Willow where, such a short time before, he'd cut their stout walking staffs.

His mind in the grip of a paralysing horror, Carl stared down at the boy on the ground in front of him, at the knife-hilt protruding from the centre of his bare chest. As he stood rooted to the spot, a small part of his brain, trying to function normally, registered surprise at the lack of blood. It seemed like forever that he stood there, hands behind him, desperately hanging onto willow-stems as he tried equally desperately to hang onto his sanity, his mind seemingly locked up, unresponsive, like one of the school computers when you had hit the wrong combination of keys.

But at last, the rational part of his mentality began to make its presence felt. Carl began to get a grip on himself, to look intelligently, albeit with a horrified fascination, at the situation he'd plunged himself into. His first, desperate wish was that he could somehow undo what was done – but Philip was dead! He couldn't undo that! And there could be no doubt – it may not have been his subject, but Carl knew enough of human physiology to know that the blade was right through the kid's heart. So, what in the name of Heaven (or should that be Hell?) was he to do? He could hardly escape with an apology, however heartfelt –'It's all right Carl, just say you're sorry and everything will be fine' – he could almost hear his father's voice from so many years before – but that would hardly suffice now!

So, the only thing he could do was to try to avoid getting caught… But how? At least, there was one thing: No-one knew he was there – he'd ridden over to the quarry on impulse. He ran through the ride in his mind; he'd not seen anyone he knew, and a boy on a bike in the evening traffic would hardly have aroused anyone's attention. If he could just get home again without being noticed, before his mother got in from work, he could say he'd been there all the time! But what if someone had called? And got no reply? He'd been in the garden – doing what? Fixing his bike, of course! He couldn't have been out on it, he'd had to refit the chain, and fix a dodgy brake!

Carl closed his eyes, forced himself to relax – there was no need to get carried away with his fabrications, that would sound funny in itself. But why should anyone even ask, if they had no reason to think he'd been at the quarry? He took a deep breath, and turned to go and pick up his bike from where he'd dropped it down the track. But then he stopped: They *would* talk to him! They would be bound to – the police would certainly talk to the boys in Philip's class, if not the whole school, and as his form prefect, he'd be bound to be questioned. But of course, they'd only know he was missing, at least, until they found his body - or, if they *never* found his body…

He had to get rid of it; but how? The lake – that was the answer! But wouldn't he float – after all, you did if you went swimming? But no, he remembered times when he'd heard on the news of divers being called in to recover people who'd drowned, so when you were dead, you must sink instead. He turned back to where Philip's body lay, and felt another surge of terror – he'd nearly walked off and left his knife in the kid's chest!

Carl walked up to him, and knelt down beside him. He took hold of the hilt, and tried to pull the knife out, but it wouldn't come; he leant forward and put his other hand on the dead boy's chest. Revulsion swept through him – *Oh God, he's still warm!* The soft texture of the youngster's skin reminded him of how it had felt under his hands as they had wrestled, and once more the horror of what he'd done threatened to overwhelm his mind. Almost weeping with sheer desperation, Carl gritted his teeth and pulled; slowly, the knife came out, withdrawing from the boy's heart reluctantly, like a snake slowly releasing its latest victim.

He gazed down at it in his hand, the blade smeared with Philip's blood – what should he do with it now? His impulse was to throw it as far away from him as he could, but the rational part of his brain was again taking charge, and he knew that if he did so, it would eventually be found, and might prove that *he'd* caused the boy's death. No, if he could avoid being connected with the quarry that evening, they'd have no reason to search him for a weapon – so it would be safest if he kept it; he'd take it home and hide it away somewhere. After he'd cleaned it. He turned and ran down from the bluff, the twenty yards or so to the lake's edge; there, he washed the knife as thoroughly as he could before slipping it back in the sheath at the back of his belt.

Standing up, Carl drew a deep breath as he turned back away from the water's edge. The thought of what he had to do sent a shiver down his spine, but he took his resolve in both hands and walked unsteadily back to Philip's body. He glanced at his watch – seven-fifteen, he'd just about an hour to do what he had to and get home ahead of his mother. Time enough, if he hurried. He put his hands under Philip's shoulders, and dragged him to the bankside, trying not to look at him. At the lake's edge, he rolled him into the water – the shore fell away quite steeply into what had once been the pit workings – and pushed him out. The body didn't sink immediately, causing Carl to panic momentarily; but he calmed himself, thinking that it would take a little while for it to go under. Turning, he caught sight of the boy's shoes and socks, felt another tremor of fear as he realised he'd nearly missed such a vital clue; he ran for them, grabbed them and threw them also into the water. And their staffs, which he'd cut from the willow - he found them, tossed them far into the undergrowth. That was everything, surely?

Turning away at last, he almost ran to find his bike, grabbing up and pulling on his own shirt as he went. Leaping aboard, he pedalled frantically down the track, but had the presence of mind to stop short of the point where it opened onto the old Northampton Road, and make sure no-one was in sight as he left the quarry. Riding home, he kept to the backstreets as far as he could – he was indoors, putting together a salad for their meal, when his mother came in shortly after eight, put her arm around him and kissed his cheek, telling him how good he was to have started dinner for her.

Chapter Four

Grancester Police Station was a solid red-brick structure of several stories in Midland Road, just around from the High Street. Over the double entrance doors, the legend 'Police' was carved in letters almost two feet high; modern fixtures such as the aluminium-framed notice boards (supposedly vandal-proof) and the current equivalent of the old Blue Lamp seemed quaintly out of place on its ornate Victorian façade.

In his ground-floor office, Jack Tremayne, duty inspector that Friday evening, sat going through the latest crime statistic report from County H.Q. Tremayne was a tall man of fifty-ish, senior uniformed Inspector at the town's police station; he cut a smart figure, always dapper, his uniform spotless and immaculately pressed. A neat pencil moustache matched his still-black hair.

A knock sounded on the door, and his opposite number in C.I.D. looked in. Keith Foreman was a few years older than Tremayne; short, stocky and greying, he was the complete opposite in his general appearance – even in a newly-pressed suit, he would look somehow vaguely dog-eared. A bluff Northerner who could at times be every bit as grumpy with his subordinates as his appearance suggested, he was never-the-less respected as a good copper of the old school, who had a knack of getting results when it mattered.

Tremayne looked up:

'Off home, Keith?' He was one of the few who could get

away with using the other's Christian name.

'Yes – I've had enough! Besides, Annie's got visitors for dinner – I'll be in deep trouble if I'm late.'

'How are you getting on with those break-ins?'

'Looks like we've got Robbie Carroll in the frame at last – I'll call the Super in the morning, see if he's agreeable to us pulling him in.'

'Had to be someone local, didn't it?' Tremayne laughed. 'No-one else would be daft enough, or desperate enough, to break into houses in that part of town!' The burglaries had all been in Warrenton, a shabby district in the Eastern suburbs of Grancester, known to all as The Warren.

'See you later – I'll be at home, but *please* don't call unless you have to!'

'Okay – enjoy your evening!'

Tremayne laughed again as his colleague closed the door – it was rumoured that his wife was the only person Foreman was afraid of. He sighed, put the crime stats report to one side and looked at his watch: Seven-thirty, and all quiet so far. Grancester was a reasonably law-abiding town as a whole, no great dramas ever seemed to occur there, but it could get busy when the pubs chucked out around eleven. He picked up the internal phone, and asked the desk-sergeant if someone could make a cup of tea.

* * *

Half an hour later, he was going through reports of a traffic accident that had happened that morning in the High Street, and wondering where his cup of tea had got to. There came another knock on his door:

'Come in!'

'Your tea, sir.'

'Oh, thanks, Sergeant.'

Frank Simmons, desk sergeant that evening, was another

copper of the same generation as Foreman and Tremayne; a tall man, but of a benign aspect which always stood him in good stead when dealing with the general public, he was an ideal 'front man' for the station. He put the tea down on a corner of the Inspector's desk.

'All quiet out there?' Tremayne asked.

'Ye-es. Edwards and Sally Brennan are checking a reported prowler up in Alderley Park – probably nothing. But we've got a missing kid.'

'Oh?'

'Twelve-year-old lad; went off after school and hasn't come home.'

'How long's he been missing?'

'He was due home by seven.'

'It's a bit early to panic then, surely?'

'Maybe; but the mother says it's completely out of character for him to be late – and it seems he's on his own, up at the old Bevington Quarry.'

'Ah… Who's on it?'

'Red Dwar…I mean, Rimmer and Jones in Delta one-seven are on their way to join the father – he's gone up there to look for the boy.'

'He's probably just lost track of the time, it's a beautiful evening.'

'Let's hope so, sir.'

Tremayne could see the same thought in his subordinate's eyes – the flooded workings of the quarry were very deep, and people had drowned there before….

'Keep me posted, Frank.'

'I will, sir.' The Sergeant went to return to his desk, but Tremayne stopped him:

'Why do people around here refer to Rimmer's car as Red Dwarf?' The Sergeant grinned:

'It's a TV show, sir, a kind of spoof space-travel thing – one of the characters is called Rimmer; he's a hologram, has a letter 'H' on his forehead so you know he isn't real. Their space-ship is called Red Dwarf, you see!'

'Oh – yes, I see.' The Inspector looked totally bewildered, despite his reply, as he asked: 'I hope this epithet doesn't creep into our radio communications?'

'Oh, no, of course not, sir!'

Some twenty minutes later, Sergeant Simmons put his head around his superior's door again:

'Rimmer just called in, sir – they're up at the quarry with the Dorman boy's father. They've found his bike, beside the access track.'

'No sign of the kid?'

'No. But he has to be still up there, somewhere.'

'Yes. He's not usually lax about time-keeping, you say?'

'No - the mother says he's always home when he's told, he's got a wrist-watch. He went up there with his best friend, a boy called Peter Moss – the Moss lad went home around five-thirty, leaving the other boy there alone.'

'He could still be okay, broken his watch, maybe – or even slipped and twisted his ankle or something.' He looked questioningly at the other, 'But you don't think so, do you Frank?' Simmons smiled:

'Me and my intuition! But no, sir, I've got a nasty feeling that this kid's in serious trouble.'

'I hope you're wrong! Let me know what develops.'

'Of course.'

* * *

Shortly after nine o'clock, the sergeant knocked urgently on Tremayne's door and burst in:

'Sir! They've found part of the Dorman boy's clothing up at the quarry, by the side of the lake!' Tremayne looked up in surprise:

31

'What? Come in, Frank, sit down.' Sergeant Simmons took the chair opposite his superior.

'So, we've got a kid, overdue at home by, what, two hours? We know he's up at the old quarry, alone; what clothing have they found, exactly?'

'A pair of underpants; they're quite distinctive, made of a camouflage material, the father reckons they are the boy's.'

'Oh Christ! What else was the kid wearing?'

'Only dark blue shorts, silver trainers and plain white socks. No shirt.'

'How the hell can he have come to lose his *pants?* Presumably, he's still wearing the rest?' Simmons frowned, his fears showing in his expression:

'There's no sign of them, sir. He might be - or they might have been better hidden.'

'You're thinking he's been attacked, Frank?'

'Has to be considered, sir.'

'Let's hope to God there's an innocent explanation for all this! Maybe he went for a swim in his pants, then left them to dry and forgot about them?'

'Maybe - but then where *is* the lad?'

'Hmmm. We'd better get more people up there. Call County, see if they can spare us the helicopter; call in anyone who's on standby – is anyone with the mother?'

'Yes. I've sent Delta one-four to the house, Sal Brennan will look after her; I've told Edwards to drop her there and go on up to the quarry himself.'

Tremayne paused, thoughtfully:

'I'm going up there myself. Keep me in touch with things.'

* * *

The Inspector's dark blue Rover swung off the old Northampton road into the quarry entrance, to be met by a uniformed constable.

Tremayne wound down the window:

'Evening, Edwards.'

'Good evening, sir. If you park with the other cars to the side there – I'll show you the way from here. It's a bit steep; and anyway, we thought we'd best not churn up the ground too much, in case…' he trailed off.

'Good thinking, constable. But, please God, we're looking at some kind of silly accident here - let's hope the kid's just dozed off in the sunshine somewhere!'

He parked the car and got out, and they set off up the pot-holed track.

They walked on in silence. As they breasted the rise and came on to the area of open ground around the bluff where Philip had been sitting, the drumming of rotor blades overhead announced the arrival of the County's police helicopter. Already instructed by officers on the ground, it began immediately to sweep the area around the lake. Tremayne turned to his guide:

'Where are our men?'

'They're searching around the lake shore, sir. Doug Rimmer has gone around to the North, and Jones and the boy's father the other way.'

'Concentrating on the lake?'

'It seemed sensible, sir. After all, that has to be the greatest hazard up here, if the boy's got himself into trouble. And we can search the rest of the area better with more men, once the reinforcements arrive.'

Tremayne nodded; the boy could have slipped and fallen into the water, maybe stunned himself - if so, his chances weren't good, if he'd been there long. But the mislaid underpants troubled the Inspector - the possibility that the kid had been surprised up here and molested by some pervert had to be considered, as the Sergeant had suggested. But still the first question remained - where *was* he?

Dusk was gathering as the Inspector and the Constable

watched the helicopter for a moment, moving slowly around the lake, its spotlight playing along the shoreline and sweeping out across the lightly rippling surface. Then, a shout went up, a whistle blew from somewhere along the Northern shore. Tremayne grabbed his handheld radio:

'Airborne Search! Give us some light on the North shore! P.C. Rimmer's got something!' The radio crackled to life in reply:

'Inspector Tremayne, sir? On our way.'

The chopper swung around from its search of the Eastern side of the lake to where Rimmer's torch could be seen directing them to the water's edge. A moment later, Tremayne's radio spoke again:

'Inspector? Rimmer, sir – I've got the boy.'

'In the water?'

'Yes, sir. I think I can reach him.'

'Constable Edwards is with me – we're on our way round to you. Is he alive?' There was a pause:

'I don't think so, sir.'

'Get him out if you can; we're on our way.'

It took the two policemen almost ten minutes to make their way around the lakeshore in the gathering gloom. When they got to Rimmer's position, they found he'd managed to get hold of the boy's body and haul him out onto the bank, and was trying to give him mouth-to-mouth resuscitation. He looked up as they approached and shook his head, an almost desperate look in his eyes.

'No use, Rimmer?'

'No, sir. I think he's been dead a while.' Aware of the distress in the younger man's eyes, Tremayne put his hand on the constable's shoulder:

'It's all right, lad, you tried. I'm sure you're right, nothing we can do is going to bring the kid back.' He got onto the radio again, to the control room:

'Delta control? – Tremayne. Can you get Sergeant Simmons

to call the duty medic and send him out here please? We've got the Dorman boy. Constable Edwards will meet him at the quarry entrance.'

'Will do, sir. Ambulance, too?' Tremayne sighed:

'Please. Although I'm afraid we're too late for that to do the poor kid much good. And we'll need SOCO, and plenty of lights. Call them, will you?'

'I'm sorry, sir'

'So am I, girl, so am I.' He turned to his companions:

'Edwards – get back to meet the doctor. Rimmer – are you okay to stay here with the boy? I'd better go to meet the father and head him off.' And into the radio again: 'Jones? Where are you and Mr Dorman?'

'Making our way back to where we started the search from, sir.'

'Okay, wait there for me. Both of you.'

He made his way back around the lake, following the constable, dreading having to face Philip Dorman's father.

Constable Jones and a tall, slim, fair-haired man of about forty-five were waiting in the clearing when Inspector Tremayne got back there.

'Mr Dorman?' The tall man just nodded, a stricken expression on his face.

'I'm so sorry, sir.'

'You're sure Philip's…?'

'I'm afraid so. One of my constables has been trying to revive him, but with no success. A doctor's on his way now.' Dorman just nodded again, not trusting himself to be able to speak.

'What about you, sir? There's nothing more you can do here, can we take you home to your wife?'

'Can I see Philip first?'

'Are you sure, sir?'

'Yes, please… I must; I can't just… go off and leave him, even if he is…' He buried his face in his hands for a moment, and then raised brimming grey eyes to meet the Inspector's 'You understand?'

Tremayne nodded gently: 'Of course, Mr Dorman. Come with me. Jones – bring the doctor round as soon as he gets here.'

* * *

Patrick Swainson, County Pathologist and duty police medical examiner, stomped up the lane with Constable Edwards twenty minutes later. A short, portly man, nearer sixty than fifty, the climb had him breathing heavily by the time they reached the clearing at the top, where they met Inspector Tremayne and a distraught but composed John Dorman.

'Ah, Edwards, thank you. Evening, Doctor. Jones – you here?'

'Yes, sir.'

'Good. Will you take Mr Dorman home to his wife, please? Edwards – wait and direct SOCO when they get here, please. Come with me, Doc.'

Philip's body lay on the lakeside still, where Rimmer had laid him; the helicopter still hovered overhead, providing the only light on the tragic scene until such time as the portable lights arrived. The doctor bent over the still form and made a hurried examination of the boy. Without looking up, he asked:

'Floating, was he?'

'Yes, doctor.' Rimmer replied: 'Caught under the bank just here. You can see where I had to pull him out.'

'Hmm.' He stood up and turned to the inspector:

'Well, you were right about one thing, he's been dead a little while.'

'How long?'

'Couple of hours or so.'

'Drowned?' Please say yes, Jack Tremayne thought to himself, please God let it be an accident!

'I don't think so. Can't be sure of course, not until I can do a post-mortem. But if he was floating, that suggests air in the lungs for a start. And look here, that could be a knife wound.' He pointed to the boy's chest, where a clean-lipped cut could be seen just to the left of the breastbone.

'Oh my God.'

'Yes, exactly. I'll get him on the slab first thing, get you some answers. Shall I see you there?'

'Not me; I'll let Keith Foreman know; it's CID's pigeon now.'

'Okay, Jack. Be seeing you.'

Chapter Five

Annie Foreman's dinner guests were just partaking of a last coffee before leaving when the telephone rang. Keith excused himself, went out into the hall and picked up the receiver:

'Foreman.'

'Keith? Jack Tremayne.'

'Oh, no! What is it?'

'We've got a body for you.'

'Oh God! What's the story?'

'It's a kid – reported missing after school today. We just fished him out of the lake at the old Bevington Quarry.'

'Sounds like an accident – your department, surely?'

'Pat Swainson's been by – he thinks not. Possible stab wound.'

'Oh Jesus! Poor little bastard! Who is it?'

'Lad, name of Philip Dorman – twelve years old. Lives in Alderley Park, goes to The Priors. Used to, I mean.'

'Okay, Jack. Do you need me now?'

'No, I don't think there's much you can do 'til morning. SOCO are on their way here; we'll send the boy's body to the mortuary as soon as we can. Pat Swainson is going to start the autopsy around nine am; I said you'd probably want to see the kid first.'

'Yes, thanks Jack. Will you be in tomorrow – could you meet me in the office around eight so I can get the background from you? I'll call Dave Russell now and get him in too.'

'Okay, Keith – I'll be there for eight.'

'Thanks – see you then.'

Keith Foreman heaved a deep sigh as he dialled a number. The receiver at the other end was lifted, and a voice reeled off the number he'd just dialled.

* * *

In a little semi-detached house in the quiet suburb of Willham Brook, David Russell was relaxing in front of the television with his wife of three years. With his recent promotion to Detective-Sergeant, they had decided to try for the family they both desperately wanted; Tracy was expecting her first child in three months time. A short, pretty woman with dark brown eyes and curly dark hair, she eased herself out of the crook of his arm where she had been curled beside him on the sofa, adjusting the bulge for comfort, as the telephone rang. David reached behind him to the sideboard, groped for the receiver, reeled off the number as he lifted it to his ear:

'Sergeant Russell? Foreman here. I need you in my office tomorrow, eight o'clock.'

Foreman's Sergeant was a younger man, not quite thirty, as tall and lean as his superior was short and stocky. He was a handsome man, with neat blond hair and warm hazel eyes; all the W.P.C.s had a soft spot for the Detective-Sergeant.

'Right, sir. What's the problem?' David Russell was careful to keep the annoyance from his voice – he'd planned to take his pregnant wife shopping the following morning, for the cot and other such essentials.

'A body, Russell. Uniform have just fished a dead kid out of the workings at the old quarry – Doctor Swainson says probably murdered. Inspector Tremayne is going to brief us first thing, and then I'm going to take a look at the body while you get started on the background enquiries. All right?'

'Yes, of course, sir.'

'I know you're supposed to be off this weekend – take the time off when this is dealt with.'

'Okay, sir. See you in the morning.' A note of resignation crept into his voice.

'Night, Sergeant.'

* * *

At eight o'clock that Saturday morning, Jack Tremayne strode into D.I. Foreman's first-floor office to find both Foreman and Russell there waiting. Without preamble, he quickly took them through the previous night's events, from Mrs Dorman's first call reporting her son missing to the removal of the boy's body to the morgue around two am. When he was done, Foreman fired off a series of questions; then the uniformed Inspector left them to it. Foreman rose to his feet:

'Okay, Russell. I'm off to the mortuary. We'll need to talk to the Dormans, but I'll leave that until we have the doctor's findings later – in the meantime, get onto the school. Talk to the staff, get any background that might be useful – was the Dorman boy at odds with any other kids, was there any kind of gang-type activity going on? This could, just possibly, be some kind of bullying escapade that got too far out of hand. Or any kind of rivalry, jealousy?'

'Okay; what about the possibility of girlfriends, sir?'

'Bit young for the old eternal triangle thing, aren't they?' Foreman interjected.

'They start younger and younger these days, sir!'

'All right, Russell; I suppose we must look at all the angles until we know better. Get a list of all the kids in his class, anyone the teachers think might be able to help. I'll call you when I leave the Doc.; we'll go and talk to the Moss boy as soon as you're done.'

At the town's mortuary, Foreman found Patrick Swainson

robed up and ready to start the post mortem, the young, slender body laid out on the stainless steel table. He stood looking down at the child for a moment:

'Poor little bugger! What a bloody waste.'

'Indeed. Good-looking boy, wasn't he?' Foreman just grunted in reply.

'So far, all I can tell you is that there are no indications on the body of any kind of struggle. Oh, the odd fading bump and scrape, but only what you'd expect to find on a boy his age. There's a little minor bruising that looks quite fresh, as if he'd maybe had a playful kind of rough-and-tumble soon before he died, but no more than that; it couldn't have been what you might call a real fight, even between kids. And no signs of restraint.'

'Any idea what killed him?'

'Can't be sure yet, but I reckon this is favourite.' The doctor pointed to the cut, little more than an inch long, near the centre of the boy's chest. He pulled the skin apart:

'That's a deep cut, no superficial scratch. I'll know better when I've had a look inside, but my guess is he was stabbed. I'm sure he didn't drown, there's been no water escape from the mouth – again, I'll confirm that later.'

'Okay, Doctor. I'll leave you to it. When can you let me know the results?'

'Oh, lunchtime, hopefully. You'll have the proper report next week sometime, but I'll call you later. Sure you don't want to stay and watch?'

Foreman shook his head with a grimace:

'Talk to you later, Doc.' He left, as the pathologist bent to his grim task.

* * *

A little later, the D.I. met his subordinate at Elwood Priors School, after paying a brief visit to the scene of the boy's murder. There he had taken a quick look around, inspecting for himself the spot where he had been pulled from the lake, and where the evening's search had come across his discarded pants; after a discussion with the forensic officer in charge of the ground search, he'd left them to it. He found Russell talking to the Headmaster in the entrance hall. The sergeant introduced his superior officer; after an exchange of pleasantries and expressions of sorrow at the death of Philip Dorman, the two policemen left in Foreman's car, leaving a team of detective-constables to complete the questioning of the remaining members of staff.

As they swung out of the school gates, Russell at the wheel, Foreman asked:

'Well, what have we got?'

'Not much, sir. Philip seems to have been quite popular, there's no suggestion that any of the other boys might have been gunning for him. They do have some instances of bullying, but the staff come down hard on that kind of thing, and anyway the Dorman kid doesn't seem to have been a target.'

'Any jealousies showing?'

'Nothing obvious, sir. It doesn't sound like he was *so* popular, or *so* clever as to have upset any of the other kids. And no hint of girlfriends.'

'Okay, Russell.' The D.I. smiled: 'You could have been right there, I suppose; he *was* a nice-looking boy. Anything else?'

'I've got that list of his classmates – fifteen of them are boarders, and I've left D.C. Parkinson to talk to them. They were all on the premises last night, so I don't expect we'll get much that'll be useful from them except a bit more background. Five are day students; they all live locally, so I thought I'd go around them later. One of them is the Moss boy, Philip's best friend, who was with him earlier yesterday evening – I assume that's where we're going now?' Foreman nodded.

'Oh, and there's one other boy the Headmaster suggested we

talk to, a Carl Evans – he's the form prefect for Philip's class.'

'Form Prefect?'

'Yes, sir. They have a system where a delegated prefect takes some of the supervisory duties over the junior forms – at assembly, times like that. They also see the kids out of their form rooms at the end of the day, so this Evans boy will have been around as they left to go home. He might know something; and he should be aware of any interplay between the kids that the masters have missed.'

'Okay, Russell. Let's go and see what Peter Moss can tell us.'

* * *

Angela Moss, a tall, dark-haired woman in her thirties, answered the door to Russell's knock.

'Mrs Moss? I'm Detective-Sergeant Russell, this is D.I. Foreman. Can we come in, please?' She stood back and waved them inside:

'This is about Philip, I suppose? Do you want to talk to Peter?'

'In a moment, Mrs Moss' Foreman replied: 'How well did you know Philip Dorman?'

'Oh, very well, really. He and Peter have been friends since they were in junior school together. The Dorman's only live a few streets from here.'

'What did you think of him?'

'He's a really nice boy, bright, thoughtful – quiet, in a way, but lively, too. He loves his cricket!' Her face suddenly crumpled, and tears came into her eyes:

'I'm sorry, I can't cope with the idea that he's…gone. It just doesn't seem possible. I can't imagine how John and Kate are coping.'

'You know what's happened, then?'

'Yes – Kate rang last night when Philip hadn't gone home – and then, on the local news this morning, they said you'd found a boy's body at the quarry. They didn't say it was him, but it was, wasn't it?' Foreman nodded:

'I'm afraid so.'

'What…happened to him?'

'We're still waiting for the post-mortem results' Foreman prevaricated.

'Was it an accident?'

'It doesn't look that way, I'm afraid.'

'Does Peter know?' Russell asked. The woman nodded:

'Yes. He was having breakfast when it came on the news at nine o'clock; he realised it was Philip before I'd put two and two together.'

'How has he taken it?'

'He's desperately upset, of course – Philip was his best friend, Peter always looked to him as the leader, as he's older by a few months – he is…was…twelve; Peter's birthday's in two weeks. God knows what kind of day it'll be for him now!'

'Can we talk to him now, Mrs Moss?'

'Is your husband home?' Foreman put in before she could reply.

'Donald is at work – he's the service manager at Frost's garage, you know, the Ford dealer. He's promised to get home as quickly as he can; I rang him when we heard it on the news. I'll get Peter for you.'

A few moments later, she returned from upstairs with her son, a slim boy with big dark eyes and thick brown hair that left no doubt of their relationship. She introduced him to the two officers, who questioned him gently but thoroughly for half an hour. The boy answered carefully, obviously struggling to remain composed at times as he sat close to his mother on the settee, but at the end of it, they had learnt nothing new. Peter had only stayed with his friend at the quarry for an hour at most; he'd left him sitting on his own up near the lakeside to come home for tea; he hadn't seen anyone else at the quarry, or near there when he'd left to cycle home. Foreman asked if anyone had known of their plans to go to the quarry that evening. The boy hesitated:

'No – I don't think so. We only decided at lunch-time; and we didn't tell anyone. Except my Mum, of course – she always likes to know where I'm going.'

'Do you own a knife of any sort, sheath-knife type of thing?' Russell interpolated; Peter shook his head:

'Only a pen-knife – one of those Swiss Army ones. It's in my room – do you want to see it?'

'No, it's okay, thanks. Did Philip own anything like that, a bigger type of knife?'

'Not that I ever saw – and he always shows me everything!'

'Would you come with us to the quarry some time, and show us just what you two did, where you went last night? Not today; perhaps tomorrow, if you're feeling up to it?' Pain rose in the boy's eyes at the thought of going back to where he'd last seen his friend, but he said:

'It's important, isn't it? To help you?' Russell nodded:

'We need you to help all you can, Peter. Even silly little things you might show us could help us to find out what happened to Philip.' Dark eyes held his for a moment, the brightness of tears rising in them:

'All right, I guess, I'll try – can Mum or Dad come with me?'

'Yes, of course!'

'Okay, then.' The boy's voice broke at last, and he turned to his mother who drew him into her arms and held him, his face hidden in her shoulder. The two detectives rose to their feet:

'We'll see ourselves out, Mrs Moss.' Foreman's voice held a depth of sympathy for the child.

Chapter Six

Nine-thirty that same morning; as Keith Foreman was conferring with the pathologist, Jenny Evans had been up for two-and-a-half hours. She'd done most of the housework, turned the weeks wash (or part of it, anyway!) from the machine into the tumble-drier, offering up her usual silent prayer as she switched it on - it really was on its last legs, but she couldn't afford a new one - and put a fresh load into the machine. A small, mousy woman, with light blue-grey eyes and nondescript wavy hair, she had that care-worn look that comes from running a household, holding down a job, and bringing up a teenager with little or no help from anyone.

She'd married Bryn eighteen years before, falling for his dark Welsh charms as a rather naïve teenager herself. They'd been happy enough, for a while; but then, when Carl was only a little boy, he'd upped and returned to his native valleys. She'd coped; there was a stubborn, self-reliant streak in her that people rarely saw - and Carl had grown into a decent son, never too selfish to stop and help with the chores, do little things without her having to ask. Like getting the salad for dinner, last night - that was typical of him!

She hurried upstairs, knocked on the door of her son's room. Carl hadn't stirred yet; she stepped quietly inside, to find him blinking at her blearily. As she put the cup of coffee down on his bedside table, he pushed himself up into a sitting position. He wore no pyjama shirt; he smiled up at her, a little blearily. Usually he'd be up and about by this time, but she said nothing; that would be asking for a fit of the teenage sulks - not that her son was really prone to such things.

'It's half past nine, Carl – I'm going down the town to do the shopping.'

'Okay – I'll get up in a minute.'

'That's okay, no hurry. Make yourself some toast or something for breakfast when you're ready.'

'Mm-hm.'

She went back downstairs – a few minutes later, Carl heard the front door slam, and then the sound of her little car starting up and driving off.

He lay there a while longer, and then climbed out of bed and pulled on a pair of jeans and an open-necked shirt. He glanced out at the overcast sky, such a change from the bright sunshine of the day before – why was it always lovely during the week while he was at school, and then grey and miserable at the weekend? But at least it wasn't raining, he thought as he pulled on a clean pair of socks. Dressed, he sat on the edge of his bed, shoulders slumped, head bowed, in thought.

He hadn't slept well at all. Soon after their evening meal, he'd excused himself and gone up to his room, uncomfortable in his mother's company with the turmoil that was going around in his mind. He'd tried reading, and found himself unable to focus on the printed words; he'd put some music on the stereo – earphones on, the partition walls of these cheap seventies houses were anything but soundproof – and found that no better ease for his troubled thoughts. Eventually, he'd given up and gone to bed after popping down stairs for a last glass of orange juice from the fridge.

There, he'd lain awake, tossing and turning, for hour after hour. To begin with, his mind was consumed with the fear that the terrible thing he'd done that evening would come to light to confront him, that he'd missed something, left some vital clue that would lead the police to the fact of Philip's death, and his part in it. He lay there in a cold sweat, forcing himself to combat his fears with cold logic: By now, the boy's body would be under water, lost into the lake's depths – all the police would know was that he'd gone missing. So, they'd talk to him? So what? All they'd want to know would be whether he, Carl, had any idea where the kid might have gone, why he might have chosen to run away. They wouldn't know that the Dorman boy was dead, they'd have no reason to ask where he'd been last night after school And if they did, he had only to stick to saying he'd stayed at home until his mother got in from work. No problem - in fact, the challenge of putting one over on the police was becoming almost enjoyable….

Feeling calmer, Carl felt himself slipping slowly towards sleep. But as he did so, he found himself dwelling on the events before Philip's death, and, deep down, regretting that he hadn't taken better advantage of the opportunity he'd had to enjoy the younger boy. Unbidden, his mind recalled the stirring of arousal he'd felt when he came across Philip lying there on the hillside by the lake, sunbathing in the nude; the tingling of repressed excitement that he had felt as he followed the other boy around the quarry, scrambling and slipping after him, watching the supple athleticism of his young body; the growing urge to touch him, so unexpectedly fulfilled when the kid had jumped on him after they'd returned to the clearing above the lake.

And then, the surge of excitement at the feel of the youngster's slim, strong body as they'd wrestled, the soft, warm texture of his bare skin, the arousing, animal smell of his sweat… And at last, the uncontrollable desire to somehow possess the slim, beautiful boy who lay on the ground in front of him, squirming and laughing, that had led him to draw his knife and brandish it above the tanned, sweat-slick chest; the intense, electric thrill that had raced through him as he thrust the blade through the kid's heart.

Carl's terror had returned then. But it was fear of himself, of the awful power of his feelings, of the idea that he could fall prey to these urges again if he found himself alone with a younger boy, might kill again in the wild insanity of the moment. Carl had long ago given up believing in God; but he had then come as close as he ever could to praying: If only he could escape the consequences of his dreadful actions that evening, he'd do his damnedest to drive out of his brain the frightful cravings he had fallen prey to – please God, he just wanted to grow up and be *normal!*

He had, eventually, slept fitfully. He still felt exhausted as he stumbled downstairs to the kitchen in his socks and put the kettle on for another coffee. He made some toast, and sat eating it at the kitchen table. His mother kept the radio in the kitchen tuned to the local station – he switched it on for some background noise, and sat there tiredly trying to collect his thoughts.

The news bulletin came on at eleven o'clock, prompting him to get up and take his plate and cup to the sink. Then, after some items of national interest, the announcer turned to local news:

'Late last night, the body of a twelve-year-old boy was recovered from flooded quarry workings just outside Grancester. He hasn't so far been named, but police say they are treating his death as suspicious; we are hoping to have more information at our twelve o'clock bulletin. An accident has closed the motorway near...'

Carl heard no more; he was plunged into near-panic. He'd got it wrong! *Damn, damn, damn!* Philip's body can't have sunk, if they'd found it so quickly! What now? He forced himself to calm down and think rationally – okay, things hadn't worked out as he'd intended. Rather than a runaway, the police knew they'd got a murder – he could hardly hope they'd think the kid had drowned, they'd be bound to spot the knife-wound – but there was still no reason for them to connect *him* with it! Oh, their questions would be different now, although... as long as they followed the obvious line, they'd be asking if there'd been any strange people hanging around the school, any odd characters poking around, trying to get to know kids, things like that. *He* hadn't seen anything, of course. He hadn't known that Philip and Peter were planning to go to the quarry after school; he hadn't been anywhere near there, himself, he'd been at home on his own…

Carl was just getting to grips with his fright, when he saw a police-car sweep by outside; another followed, and he heard the screech of tyres as they braked to a halt. His panic flared again – *they know; they've come for me!* – he stood rigid, his hands frozen to the edge of the sink; but no knock came at the door. Screwing down his courage, he leant forward to peer through the window, along the street. The two cars were a few doors along; he was in time to see them pushing a young man he recognised into the back of one of them. He relaxed, almost crying with relief.

* * *

When his mother returned with her shopping, Carl had again retired to his room, wrestling with his self-doubt, and his fear of his awful, unnatural urges. She smiled to herself at the sound of a great orchestra reverberating through the ceiling; Carl had sought comfort and reassurance subconsciously in the soaring affirmation of faith that is Mahler's second symphony. Jenny Evans didn't know one symphony from another – she didn't notice when, uncomforted by the 'Resurrection', Carl switched to the almost unbearable poignancy of the tenth. She wished her son would go out more, that he had more friends – but he seemed quite content with his own company much of the time, although an occasional friend would come by, mostly boys from his class in school, sharing the difficulties of some piece of homework.

He joined her for a late lunch, seeming quiet and withdrawn over his cheese and onion sandwich, then returned to his room and his music as she began to prepare the dinner for later.

Chapter Seven

It was mid-afternoon before the two detectives grabbed a sandwich apiece from the canteen, and a mug of coffee, and headed up to Foreman's office once more. They'd barely sat down when an authoritative knock came on the door, and the Pathologist strode in. He took one look at the rather unappetising-looking sandwiches:

'Enjoying life's little luxuries, I see.'

'Hullo, Doc.' Foreman said with his mouth full of tuna and mayonnaise: 'Take a seat.'

The Doctor took the chair in front of the desk; Russell perched on the edge:

'What have you got for us?'

'My first guess was right, the boy was stabbed. One blow, straight and level, right through the heart.'

'Well, at least it was quick.' The doctor raised his eyes and gave Russell a very strange look; the D.S., surprised by Swainson's intense expression, expostulated: 'What did I say?'

Swainson relaxed and gave him a grim smile: 'You're quite right – death was as good as instantaneous.'

'What else can you tell us?' Foreman asked. Turning to face him, the doctor went on:

'I wasn't quite right when I told you earlier that there were no other marks – there was some abrasion of the heels. I'd say that he was dragged by someone holding him under the armpits, presumably to dump him in the lake.'

'He was dead by then?'

'Oh yes. As I told you, he could have had a bit of a rough-and-tumble shortly before he died, but it can't have been anything serious. There's no sign of any *real* struggle.'

'He didn't fight for his life, then?' Russell interjected.

'It wouldn't appear so. And there's no sign of him being bound, or restrained in any way, that I can find, either.'

'What sort of knife are we looking for, Doctor?' Foreman asked.

'You haven't got it, then?' The Inspector shook his head.

'Sharp on one edge, at least six inches long – it went right through his chest and just touched one of his vertebrae. Straight blade.'

'Kitchen knife ?'

'No, heavier, I'd say. Sheath knife, Bowie knife, that kind of thing.'

'We haven't found any traces of blood at the quarry?'

'I don't suppose you will! The boy was dead almost as soon as the knife went in, there would have been very little blood escape, if any. No blood pressure, see? Especially if the knife was left in the wound rather than being withdrawn straight away.'

'Oh – yes. Doesn't help us find just *where* he was killed, though.'

'Close to the lakeside, I'd assume – as I said, he wasn't dragged far. Hasn't the ground search given you any indications?'

'Not really. There's grass over most of the area, as you saw - doesn't hold traces very well. And what there is, is too confused to help much.'

'I see.'

The pathologist sat back in his chair, a slightly worried expression on his face.

'There's something else, Doc?'

For the first time, the doctor appeared hesitant:

'Yes. It's that knife-wound. There's something about it I don't like - it was level, almost parallel to the ground. And so accurate.' He paused; then went on, getting to his feet again:

'If you stab someone out of the blue, so to speak, you usually hold the knife like this, and thrust up' He demonstrated, picking up a ruler off of the desk: 'or like this, and come down' another demonstrative blow. He paused again: 'The blow that killed the Dorman boy looks too careful, precise even. As if the killer took his time about it.'

'You're assuming he was standing up - was that the case, can you say?' asked Foreman.

'No, I can't. But it doesn't make much difference - given the location, the other obvious possibility would be that he could have been lying on the ground, perhaps held down; there is some indication of that, a few minor abrasions, a couple of tiny punctures on his back, from stones or whatever, so I'd say it was a possibility. But even then, the same applies - a spur-of-the-moment blow would tend to come downwards, in relation to the body…' He knelt on the floor of the office to demonstrate: 'In this case, the killer must have held the knife over the kid's chest and pushed down, so…'

'So the boy must have… known what was coming?' Russell sounded shocked.

'That's the way I see it.' Swainson climbed to his feet, brushing the dust from the knees of his trousers.

'Poor little sod!' put in Foreman 'he must have been terrified!'

'Perhaps that's the answer' said the Doctor: 'He must have been rigid with fear. Otherwise, why not run, or fight?' Foreman's expression took on a hard determination:

'It sounds as of our killer is a brutal son-of-a-bitch. To hold a decent kid like Philip Dorman at knife-point and casually line the blade up before… Jesus Christ!'

All three men sat in stunned silence for a moment. Then Foreman asked:

'Had he been assaulted?'

'Not that I can say. He certainly hadn't been raped, and there's no physical indication of any other assault. He could have been molested, of course, without there being anything for me to find, if the attack was carefully done. We've sent his shorts to the lab, the tests might show something, when I get them.'

'So it could be that our killer was sexually motivated, even if you've no proof?' Russell asked.

'Quite possibly.'

'Okay, thanks, Doc. You'll send on your report?'

'Next week. See you later.' Swainson gave them a casual salute, and left the office.

Russell looked at his discarded sandwich, and shook his head:

'I don't feel hungry any more.'

'Nor me. God, what a mess! It sounds more and more as if we've got a particularly nasty pervert out there.'

'It's difficult to see what else we can be dealing with, isn't it?'

'Yes. There's no other motive, unless something comes to light that we don't know about yet.'

'There aren't any known perverts around here, are there?' The Sergeant asked.

'The only one I know of is that guy who was jailed for molesting little girls about ten years back. He's out again now, but he doesn't seem to have put a foot wrong since. Anyway, this is hardly his style, is it?'

'No, I guess not.'

'If only there was some kind of register of all these sex offenders, Russell – if we could tap into a record somewhere that would tell us if there's anyone out there who fits our M.O. It could as easily be someone from Cornwall or Inverness as a local, and we've no way of checking!'

'Isn't the Federation trying to get something like that set up, sir?'

'Yes – I'm on the committee that recommended it, but you

can't get government to move until they've weighed all the pros and cons. And all the do-gooders are against it, of course, say it'll infringe their human rights - though why perverts who prey on innocent kids deserve any human rights is beyond me!'

'Shall I try Scotland Yard, sir?'

'Yes, do, Russell. Ask them if they know of anyone who likes to molest little boys and then uses a knife on them.'

Both men sat in silence for a moment, contemplating the depths to which human nature could sink. Then Russell said:

'The way the kid didn't try to run, or fight – it sounds as if the killer was someone he knew? And trusted?'

'That might fit, but who, Russell? The only possibilities would be a teacher at the school, or one of the parents, his own, or the Moss boy's. Doesn't seem likely, but you'd better check the backgrounds of all of 'em. We're doing a house-to-house?'

'Yes, right now. They might come up with another possible, someone the kid was friendly with - I'll check out anyone who might fit the bill.'

'Okay, Russell. You're going to see the remaining boys in Philip's class?'

'Yes – there's four more to go, day students – they all live locally.'

'Let's go and see the Dormans first. I'm not looking forward to this, Russell.'

'No, sir.'

* * *

The Detective-Inspector knocked at the door of number 14, Alderley Park Avenue, a smart detached house in one of the more expensive parts of the town. A small woman with black hair and blue eyes bright with sorrow, in a black top and slacks, opened it to them.

'Mrs Dorman? Detective-Inspector Foreman. This is

Detective-Sergeant Russell. May we come in?'

'Please do, Inspector.' She held the door for them, and then led them into a well-furnished sitting-room. John Dorman, looking rather dishevelled, raised his eyes to them distractedly.

'I can't tell you how very sorry I am about your son' Foreman began. Mrs Dorman averted her eyes for a moment:

'Thank you, Inspector. It's... so difficult for us. John especially; he thinks – thought – the world of Philip.'

At this, John Dorman rose unsteadily to his feet with a mumbled apology:

'Will you excuse me for a few minutes? I'll be right back.' He left the room.

Foreman stared after him:

'Would it be better if we came back another time, Mrs Dorman?'

'No, please' She gave him a bleak smile 'It's most important now that we do all we can to help you. You must forgive John: He dotes on all the children, of course, but... Philip was our oldest son, and he's the spitting image of his father. They were so close – I don't know how John will cope...' She sat heavily on the sofa, staring unseeingly into the distance. After a moment, Foreman asked, gently:

'You have other children?' Kate Dorman raised her head, tears glistening in her eyes:

'Yes, Inspector. Caroline's nineteen; she's studying in Bristol. I rang her this morning, she's on the train home, I'll have to go and pick her up shortly from the station. And Andrew – he's eight. He's up in his room; he worships – worshipped – his big brother...' She dissolved into tears again; Awkwardly, Foreman pulled out a clean handkerchief and handed it to her.

At that moment, the door opened, and John Dorman returned, his arm around the shoulders of a little boy, black-haired and blue-eyed like his mother. The child broke free and walked over to the sofa – climbing into his mother's arms, he kissed her on the cheek and whispered:

'Don't cry, Mummy – please?' She kissed him back, and raised her eyes again, once more composed, to the two policemen. Her husband came and sat beside her, slipping his arm protectively around her shoulders; but looking at them, Russell wondered who, in fact, was deriving comfort from whom. The two officers were just taking the chairs she indicated with a wave of her hand when the telephone on the low table by the end of the sofa rang. John Dorman reached out for it:

'Hello?'

'Caroline, Darling! Where are you?'

'Yes, I know, sweetheart.'

'We'll come and pick you up…'

'Tell her my Sergeant will collect her' Foreman cut in.

'Caroline? A policeman will come to get you, Sergeant…?'

'Russell.'

'Sergeant Russell. All right, Darling?'

'See you in a little while, then.' He replaced the receiver.

'From the Main Line Station, sir?' Russell asked.

'Yes, down the end of Midland Road' Mrs Dorman told him.

'She knows what's happened?' Foreman asked.

'Only that Philip's been killed, no more.'

'Okay, off you go, Russell.'

The Detective-Sergeant let himself out and drove off. In the house, Mrs Dorman turned to Foreman:

'How did Philip die, Inspector?' Foreman drew a deep breath:

'It was very quick. He was stabbed; he must have died instantly.' She closed her eyes in pain, drew a sharp breath:

'That's some small consolation, if he didn't suffer.' She sighed deeply: 'But why? For God's sake, why should anyone want to kill a little boy?'

'I can't answer that, Mrs Dorman. There are some…very strange people out there. Very few of them, thank goodness, but they do exist.'

Visibly taking a grip on herself, she asked in a hushed voice:

'Had…anything else… been done to him?'

'Not that we can tell. But we can't see any other motive, at least so far.'

She nodded; silence reigned for a moment, before Foreman ventured to begin his questions.

By the time Russell returned with the eldest daughter, the Inspector was beginning to feel almost frustrated; his questioning had elicited nothing useful. No, they could think of no reason why anyone would attack their son. No, he didn't have any friends or acquaintances that they were doubtful about. No-one had ever made any threats against any of the family. They were more than happy with his schooling, and the teachers there. They knew that he and Peter frequented the old quarry; they'd been concerned about the boys' safety, with the deep water in the lake, but John Dorman admitted that he, too, had gone there regularly as a boy, so he hadn't felt he could forbid his son from doing so.

Foreman had asked if Philip had owned any kind of hunting knife or similar weapon; neither parent knew of any such thing, and his mother said that he hadn't been the kind of boy to hide things away from them. Kate Dorman had taken the Inspector up to the boy's room - he gave it a cursory look-over, asked for and received her agreement that he would have a forensic officer check it over properly later in the day. Downstairs again, she had sought out a copy of Philip's last school photograph for him, and gave her permission for it to be released to the press. She sat down again, and the eight-year-old climbed back onto her lap, easing his arms around her neck and clinging close to her.

The door flew open, and a tall, slim girl, blond and blue-eyed, in a smart red leather mackintosh, rushed in and flung her arms around her father, who had stood up to greet her:

'Oh Daddy! How horrible! The Sergeant told me what's happened!'

'Russell!' Foreman barked; the girl turned to him:

'Oh, don't be cross – I made him. I had to know; and I didn't

want Daddy to have to tell me, I know how hurt he is already…'
She looked into her father's eyes, and they both burst into tears,
hugging each other tightly.

Foreman turned to his deputy:

'Come on Russell, let's leave these good people in peace.
We'll let ourselves out, Mrs Dorman.'

'Thank you, Inspector. We'll be here if you need us again.'

'Thank you – and…'

'I know.' She smiled sadly up at them over the little boy's
head as they turned to go.

Chapter Eight

A little after six o'clock: Jenny Evans had just called up to her son that dinner would be ready soon, when a knock came at the door. Outside stood two men she didn't recognise:

'Mrs Evans? Detective-Sergeant Russell. Could we have a word with Carl, please?' He smiled reassuringly at the worry on her face: 'It's all right, just a matter of routine, he's not in trouble or anything.'

'Oh… yes, of course. Come in.' She led them to the sitting room, calling up the stairs again:

'Carl? Come down a minute, love, there's someone to see you.'

In his room, sitting quietly after the conclusion of the music, Carl had heard the knock, and somehow known what it meant. He paused to compose himself, and then went downstairs, to be confronted with two strange men in the living-room:

'Carl? I'm Detective-Sergeant Russell; this is Inspector Foreman. We just need to ask you a few questions, if you don't mind?' Carl put a puzzled look on his face:

'Okay, I guess. What's it about?'

'You go to Elwood Priors School?'

'Yes, I do.'

'He got a scholarship!' his mother put in proudly; Carl smiled indulgently at her.

'Do you know a boy called Philip Dorman?'

'Yes, he's in my class!'

'In your class?' The older policeman interjected.

'Not in the same class as me, he's only a kid; in the class I look after, as form prefect, you know?'

'Yes, we know. I'm afraid Philip's dead.' Russell spoke quietly.

'Dead? How? Wait a minute, there was something on the news – in the quarry?' Russell nodded.

'Was he drowned in the lake?' Russell's nod became a shake of the head:

'No – he was killed, murdered.' Carl sat down with a bump in one of the armchairs, acting shocked and upset:

'Oh, God! I… Oh!'

'It's okay, Carl, relax for a moment – we need you to tell us what you can about Philip, his friends and so on – Mrs Evans, could we all have a cup of tea, do you think?'

She nodded distractedly, and went to the kitchen. Carl looked up at the two officers and took a deep breath: 'Okay – what can I tell you?'

'Are you sure you're all right?' Carl nodded; Russell went on with his questions: 'We know that Philip went up to the old quarry after school yesterday, with Peter Moss – you know him, too?'

'Yes – he's Philip's best mate.'

'Did you know that they were planning to go there?'

'No – should I have done?'

'No, of course not; we thought you might have heard them planning it, that's all. So you wouldn't have any idea whether anyone else knew their plans, then?'

'No.'

'Philip wasn't… unpopular, with anyone at school, was he?'

'Not that I knew – quite the opposite, really. He seemed to get on with everyone. He's a clever kid, really quick – he even pokes fun at me sometimes!'

'You don't mind that?'

'No! It's only for a laugh, he's never nasty with it. I think everyone likes - liked – him.'

Jenny Evans returned to the room with a tray of teacups and a mug of coffee for Carl. As she passed them around, Russell asked Carl:

'Have you seen anyone unusual at school lately?'

'No.'

'No-one hanging around, maybe? No strangers?'

'No, not that I recall – there's always a few parents, come to collect some of the younger kids, by the gates when we go home, but I don't remember seeing anyone different. Most of the boys are boarders, anyway – but I suppose you know that?'

'Yes. Thanks, Carl, that's about all – Oh, one thing; were you out at all yesterday evening? After school?'

'No; I came straight home – I was here until Mum came in from work.'

'When was that?'

'Oh, just after eight.'

'That's right, I finished my shift at the supermarket at eight, and it's only a few minutes away.' Jenny confirmed.

'All right Carl, that's all. Thank you for your help; I don't suppose we'll need to talk to you again. Thank you, Mrs Evans, I hope we've not intruded.'

'Not at all, Sergeant. You don't know who could have done it?'

'Not so far, Mrs Evans. It's early days – we've a number of lines of enquiry, as you can imagine, but no firm suspicions as yet.'

'I hope you catch him. I can't imagine what sort of person would want to kill a little boy, like that.' Foreman shook his head:

'It beggars belief, doesn't it?' He finished his tea: 'Come on, Russell, we've work to do, no time to sit drinking tea!'

'Yes, sir.' The Sergeant quickly drank off his own cup.

As they left the room, Carl sat back and heaved a sigh of relief – that had gone okay! When Jenny Evans returned from showing the two police officers out, she found her son still slumped in the armchair, lying back with his eyes closed.

She leant over him, and slipped an arm around his shoulders:

'You all right, love?' Carl opened his eyes and raised them to meet his mother's; he nodded:

'Yeah – I'm okay. It's just a bit of a shock.'

'It must be.' She bent to kiss him on the top of his head; he smiled up at her:

'Come on, Mum, let's have dinner.' She ruffled his hair fondly, got up and went through to the kitchen.

Carl sat still for a few moments; rather than feeling distressed, he'd actually been offering up a silent prayer of thanks when she'd returned, relieved that what he thought would be the worst moment of his ordeal was over. It was beginning to look as if he would indeed escape retribution for his impulsive actions – all he had to do was keep his head and hang on, it was obvious the two policemen had had no idea that he'd had anything to do with Philip's death! The thought that he'd fooled them gave him a surge of pride, brought a secret smile to his face. He got up and followed his mother.

Jenny took a casserole out of the oven and dished up two portions, adding boiled potatoes to each plate after she'd drained them over the sink. Putting one plate in front of her son, she said:

'I'm sorry, love; the potatoes are a bit over-done. Those two upset my timing!' Carl just smiled at her. To change the subject, she asked:

'You heard about our other bit of excitement today?'

'What was that?'

'While I was out this morning; Old Mr Johnson next door caught me as I got back and said the police had arrested the Carroll boy. You know the Carrolls, along the street? It seems they think he's responsible for all those burglaries around the estate.'

'Oh, is *that* what it was about? I saw the police cars, when I was getting my breakfast. That was just after the news had been on the radio.'

Jenny looked at her son, concern in her eyes: 'That's when you heard about that boy; Philip, was that his name?'

'Yeah – but I didn't know it was him, then. I guess it never occurred to me it might be someone I knew, even.'

'You knew him quite well?'

'Yeah, as well as any of the kids in that form. He kind of stood out, always making the other kids laugh; he does – did – a great impression of Frankenstein!'

'Who?'

'Doctor Frankham, the Head – he had him down to a T!'

She shook her head: 'Why would anyone want to kill a boy like that? I just can't understand it.'

'Nor me, Mum. I can't imagine anyone having anything against him – not like Peverill, in my year, if someone stuck a knife in that arrogant bastard they'd be doing us all a favour!'

'Carl!'

'Sorry.' he smiled contritely; they lapsed into silence. The meal over, Carl cleared away the plates:

'I'll wash up, Mum.'

'Thanks, love – are you sure you're okay?'

'I'm fine – really!'

Chapter Nine

When Foreman and Russell got back to the station, Frank Simmons was on duty at the desk again:

'Inspector? The Super would like to see you, sir.' Foreman turned to his Sergeant:

'I'll join you in my office, Russell.'

'Okay, sir.'

He knocked at the Superintendent's office door, and entered at the gruff 'Come!' from inside. Superintendent Charles McFadden was the Senior Officer in charge of the Grancester division of the County Constabulary; a short, wiry Scot, his once-red hair now fading to a kind of rusty grey, he was as finicky about his turnout as was Tremayne, and regarded his senior C.I.D. officer's appearance as a kind of personal affront:

'What's this to-do with the murdered schoolboy, Inspector?' The once-broad Glasgow accent had mellowed after nearly twenty years in the midlands.

'As I expect you know, sir, Uniform recovered his body from the old quarry out towards Bevington last night. He was stabbed, and dumped in the lake, according to Pat Swainson. No obvious motive, no murder weapon as yet, although I'm hoping the report of the ground search at the quarry's on my desk now. No obvious suspects, either.'

'Hnh. All very obscure, by the sound of it. Ye'll be needing the divers, I expect?'

'If we've not got the weapon so far, yes, if you're agreeable, sir?'

'No choice is there? Call them in, and hang the expense! Right now, as you might imagine, the press are clamouring for a story.'

'I'm sure they are, sir. All right if I get them together, tell them we're working on it, following up leads, the usual?'

'Fine. Keep 'em off our backs, but don't let 'em know we haven't a clue, will you? Ye'll appeal for witnesses?'

'Yes – and I'll talk to the Dorman family, see if they'll come to a press conference, put out an appeal as well; it always gets better results if the grieving parents are seen on TV. Perhaps tomorrow?' The Superintendent regarded his C.I.D. chief with a twinkle in his pale blue eyes:

'You're a cynical bugger at times, Foreman! But yes, if they'll do it. Keep me informed, won't you?'

'Of course, sir.'

* * *

Back in his own office, Foreman asked his subordinate:

'Anything from the ground search, Russell?'

'Not really, sir. No tracks or traces on the ground, at least nothing that SOCO can interpret as useful – it hasn't rained for, what, a week or more, and it's so dry up there... No trace of a knife, or of the kid's shoes and socks.'

'They'll all be at the bottom of the lake, no doubt. The Super's just given me permission to call in the divers.'

'That's good; they'll start tomorrow, will they?' Foreman gave him a rare grin:

'Yes - not that they know it yet! I'll give 'em a call in a minute, tell 'em the good news about their overtime.' Russell laughed, then went on:

'They did find two sticks, lengths of wood, cut from one of the old willow trees near the lake, thrown into the undergrowth -

forensic are taking a look, but they didn't sound hopeful of finding anything on them. And there's no reason to connect them with the lad's death.'

'No reason not to, either! Freshly cut, were they?'

'Apparently - within a day or two, they say.'

'Okay - we'll see what forensic make of them, if anything. They've got the kid's shorts?'

'Yes - preliminary tests show no traces from them, though, no sign of blood, or semen, nothing to give us a hint of a motive. And his watch - SOCO took it off of his wrist at the scene.'

'Ah! Time?' It was Russell's turn to grin:

'No luck, sir! It's one of those waterproof models; it was still running, unfortunately!'

'Hnh! And nothing useful from the house-to-house?'

'No, sir. The locals seem to have liked the boy – they all say the same, that he was a good kid, cheeky at times but never malicious. And the family's well-liked, too.'

'No suggestion of any strangers hanging around the area, watching the local kids, anything like that?'

'Nope. And no hint that the boy could have been in with any undesirable types, as far as we know.'

Foreman leant forward on his desk, chin in his hands:

'So what have we got? A twelve-year-old kid, attacked and killed some time between five-thirty when his friend left him at the quarry, and what, seven? We must assume that he'd have left for home by then if he'd been able to. No witnesses, no weapon. Everyone says what a nice kid he was, no-one seems to have any kind of grudge against him, he wasn't a target for bullies, so I think we can rule out any kind of kid's quarrel that went too far, don't you?'

'It doesn't seem likely, does it?'

'No sign of anyone with anything against the family, so it's not likely that the killer was trying to get at the parents by killing their son. So?'

'So we come back to the obvious possibility, sir. It almost *has* to be a sex attack, doesn't it? I mean, the kid has to have been stripped at some point, to end up without his pants, doesn't he?'

'Yes; but did someone else strip him, or did he do it himself? Did he undress and go for a swim in his underpants, then take them off to dry while he put his shorts back on? If it was a paedophile, it was a very clever one – he's left us little if anything to go on. He's restrained himself remarkably – no semen to be found. Must have only molested the boy before killing him, and that so as to cause no bruising or other marks.'

'Callous son-of-a-bitch, too, if the doctor was right.'

'Yes – it doesn't bear thinking about, how that kid must have felt as he saw the bastard lining the knife up to kill him.'

'Perhaps he was unconscious?'

'Not if Doc Swainson's right – no sign of it.'

'Could he have been drugged?'

'Seems unlikely, given where they were – how would the killer have administered it? Anyhow, the P.M. will tell us, when they finish the tests. I expect the kid had been held at knife-point from the start, and was just playing along to try and avoid getting hurt.'

'I dare say.' Russell paused, and then went on: 'And yet the killer made no effort to hide the boy's bike, did he? He must have known we'd be searching for the kid when he was reported missing, and would go there to look – unless he didn't know that *we'd* know Philip had gone there, of course… or he knew he'd be well away from the area by the time we did?'

'Someone passing through, you mean? An opportunist, sees a nice-looking kid on his own, grabs him and kills him for a quick thrill before driving on? Maybe.'

'I wonder if that's it, sir? I've heard, or read somewhere, that some types of pervert actually get off on killing their victims. It's all part of their…you know, it turns them on?'

'Yes, you're right, Russell. I've heard mention of it before –

there're people, so the shrinks reckon, who get as much of a thrill from killing as from sex. More, even, in some cases. Might explain the callousness of the way he stabbed the kid.'

'It's beyond belief, isn't it? That anyone could actually do that.' Russell broke off for a moment: 'So? Where do we go from here, sir?'

'I'm going to call the press together shortly, give them the basics of what we know, ask them to broadcast an appeal for witnesses. And I'll talk to the Dormans, see if they'll do the same some time tomorrow. Uniform will broaden the search at the quarry in the morning, see if they or the divers can find us the weapon – if it's still there, I'm betting it's at the bottom of the lake. And we'll continue with the house-to-house around Alderley Park. I don't think there's anything more to be learnt from the school, do you?'

'No, sir. It doesn't seem to have any connection with them.'

'Okay, Russell. I'll go and see the press. You get off home to your wife.' Foreman glanced up at his junior:

'She's expecting, isn't she?'

'Yes, sir!' Russell smiled proudly 'Three months to go!'

'All right, lad. Get yourself home to her – and tell her I'm sorry to have dragged you in here for so long today.'

'Thank you, sir – I'll tell her' Russell was pleasantly surprised to see a rare smile on his superior's face 'See you tomorrow, sir?'

'Nine o'clock on the dot, Russell!' Foreman had turned back to the papers on his desk.

'Yes, sir!'

When the Sergeant had left, Foreman lifted the internal phone and asked Sergeant Simmons to let the press know he'd talk to them in half an hour. Then, on the outside line, he dialled the Dorman family home. Kate Dorman answered; he explained, feeling uncharacteristically nervous, what he wanted, but she replied immediately:

'Of course, Inspector - we'll do all we can to help.'

'It could be… difficult, for you?' He heard her sigh over the wires:

'I know.' She paused: 'We'll be there, Mr Foreman. Just… just get the bastard who killed our son!' The phone went down, as her voice broke with anguish. Foreman ran a hand over his face as if to wipe away her pain, then dialled the control-room to call in the diving team.

In the ground floor press room, he gave the waiting reporters the information they'd been pushing for. With the dead boy's details, he handed out copies of his last school photograph, and appealed for anyone with information that might help to contact the C.I.D. office, particularly anyone who was in the vicinity of the abandoned Bevington quarry the previous evening. He answered a few questions, being carefully non-committal about the details of the investigation; when the reporters had left, he too went home to his wife, and a late dinner.

Chapter Ten

At nine o'clock on Sunday morning, David Russell walked into his superior's office, to find Foreman already behind his desk, looking through reports relating to the Dorman case. He looked up:

'Morning, Russell.'

'Morning, sir – anything new?'

'No. Uniform have called off the ground search of the quarry, at least for the moment. They've covered the entire area now, and I want to take the Moss boy up there today, get him to talk us through what they got up to on Friday. Come on.' He stood up, and the two men went down to the car park behind the station and got into Foreman's silver Volvo estate car.

In Alderley Park, they called at the Moss home in Turner Close. Donald Moss opened the door to them; a stocky, greying man with a receding hairline, he ushered them inside:

'I'm sorry I missed you yesterday, gentlemen - I'd already gone to work before we heard about Philip.'

'That's quite all right, sir, it was mainly Peter we needed to talk to, as you'll understand' Foreman replied: 'Is he up to coming to the quarry with us, today?'

Moss hesitated before answering: 'He is, but… please treat him gently? He's absolutely shattered by what's happened, and I don't want him upset any more than is necessary.'

'Of course, sir. I wouldn't put him through it if it weren't important.'

The man nodded, and turned away, going up the stairs and knocking gently on the door of the boy's room. Peter emerged, composed but red-eyed, and followed his father downstairs.

During the drive, Russell turned in his seat to speak to the boy:

'Okay, Peter, can I go through what happened on Friday with you? You and Philip were at school as usual?'

'Yeah – it was only an ordinary sort of day, nothing special.'

'You arranged to go out together after school?'

'Yeah – at lunchtime. We both take a packed lunch; we have to eat in the refectory with the boarders. While we were eating, we talked about what to do later.'

'Who suggested the quarry?'

'I'm not sure, I think I did. But it was somewhere we go quite often, so it wasn't, like a big discussion, you know?' He glanced at his father: 'Dad doesn't like us going there, he's afraid it's dangerous.'

Donald Moss put his arm around his son's shoulders: 'I was afraid they'd get into trouble, fall in the lake or something - that water's very deep in places. I never dreamt anything like this could happen.'

'Who was at the table with you?'

'Only the others in our form – oh, and Evans of course. He's our form prefect.'

'Did any of them know you intended to go to the quarry later?'

'We didn't talk about it with them, no.'

'Could they have overheard?'

'Maybe; but it gets quite noisy in there. And they were all talking to each other, you know?'

'What about Evans?'

'Oh, he was at the other end of the table. He couldn't have heard what we were talking about if he'd wanted to!'

'And you didn't discuss it again during the afternoon?'

'No, not that I remember.'

'And at the end of your lessons?'

'We went back to our form room, put our books and things away, and went home.'

'You didn't talk about going to the quarry then?'

'No – Philip and I cycle home together, most of the way - we talked about it then. We didn't say goodbye until the end of Shakespeare Drive – I turn off to go home, and he goes on to get to Alderley Park Avenue, where he lives. We met up there again when we'd both got changed at home.'

'So as far as you can tell, no-one knew you were going to the quarry?'

'That's right – why's it so important?'

'Because it means that no-one could have gone there deliberately to find you or Philip, if they didn't know you'd be there.'

'Oh, yeah - I see.'

'Did you two go there regularly, after school? Would anyone have guessed that you might be there?'

'We used to go there mainly at the weekend – after school, we've usually got homework, and there isn't really time. We went Friday because, with the exams over, we hadn't got any homework, and it was a nice day; We'd have had plenty of time, but I forgot Dad's boss and his family were coming for dinner. That's why I had to come home.' He paused, looking up at Russell with tears brimming in his eyes: 'If I'd stayed there with Philip, would he have been all right?'

'I can't tell you, Peter' Russell gave the boy a sympathetic smile: 'We don't really know what happened after you left.'

Foreman swung the car into the quarry entrance. They parked at the bottom of the lane and got out to walk up towards the clearing beside the lake:

'Can you tell us what the two of you did when you got here, Peter?' Foreman took up the questions to the boy.

'We left our bikes – a bit further on – just up there. It's too steep to cycle right up, although we've tried sometimes.'

'Philip's bike was still there when they found it, sir.' Russell put in.

'Yes - I saw it there yesterday. Then what, Peter?'

'We walked up to the top of the mountain – that's what we call it, you see.'

'Up to the ridge overlooking the water?'

'Yes, that's right.'

A few minutes later, the little group emerged onto the bluff above the lake. By its edge stood the diving team's Land-Rover; several men were clustered around it, others, in wet suits and aqualungs, floated a little offshore in an inflatable dinghy. Foreman turned to the boy:

'What did you do then?'

'We went off exploring – well, pretending to. We know our way around here pretty well already, really. We went round that way' he indicated toward the South and East of the lake: 'It gets very hilly over there, all steep hills and narrow valleys, great fun to climb around in.'

'Is that anywhere near the road, outside?'

'Not really – you have to go that way' he pointed South-West: 'to get to the fence along the road. Even if you get near the fence, where we were, it's only fields the other side.'

'You didn't see anyone else while you were here?' The boy shook his head:

'No – no-one at all.'

'And when you had to leave?'

'We came back here – I asked Phil if he was coming back with me, but he said he'd stay here on his own for a while. When I left, he was sitting just there on top of the ridge, looking out over the lake. He's always making up stories in his head, really clever ones; I guess that's what he was doing then. He says he wants to be a writer when he grows up…' The boy's voice faltered: 'I mean, he did…'

Hit anew by the reality of his friend's death, Peter turned to his father, tears again spilling down his cheeks, and flung himself into his arms. Donald Moss cuddled his son close, murmuring reassuringly. He looked up at the Detective-Inspector:

'Can we go home now? Please?' Foreman nodded sympathetically.

* * *

Just before three p.m., the press room at the police station was crammed with representatives of the press, from the local newspapers to the national dailies; TV news crews were lined up, their cameras at the back of the room. On the dot of three o'clock, Superintendent McFadden led the family in to their seats; to Foreman's surprise, both children were with them. Caroline had refused to stay away, and their mother had insisted on bringing Andrew rather than leaving him at home with a babysitter. John Dorman looked pale and drawn as he sat in one of the chairs placed side by side behind the table on which stood the bank of microphones; his wife seemed more composed, but showed the strain of events in her eyes as she sat beside him. They were flanked by McFadden and Foreman; Andrew sat on his father's lap, and Caroline stood behind her parents, one hand protectively on a shoulder of each of them. The eyes of the gathered press were largely on the girl in the simple black dress, her beauty undiminished by the solemnity of her expression. Behind, their backs to the wall, stood a uniformed constable and a WPC.

The Superintendent introduced the Dorman family to the press, and briefly summed up the situation: 'Mr and Mrs Dorman's twelve-year-old son, Philip, was attacked and killed on Friday evening, at the old abandoned Bevington Quarry. He'd gone there to play with a school-friend, but the other boy had had to go home, leaving Philip alone, at around five-thirty. When he didn't turn up for his dinner by seven, they became suspicious and telephoned the other boy, who said he'd left Philip at the quarry. Mr Dorman began the search for his son, while Mrs Dorman called us. The child's body was recovered around ten p.m. that night; he had been stabbed to death, and thrown into the flooded workings.' He paused, to glance at the couple beside him, concerned for their response to his blunt description of events: 'Despite their obvious distress, Mr and Mrs Dorman have agreed to meet you all, to ask for the help of the public in tracking down their son's killer. Mrs Dorman?'

Kate Dorman raised her eyes from the table, but hesitated before speaking:

'Philip was a perfectly ordinary boy, bright, lively, like any twelve-year-old... He was doing very well at school; his teachers liked him; so did everyone he met. He would never have hurt anyone... Why anyone should have... done this to him, we have no idea.' She spoke slowly, hesitantly, pausing frequently as if to collect her thoughts. 'We need your help. If anyone knows anything, anything at all, that might help the police to find out who killed our boy, please, *please,* come forward and talk to them. You cannot imagine what we are going through... The effect this is having on little Andrew' she paused to smile down at her younger son: 'Or on our daughter Caroline. If you *can* help, I beg you, please do, as quickly as possible, so that we can try to get over this awful tragedy... Inspector Foreman will tell you what he needs to know – please listen, and call him if you know anything at all that might lead him to Philip's murderer.' She reached across and took her husband's hand; John Dorman had sat throughout, his face averted - now, he looked up to give her a wan smile which she returned, encouragingly.

Foreman took up the reins:

'We know Philip was alive at five-thirty on Friday. We need to hear from anyone, anyone at all, who was anywhere near the old quarry between around five o'clock and ten o'clock that same evening. The quarry is situated South of Grancester, just beyond the bypass, off the old Northampton Road; the only access to it is from that road, via a track which leads up to the old workings. The gate at the bottom has not been locked for many years, and local people, mainly children, have been using it as a kind of unofficial playground for as long a anyone can remember. So if you were anywhere near there on Friday, please come forward so that we can not only build up a picture of the people who were moving in the area at the time, but can eliminate the innocent from our enquiries. If you were passing on that road during those times, please contact us, even if you saw nothing; that way, you will help us to begin to understand the sequence of events' He continued by giving out the relevant contact phone numbers.

McFadden then asked for questions. Various reporters questioned Foreman about the current state of the investigation, to which he replied that enquiries were proceeding, following several possible leads, but that it was too early to suggest that any arrest might be imminent. One asked if he thought this was a sex attack; he gave a non-committal answer, saying that the results of tests were still awaited. The questioning then switched to the Dorman family, concentrating on what sort of kid Philip had been, his schooling, his hobbies and so on. Then a few questions were directed at Caroline, probing into her life at university; she had to lean forward to reach the microphones in order to answer. Then, one reporter from one of the tabloids asked her if she had a boyfriend: For a moment, she didn't reply; then her anger surfaced in her expression, she leant forward to the microphones:

'What the hell does *that* matter? You're asking a lot of stupid questions about things that don't matter at all!' She grabbed a picture of Philip from off the table: 'The only thing that matters to *me* is that this is my little brother – *and I'm never going to see him again!* And if the police don't get the bastard who did this, it might be *your* little brother, next time!'

She stood defiant for a moment; then, as tears ran down her cheeks, she turned and fled from the room. At Foreman's nod, the WPC followed her.

There was a stunned silence, only broken when McFadden, his Glaswegian brogue more noticeable than was usual, spoke:

'Well, gentlemen, there's no' much more we can say just now, I think.'

In the briefing area behind the press room, they found Caroline sitting with the WPC's arm around her, looking a little more composed again. She looked up at the Superintendent:

'I'm sorry, I shouldn't have lost my temper like that. I know you need them to help; I hope I haven't spoiled things?'

'Far from it, lass!' McFadden smiled down at her: 'If the truth be told, you probably did more to help in those few seconds than all our calm, reasoned talk. You'll be all over national television tonight, and on every front page in the morning! That is, unless you'd prefer we tell them not to use it?'

'No – if you really think it might help?'

'I'm sure of it! You'll have the whole country in tears, my girl, and when people see how much you hurt, they'll be climbing over each other to help!'

* * *

And true enough, Caroline's outburst at the press conference was the lead story on the news bulletins that night. Over in the Warren, the news came on just as Jenny Evans was dishing up a meal for herself and her son. When Caroline let rip at the reporters, Carl sat staring at the screen for a moment, and then buried his face in his hands. His mother put down the plate she was carrying, and hastened to put an arm around his shoulders. He put one hand over hers, and looked up:

'Sorry, Mum. It's just – he was such a good kid…' She kissed his hair:

'I understand, Carl. Don't worry, love, they'll catch the man who did it, I'm sure.'

'Yeah – I hope so, Mum.'

The teenager struggled to force down any of the meal she placed in front of him. The girl's televised outburst had brought home to him, in a way he hadn't expected, the awful effect of Philip's death on his family; something which, in his growing sense of self-congratulation at the fact that he seemed to have got away, literally, with murder, he hadn't even considered. Now, his quiet elation evaporated, leaving him shocked and afraid once more.

All that evening, he found he couldn't settle to anything – television, music, books, anything. And that night, again, he slept badly, tormented by his dreams.

Chapter Eleven

Eight-thirty on Monday morning saw the two detectives conferring briefly in the D.I.'s office. Russell's first words as he entered, carrying two mugs of coffee, were:

'Hello, sir – seen the morning papers?'

'Some of them, yes.'

'She certainly made the front pages, didn't she?' he asked, as he dropped a copy of the Daily Mail in front of his superior.

Foreman glanced down at the paper: Under a banner headline which read 'TEARS OF AN ANGEL' practically the entire front page was given over to a picture of Caroline. The photographer deserved a medal, if only for having the presence of mind to press the shutter at the precise moment when, as she finished speaking, the girl had looked up straight into the lens of his camera. As a result, she seemed to be standing there in her smart, simple black dress, gazing out at the reader, the anguish of her family written clear on her pretty face, tears welling from her blue eyes as she brandished the picture of her brother. The Detective-Inspector picked it up and began to read aloud:

"At yesterday's press conference, Caroline, beautiful nineteen-year-old sister of murdered schoolboy Philip Dorman, lost her cool with the gathered representatives of television, radio and the press. Her outburst, directed at a particularly inane question put to her by a reporter from another newspaper, in fact served to remind us all of the depth of the tragedy which has befallen this close-knit family. Therefore, in a effort to help the police, in the persons of D.I. Foreman and his team, to track down the callous pervert who has deprived them of their beloved son and brother, this paper is offering a reward of ten thousand pounds for information leading to the capture and conviction of the killer.' Lay it on a bit thick, don't they?'

'They do, sir – but if it helps…'

'Yes, indeed, Russell. And I've the feeling we're going to need all the help we can get on this one.'

'Yes, sir. Anything in from the appeals?'

'We've had a lot of calls, for sure. Mostly after they showed her tearing a strip off the press on the TV news! I'm in court this morning – it'll keep you out of mischief correlating everything. I should be done by lunchtime – I might look by the forensic labs on my way back, see if they've got anything useful for us yet.'

'Okay, sir. See you later.'

* * *

The Detective-Sergeant spent some time going through the details of the various calls received by the incident room following the appeals by TV, radio and in the papers. Most were from motorists, calling to say that they had been on the Old Northampton Road during the relevant period on the Friday evening. Some had reported seeing other vehicles; one had mentioned seeing a boy on a bike. Several calls appeared to be the usual crack-pots who always surface at such times; a few were from concerned citizens, blaming the council for not closing and securing the old quarry, and telling the police that many local kids frequented the site in the holidays - a fact which they already knew, of course.

Around eleven, a uniformed constable knocked and put his head around the door:

'There's a girl asking for D.I. Foreman, Sarge – do you want to see her?'

'Who is it?'

'Says her name's Caroline Dorman.'

'Oh, right – send her in, would you?'

A moment later, Caroline walked into the office; Russell motioned her to a seat.

'Good morning, Sergeant.'

'Morning, miss. How are you feeling?' She smiled, a little shakily:

'Not too bad, considering, thank you. But I'm afraid my mother's not so good – she collapsed last night, and we had to get the doctor. She'd been bottling it all up, trying to stay strong for my father's sake. The doctor gave her some sedatives; she's a bit better this morning.'

'Oh, no! I'm so sorry. She'll be all right?'

'The doctor says so – it was just the stress, he said. But I feel rather guilty – I think it was what I said to that reporter, about never seeing my brother again, that brought it home to her.'

'Perhaps, in the end, it will be better for her to be able to give in to her feelings for a while; as long as your family can cope – let me know if there's anything we can do to help, won't you?'

'Thank you, Sergeant – I'm taking charge for the moment! But I'll remember that offer.' She gestured at the papers lying on the desk:

'It seems your Superintendent was right, wasn't he?' She gestured at the paper, still lying on the desk, a shy smile on her face.

'It certainly seems as if you're quite the star of the show!'

'Not the way I would have chosen to achieve my five minutes of fame, though.'

'No, I'm sure it isn't, miss. But it does seem that you've got everyone's attention.'

'Have you had many calls, Sergeant?'

'We've been inundated, miss.' he gestured at the pile of statements in front of him.

'Anything useful?'

'Well, good and bad, to be truthful. We're getting a very clear picture of traffic movements, such as they were, on the road past the quarry. But the bad news is that nothing is coming to light which you could call suspicious. Where there are sightings of other vehicles, they correlate with other people who've called in themselves. Except for two.'

'Oh?'

'Yes, but they don't seem to help. One is a bright red Jaguar roadster with personalised number-plates, although the man who reported it didn't get the actual number - hardly the kind of thing you'd choose to drive if you were up to no good and trying to be inconspicuous! And the other followed the driver who reported it right into town, not stopping anywhere near the quarry. Oh, and there was a mention of an older boy on a bike, in the general area, that we haven't been able to trace as yet, but I doubt if there's any connection.'

'Oh, I see. Tell, me, Sergeant, you *are* going to catch the man who killed my brother? Truthfully, please?' She had seen the hesitant look in his eyes. Russell paused, not sure of just how honest to be with the girl. Despite her outburst the day before, she seemed to be level-headed enough to cope with the reality of the situation:

'Well, miss…'

'Caroline, please!'

'Well, the truth is that we haven't a lot to go on at the moment. We haven't found the weapon; we only have a broad idea of what actually happened to your brother after his friend left the quarry. We don't even know for sure that he was… you know…'

'Sexually assaulted, Sergeant! Please don't think you have to euphemise for me, I'd rather have the truth, even if it does hurt.' Despite her words, pain darkened her blue eyes.

'All right, miss – Caroline. We're hoping that the lab tests will give us more; we should have them in a day or two. But until then, to be honest, we're rather groping in the dark.' She sat back in the chair, trying to cope with the idea that her little brother's killer could possibly escape justice. Looking up at the Detective-Sergeant, she said:

'Thank you for being honest with me. I know you and the Inspector are doing everything you can to find out who did this.' She took a deep breath: 'One more thing – can you tell me when we might be able to bury Philip?'

'That's really up to the Coroner – he'll have to hold the inquest first, but if we're happy that there's nothing more we can learn, and tell him so, he'll probably release him for you straight away. That could be a week or two, maybe.' Caroline looked across at him, tears beginning to well up again. She quickly dabbed them away, and smiled at him:

'Thank you again, Sergeant! It will help Mum and Dad to cope, if we can at least get the funeral over with.' Russell looked at the girl opposite him, sorrow for her and her family momentarily choking him. He cleared his throat:

'If you don't mind me saying, you seem to be handling this very well, considering?' She smiled at him, a hint of her natural beauty returning to her face:

'I take after my Mother, Sergeant! We're the cool, calm, collected ones – as a rule! Mummy will be back to normal, too, before long; things had just got too much for her. Even we Dorman women have our limits!' Russell smiled back at her.

'But it's poor Daddy who can't manage' she went on, averting her eyes: 'He and Philip were so close... Oh, I know he loves me and little Andrew very much, but Pip was so much like him. Not just in looks, they liked the same things... He's so desperately upset, I don't know if he'll ever get over this...' her voice trailed off. Then she looked up, in charge of herself once more:

'Anyway, I must go and let you get on. I've held you up quite enough – but please let us know how things develop, won't you?'

'Of course we will, Caroline. Tell your parents we are doing all we can; we won't let go until we *have* got the man who killed Philip.'

It was mid-afternoon when the Detective-Inspector returned to his office. Russell filled him in on the results of the appeals, repeating what he'd told Caroline earlier. Foreman, in his turn, told his Sergeant that the forensic technicians were still going over the dead boy's shorts, but despite further tests hadn't found anything that might be of use. The only fingerprints on Philip's bike had proved to be his own or Peter's, as they might have expected, and the two freshly-cut poles had added nothing - even if it was a possibility that they had been cut and trimmed with the same knife that had killed Philip, they had no definite evidence to connect them with the crime. Russell had called the pathology lab, to be told that they had found no traces of drugs in the boy's system, or anything to support the theory that he'd been assaulted sexually.

'It still looks as if we're getting nowhere fast, Russell' the D.I. summed up.

'I had a visit from Caroline Dorman earlier. Wanted to know how we'd done on the appeals; and when they might have the boy's body for burial.'

'How is she holding up, after the tongue-lashing she gave the press?'

'Very well, I'd say, sir. Quite in control. But I'm afraid Mrs Dorman isn't so good – apparently she collapsed from the stress last night. The doctor's been; Caroline says she'll be okay.' He paused, went on: 'That's a very pretty girl, too. Seems dreadful that something like this should happen to a nice family like the Dormans, doesn't it?' Foreman nodded sympathetically:

'Sometimes I think there's no justice in the world, Russell. There're kids, in the Warren, for example, who're allowed to just run wild, as if no-one cares a damn about them - but it always seems to be the ones that are truly loved and cherished that have to suffer. And the families who love them who have to go through horrors like this. It's our job, Sergeant, to try and redress the balance a bit!'

'We'll just have to do our damnedest to catch the bastard, won't we, sir?'

Foreman heaved a sigh: 'Just keep praying for a break, Russell!'

Chapter Twelve

For a few days, the investigation surrounding the murder of Philip Dorman proceeded on a routine level, without any real progress being made. The divers had recovered the boy's shoes, and one sock; the forensic team had turned up their noses, expecting nothing after they had been in the water for so long, and, indeed, nothing was precisely what they found.

Then, on the Thursday morning, D.S. Russell picked up the telephone as it rang:

'C.I.D., Sergeant Russell.' He paused, listening:

'Okay, great! Thanks for that.' Replacing the receiver, he got up and went through to the D.I.'s office.

'Sir! Vehicle registrations reckon they've found our red Jag!' Foreman looked up:

'Oh?'

'Yes! It belongs to a Harvey Williams, he's some kind of financier in the City. Lives in the old manor house at Great Thornwood.'

'Hm. They took their time, didn't they?'

'Oh, I don't know - we didn't have any part of the number, did we? But, as the fellow said on the phone, red Jag roadsters aren't that common, especially with personalised plates, and this is the only one registered anywhere near here that fits the description. Shall I check it out?'

'Yes, do, Russell; but I can't see him having anything to

do with the boy's murder, can you?'

'Maybe not – You wouldn't drive around in something as conspicuous as that if you were on the prowl for a kid to molest, would you? Anyway, I'll get onto the owner right away.'

'Right. You could stop by the school as well, ask the Head to try to find out if any of their boys were out and about in the area of the quarry that evening – we've still got that sighting of an older boy on a bike, haven't we? I'm going to contact all the other schools in the area, ask them to appeal at their assemblies or whatever, see if we can't eliminate this kid on the bike. And tell them to warn all the kids to be on their guard – with the holidays coming up, if this bastard's still around…'

'Good idea, sir. I'll get onto the Jag. owner now.'

* * *

A little later, the Detective-Sergeant drove in through the gates of Elwood Priors in a C.I.D. car. He went up to the reception office, and asked to speak to the Headmaster. A few minutes later, Dr Frankham, a cadaverous figure wearing his black academic gown over a smart grey suit, strode into the entrance hall and greeted him:

'Good morning, Sergeant! Sorry to keep you waiting; won't you come through to my office?'

As they walked through the finely-panelled corridors to the Headmaster's office, Frankham asked the officer:

'Are you any closer to arresting Philip's murderer?'

'Not really, I'm afraid, sir. We're working on a number of leads, as you might expect at this stage, but none of them look too promising. I'm here at the moment to ask you to do something for us, if you will?'

The two men turned into the Head's office – Frankham gestured the Sergeant to a seat, and sat himself behind the heavy, old-fashioned desk:

'What can I do for you, Sergeant?'

'Two things, sir. Firstly, I'd like a quick word with the Evans boy, if that's possible?'

'From the lower sixth? Yes, I don't see why not – can you wait about ten minutes, until the morning break? We won't disturb his class that way, and I can have word sent for him to come here at the end of his present lesson.'

'Yes, that'll be fine, sir.' Frankham picked up the phone on his desk, and asked his secretary to locate the lower sixth and have a message sent to the teacher in charge to send Evans to his office at break. Putting the phone down, he looked up at Russell again:

'And the second thing, Sergeant?'

'At your next school assembly, could you ask if any of the boys were out on a bicycle on Friday, on the Old Northampton Road near the bypass, at about seven-thirty? We've had a report of a youngster on a bike seen there, and we'd like to trace him, if only for elimination purposes, you understand?'

'Of course. You're asking all the schools around here, I take it?'

'We are, sir. The driver who saw him says the lad was about fifteen or thereabouts, but he didn't take much notice of him, so we haven't got any real description of him or the bike.'

'Do you think Philip's killer is still around here?'

'Truthfully, sir, we have no idea. We've no suggestion of any real suspects locally, but no proof that it was someone from out of the area, either. Although, if it was someone who went up to the quarry in the hope of finding a lone kid there, that suggests local knowledge.'

'Should I be warning the boys to be careful, then?' Russell laughed:

'You're way ahead of me, sir! That was my next suggestion. Can you do that as well, tell them to be wary of strangers, the usual things, especially through the summer holidays? And to avoid the old quarry for the time being, at least?' It was the Headmaster's turn to laugh:

'That'll be popular with the local boys! The quarry's been a kind of unofficial adventure playground as long as I've known it! We already warn our boys of the dangers of the place, the steep slopes, the deep water and so on, but I'm sure that only makes it more attractive for them!'

'You've been here for a while, sir?'

'Yes; I started teaching here nine years ago, and I've been Head for, oh, four years, at the end of this term. Yes?' The last was in response to a knock at the door, which opened to admit Carl Evans.

'Come in, Evans. The Sergeant here would like a word with you.'

A look of concern, verging on fear, crossed the boy's face, which Russell noted; but the teenager's voice was firm when he spoke:

'Yes, sir. Is this about Dorman, Sergeant?'

'Yes, Carl. Please don't worry, it's just to confirm what you told us the other day. You said you went straight home from school?'

'Yes, that's right.'

'And you stayed there until your mother came in from work?'

'Yes?' The boy was beginning to sound puzzled.

'Did anyone come to the house in that time, or telephone, or anything?' Carl shook his head, smiled; he had recovered his self-possession quickly, and now felt again that buzz that came with the challenge of out-witting the police:

'You're asking if I've got an alibi?'

'I wouldn't put it like that, Carl' Russell echoed the smile 'It's just that we have a motorist who's told us he saw a boy on a bike near the quarry, about your age, and I just wanted to be sure we had everything right about what you told us.'

'Oh, okay.' The boy looked thoughtful: 'Well, when I got

home, I changed out of my uniform, and then I did some work on my bike, in the garden – it's a bit old' he smiled ruefully 'and the chain had got loose, so I fixed that, and gave it a grease-up and adjusted the brakes. Mum wanted to get me a new one, but I said I'd hang on; I'd rather she put the money towards a little car when I'm old enough to learn to drive. So I wouldn't have heard anyone at the door, then. The phone didn't ring at all, that I remember. So I suppose I'm still a suspect?'

Russell echoed the boy's grin: 'No – it's just that we have to dot all the I's and cross all the T's in this job! You don't know if any other boys from the school were out that way, on Friday evening?' Carl shook his head:

'No-one's said anything about being near there - and it's been the big topic of conversation all week, as you can imagine.'

'Okay, Carl. I'm sorry to interrupt you at school, but I needed to talk to Dr Frankham as well, and it saved me a journey. Thank you for your help again.'

'That's all right, Sergeant. Can I go now, sir?' he asked the Headmaster.

'Yes, go on, Evans. Oh, before you go – how are the boys in 1A? How do they seem to you?'

'Okay, really, sir. They're a bit subdued, as you can imagine, and of course Moss is still away. But they're all right.' He nodded to the policeman, and left for his next class.

'He's a good boy, Evans. Very good as a form prefect, seems to enjoy working with the youngsters. Rather quiet and introspective, perhaps, bit of a loner. Clever – he wants to be a civil engineer, could do very well, we think.' The Headmaster mused.

'We can trust his story, do you think?' Frankham looked up:

'Oh, I would think so, Sergeant. I can't imagine for a moment that he could have had anything to do with this terrible business.'

* * *

On the Old Northampton Road, beyond the village of Bevington, lay the Thornwoods. First the hamlet of Little Thornwood, a couple of miles past Bevington; and then, some three miles farther on, the larger settlement of Great Thornwood, with its Georgian Manor House and part-Norman Church set at opposite ends of the expansive village green.

Harvey Williams was pottering in his front garden, tidying up the roses, pulling the occasional weed from their beds, when he saw the CID car pull up outside. A heavily-built man of average height, grey-haired, with a bristling handlebar moustache, Williams had retired after over thirty years in the Royal Air Force with the rank of Air Commodore, to take up a directorship with the City finance house which had been started by his father many years before. Now, he enjoyed a relaxed and more than comfortable lifestyle, only needing to attend board meetings and other commitments once or twice a week.

He rose from his knees, brushed the dirt from his moleskin trousers and old, patched sports jacket, and shook the hand of the plain-clothes officer who emerged from the driving seat:

'Good morning, sir. Detective-Sergeant Russell; I rang you earlier?'

'Yes, of course, Sergeant – come in.' Williams led the way through the heavy old oak front door, along the hall and into the dining room, resplendent with Georgian wood panelling:

'So, Sergeant - what can I do for you?'

'You are Mr Harvey Williams?'

'Yes, I am.'

'And you own a red Jaguar XJS roadster?' Russell reeled of the registration number.

'Yes, that's mine! My little toy, my wife calls it!'

'Were you in that car, driving in towards Grancester last Friday evening, sir?'

'Yes, I was – we were going to the White House Inn for a meal, myself and Joannie – that's the wife, you understand.'

'What time was that, sir?'

'Oh, now – our table was for seven-thirty, we left here around a quarter to…'

'So you'd have passed the old quarry the other side of Bevington about what, seven o'clock?'

'Just before, probably' he paused, a look of sudden realisation coming into his eyes: 'Is this to do with that kiddie who was killed there, Sergeant?'

'That's right, sir. Someone reported seeing your car, and we're trying to trace all the vehicles moving on that stretch of road around that time – haven't you heard the appeals we put out for people to come forward?'

'No, I'm sorry, Sergeant – we heard about the case on the news, of course, but I suppose it never occurred to me that we were near there at the time. You think he was killed around the time we were passing?'

'Yes, sir; between five-thirty and seven, we believe.'

'Oh, my God! I am sorry, I hope I haven't caused you too much trouble? The car's a bit noticeable, I expect you found us quite easily.'

'It wasn't too difficult, no, sir. Can anyone vouch for your movements, at all?' Williams grinned through his moustache:

'Suspects, are we? Wait 'til I tell Joannie! She can confirm when we left here, of course, and she was with me all evening. The Hotel will confirm when we arrived, the Maitre d' knows me quite well, and he showed us to our table himself. You'll be checking all this, of course?'

'Of course, sir! But I'm sure it's only for the record.'

'As long as it's not *my* record! Wouldn't go down well in the City, a murder conviction!'

'I'm sure it wouldn't, sir.'

'Hold on a mo – I've just remembered something: There was a car – the quarry entrance is just near the bypass, right?'

'That's right.'

'There was a car there, parked, in the end of the lane. A silver Vauxhall. With a number on the door.'

'A number?'

'Telephone number – that local taxi firm, they have a red panel on the doors with the number on. Don't know the name, I'm afraid, never use them. Rather play with the Jag. you know!'

'And this would have been just before seven o'clock, sir?'

'That's right, Sergeant. I hope that helps?'

'We'll check it out, sir.'

'Let me know how you get on, will you? And Sergeant – is there anything I could do? For the family? Got a few bob stashed away, you know.'

'I think they're okay, sir, but I'll tell them.'

'Do that – mean it, you know!'

'I'm sure, sir – thank you. I'll keep in touch.'

In the car, Russell sat in thought for a moment - a taxi with a red panel on the door sounded like the firm who were based down near the railway station somewhere. Supercars? No, Supercabs, wasn't it? He radio'd in, confirmed the name and address of Supercabs Taxi Service, and then drove straight from Thornwood Manor to their Midland Road office. There, the girl on the desk, a well-dressed, attractive brunette, sent him straight in to the proprietor, James Martin. Martin, a somewhat nondescript figure in well-worn casual clothes, stood up and shook the Sergeant's hand as he entered, and waved him to a seat:

'What is it, Sergeant?'

'You have a silver Vauxhall in your fleet, sir?'

'Two of them - we bought them new last year.'

'We're interested to trace their movements on Friday evening of last week, sir.'

'Oh? What's it about?'

'You'll have heard of the boy murdered at Bevington Quarry?'

'Of course.'

'We have a report of one of your cabs, a silver Vauxhall, parked in the entrance to the quarry about the time he was killed.' Martin looked at the Sergeant for a moment, and thumbed his intercom:

'Mary? Can you dig out the despatch records for Friday, please? I want to know where 142 and 143 were, from about five o'clock on.' He looked up at Russell again, questioningly; the D.S. nodded. The girl's voice crackled from the speaker:

'143 was in for service Friday, Jim, but I'll get 142's details.'

'Thanks.' He turned to Russell again:

'That's right, one was at the dealer's for service – Mary'll have the other one's calls for you right away.'

'You don't have any other silver Vauxhalls?'

'No. We have two more, but they're blue. The only other silver car we've got is the big Cadillac that we use for weddings and the like, and I don't suppose your witness would mix that up with a Cavalier!'

'I'm sure this man wouldn't, sir!'

'Oh, thank you, Mary.' The girl had entered the inner office and placed a computer-printed sheet on Martin's desk; she smiled at Russell and returned to her post.

'Let me see... Alan was in 142 on Friday – Alan Broadbent, he's one of our full-time drivers, usually does Fridays and Saturdays and then other days as required; he's off today, as it happens... This list gives all the radio calls to and from 142 during his shift on Friday, two p.m. until ten; do you want to take it and go through it at your leisure? Mary's run it off it for you.'

'If you don't mind, sir? There's quite a lot here.' he looked at the sheet as Martin handed it over, and then up at the other man:

'And could you give me Mr Broadbent's address? We'll need to talk to him, as well.'

'Of course; I'll get Mary to make a note of it for you. Pick it up on your way out.' He hesitated: 'Do you think there's any connection, Sergeant?'

'I doubt it, sir; but we have to tie up all the loose ends.'

'Yes, of course. I hope you get the bugger that did it!'

Chapter Thirteen

It was around two o'clock when Russell got back to the police station. He went straight to Foreman's office:

'Here you are, sir – I picked up some sandwiches in Tesco's, they're a bit more palatable than the ones from the canteen!'

'Good thinking, Russell! Come on, I need to get out of here for a while.'

They went down to the station car park, and got into Foreman's Volvo. Driving out of the gates, Russell asked:

'Where are we going, sir?'

'Up to the quarry, Sergeant.'

Neither man spoke again until Russell had parked the car in the quarry track, and they were walking up towards the lake. Foreman had eaten his sandwiches in the car; now, Russell opened his pack and began to munch hungrily.

'What did you find out from the Jag owner, Russell?' The Inspector asked his subordinate.

'He admits that he drove by there, just around seven, sir. He was taking his wife for a meal at the White House; the Maitre d' confirms that they arrived about twenty past. But he says they saw a car in the entrance to the quarry track.'

'Does he, by Jove! What sort of car?'

'A silver Vauxhall, sir, a taxi. I've traced it to Supercabs, and got their despatch records for it on my desk. I'll go through them and try to work out how the timings fit in.'

'Excellent, Russell! This might be the breakthrough we need! Who was the driver, do we know?'

'Yes, sir. One of their regulars, an Alan Broadbent; I've got his address, too, but I thought we'd best see what the record tells us before speaking to him.'

'Yes, good work. Is anything known against this Broadbent?'

'I've put a call in to Central Records, sir; there's nothing shown locally.'

They reached the top of the track, and stood for a moment looking out over the lake. The Inspector heaved a sigh, and sat on the bluff – had he but known it, virtually on the very spot where Philip Dorman had sat, next to Carl Evans, before the playful brawls that had led to his death. Silence reigned for a few minutes; Russell finished his sandwiches. Foreman looked up at his junior officer:

'I hope this taxi business gets us somewhere, Russell. We don't seem to be making any progress, otherwise.'

'Sir?'

'Well, let's face it, we haven't got the murder weapon, we haven't got any suspects, unless your taxi-driver fits the bill, and we haven't really got a motive, have we?'

'No more luck with the divers, then, sir?'

'No! Two days, at a horrendous cost, and two trainers and a sock to show for it! McFadden's quietly doing his crust, as you can imagine - I still think the knife's probably down there, somewhere, but they can't find it.'

'Do they know where to look?'

'Yes; Apart from our assumption that the boy was killed somewhere around this area, the Met. Office confirms that the wind direction would have taken the body to just about where Rimmer found him, if he'd been thrown in along this bank somewhere.'

'I reckon we've got to assume the motive was sexual, don't you, sir?'

'In all probability, Russell – but we've no actual *proof* of that, have we? Forensic haven't found any trace of semen on the kid's clothes, or any other traces to suggest a sex attack, any more than the post-mortem showed on his body. We're assuming, largely because he'd managed to lose his underpants, that it was sexual. And, because we can't find any other motive. But… I don't know. Nothing seems to fit, somehow.'

'I know what you mean, sir.'

'Do you, Russell? When you've been in this job as long as I have, you get a kind of feeling when you're barking up the wrong tree. But I'm damned if I can see another one this side of the bloody horizon! Frank Simmons is supposed to be the one with the intuition, but this whole case just feels wrong, somehow.' He paused, and then went on: 'The only really viable theory we can offer is that Philip was spotted, purely by chance, by a roving paedophile, who proceeded to stab him after no more than a quick feel! Perhaps your idea was right, perhaps *killing* the boy was his big thrill – but even then, it seems remarkable that there's no trace of any actual sexual activity. If your cabbie *is* the killer - or whoever it turns out to be - proving the motive could be the most difficult bit.'

'I suppose so, sir.' Russell hesitated, and asked: 'What about the Evans boy, sir?'

'What about him?'

'Could *he* have done it? I thought I'd ask him about any kids being near the quarry that evening, while I was at the school, on the off-chance he might have overheard something. It's just that, when he came into the Head's office this morning, he looked quite – shocked, frightened almost, to see me. And he doesn't really have an alibi, does he?'

'A sixteen-year-old, stab another kid in cold blood? Unlikely, I'd have thought. We can't place him at the quarry, nor do we even have any reason to think he might have been there. And let's be honest, if you were sixteen, just had a school-mate stabbed to death, and suddenly found yourself confronted with the might of the local constabulary, you'd probably be a bit disconcerted, too!'

'Yeah – I guess so.'

'Oh, come on, Russell – back to the office. I'd just hoped that coming up here would somehow inspire me with some idea of what happened to that kid after his mate went home. I'll leave you to get those radio calls checked out, see if the cabbie could have done it; I'm going to pay a courtesy call on the Dormans.'

'Right-oh, sir.'

Chapter Fourteen

The following morning, Russell came into the D.I.'s office in a state of some excitement:

'I think we're onto something, sir!' Foreman looked up from the papers on his desk:

'Oh?'

'Yes! I went through those taxi records last night...'

'Taking work home with you, Russell?' The Sergeant had the grace to blush:

'Well, we needed a break, sir! - and I didn't get time yesterday afternoon. Anyway, look at this:' he laid the computer-printed sheet in front of his superior:

'Broadbent came on duty at two o'clock, right? He was quite busy through the afternoon, one trip to Northampton, then round and about the town here, none of which interests us much. But then, look here – around five o'clock, he took this fare to Culver Street, in the Warren, the old part of what used to be the Council Estate. He called in to say he was free, but there's no pick-up for him. Then, he's got this one, from the railway station, timed at 5.17pm - must have picked it up as a casual - he drops them in Little Thornwood – that's on the old road, between Bevington and ...'

'Yes, yes, I know where it is, man! Get on with it.'

'Well, anyway, he calls in to say he's dropped them off at 5.46; and then look – the next call is at 6.55, when the office asks him to go to Taverners Drive, on the new Glebe Farm Estate, and he says he's on the old road still, near Bevington!'

'So what you're saying, Russell, is that he has an hour or more unaccounted for, and that in the immediate vicinity of the quarry?'

'Exactly, sir! And he's got previous, a conviction for violent affray when he was a teenager. He's got to be our man, hasn't he?'

'Let's not jump to conclusions, Sergeant! No-one else except the man in the Jag. saw his car there, remember.'

'Yes, but he only needed to drive a little way up that lane to hide it, you know how overgrown it is! And if Harvey Williams saw him just as he was leaving – the time would be about right, wouldn't it?'

'Okay, Russell, you might be right. I think we should pull him in for questioning, don't you?'

Downstairs, the two men collected a Ford Granada from the C.I.D. pool, and drove the short distance to Alan Broadbent's address in Denbigh Street, one of the old terraced streets off of Midland Road. They got out of the car outside the drab-looking property, and knocked on the door, which opened to reveal a man in grubby trousers and an open-necked shirt, balding, and somewhat overweight:

'Yes?'

'Mr Alan Broadbent?'

'Yeah; who's askin'?'

'I'm Detective-Sergeant Russell, and this is Detective-Inspector Foreman.'

'What d'you want?'

'We need to talk to you, Mr Broadbent; it's about the boy who was murdered a week ago, at the Bevington Quarry.'

'What the 'ell's that got to do wi' me?'

'If you'd like to come down to the station with us, we can explain, and discuss it with you.'

'I'm not sure I wanna talk to *you,* though! I tol' you, I don't know nothin' about that; I din't know the kid, or anythin'.'

'We'd still like you to come with us, please.'

'You arresting me? What the 'ell for?'

'No, sir' Foreman took a hand: 'We could, of course, but it saves the paperwork if you'd just volunteer to help us, you see.' Broadbent stiffened as if ready to throw a punch at the D.I., a furious look on his face. But then he relaxed:

'Don't suppose I got much choice, have I? Okay, then, I'll jus' get my jacket.'

Russell held the back door of the car open for the taxi-driver to get in, and then, at Foreman's gesture, got in beside him. With the D.I. driving, they headed back to the station. The journey was conducted in silence, until Broadbent broke it to tell them that he was due to start work at two; Russell reassured him that they would let Martin know to arrange for a stand-in driver, in case he couldn't make it. At the police station, the Sergeant took Broadbent down to the custody suite and went through the necessary formalities, telling their suspect that they would be down to interview him as quickly as possible; Foreman went up to the office, to go over the relevant details in his mind before the interrogation began.

The taxi-driver was left fuming quietly in a cell for quite a while. Broadbent had had a few brushes with the law in the past, but even so, he still found the wait in confinement a daunting, unnerving experience. Brought up in one of the rougher districts of Corby, when the steelworks were going full-chat and it was the kid without a Gorbals or Ulster accent who was the odd one out, he'd been a tough nut as a teenager, and his short fuse had got him into trouble a number of times. It was what had led Jacky to leave him, taking the girls with her - he loved his two daughters, but even so, his temper had a way of getting the better of him, and sitting there, with nothing to do but worry about what the two detectives wanted with him, he felt his anger growing once more.

It was some while later when the two detectives came down to lead him from his cell to an interview room. They sat at one side of the table, the suspect facing them; Foreman inserted two blank tape cassettes into the recording machine, and switched it on:

'Interview with Mr Alan Broadbent, in connection with the murder of Philip Dorman on Friday, July 5th. Interview commenced at' he glanced at his watch: '11.17 am, July 12th; present, Detective-Inspector Foreman and Detective-Sergeant Russell.'

Broadbent interrupted, bottling up his anger, knowing that to show it would only make matters worse:

'I wan' to call my ex-missus – I'm s'posed to pick me kids up in the morning, it's their weekend wi' me. I should let 'em know if they can't come; and I don't need the grief the bitch'll gi'me if I don' turn up.'

'We'll deal with that after the interview, Mr Broadbent, if that's all right? I'll make sure you can call her. Now, Sergeant?'

'Mr Broadbent, you work for Supercabs Taxi Service, of Midland Road, Grancester?' Broadbent nodded; Russell told him:

'Please answer verbally – for the tapes, you understand.'

''Kay – yeah, I work for them.'

'Last Friday, the fifth, you were driving their silver Vauxhall, the car known by the numbers of its index mark as car 142?'

'Yeah, I was.' So it was the car they were interested in?

'At about seven in the evening, that car was seen parked in the entrance to the old quarry, on the road towards Bevington village – is that correct?'

'What? Oh, yeah, tha's right! Despatch called me to go to an address on the new estate, Glebe Farm they call it, and I din't know where it was, so I pulled over to write down some directions. I was just passin', and it was a handy place to stop.'

'Where were you coming from, Mr Broadbent?'

'I'd just dropped the old biddy in Little Thornwood, down the road. I was on me way back to town.'

'I should tell you that we have the despatch records from Supercabs office; and those records show that you dropped the fare in Thornwood at about quarter to six. They called you with the Glebe Farm pick-up at around five to seven – that leaves a gap of more than an hour. Can you tell us where you were during the intervening period, please?'

Broadbent looked astounded; he sat back for a moment, his mouth open:

'What? What the 'ell are you talkin' about? I'd only just left Thornwood, I was drivin' straight back! I stopped for a coupl'a minutes, no more, to scribble down the directions, then I drove inter town!'

'That's not what the records show, Mr Broadbent.'

'Well, they're bloody-well wrong, then!'

'I'm sure you're aware that these records are required by law, and they have to be kept meticulously. Are you saying that the records kept by your employer are inaccurate, or that they have been tampered with?'

'How the 'ell should *I* know? S'not *my* job to keep 'em – I'm just tellin' yer, they're wrong, this time, tha's all. I dropped the old girl in Thornwood, and came straight back inter town, I tell you!'

'How could it come about that the records don't tally with your recollection of events?'

'I tell yer I don't know! Are you sayin' I'm wrong, I'm hidin' something? What's the bloody record say, then?'

'The despatch records suggest that you dropped the fare in Thornwood earlier, as I told you just now. Which means that you were in the vicinity of the quarry where the boy was killed, and cannot account for at least an hour of your time.'

'What? *What?* You're tryin' to say *I* killed the poor little bugger, aren't you? Don' be so bloody stupid! How old was 'e? Twelve, wan't it? For God's sake, my youngest girl's twelve, too – do you think I could cold-bloodedly kill a kid the same age as my little girl?'

'We don't know, Mr Broadbent – that's what we're trying to find out.'

'Well, go'nd check those bloody records again, then! They're wrong, I'm tellin' yer!'

'So what did happen, then?' Broadbent's anger had given way to a feeling of near-panic, now - could these two pin the kid's murder on him? Surely not - but he held no great trust in the integrity of the police force:

'Oh God, let me think – the last trip I 'ad before me break was the ole geezer; I took him from the town out ter the Warren. Despatch hadn't got nothin' for me, so I went to Jack's Caff, in Midland Road, 'ad a sandwich an' a mug o' tea. Must'a been there 'bout half an hour, mebbe more. Then I went to the railway station – you offen get casuals there, that time o' night – waited a bit fer the train, and then I got the old biddy from Thornwood, back from 'er shoppin' in London. That must'a been about quar'er past six; I dropped 'er off, then got the call for Glebe Farm on me way back.'

'You had a break, then, from about five o'clock, until you picked up this old lady at the station, at about six-fifteen?'

'Yeah, that's about it. From mebbe ten past five, I'd say.'

'But the despatch records only show the gap we've told you about, Mr Broadbent?'

'Well, they've cocked it up some'ow, 'aven't they? Here, let me see…' he pulled the printed sheet towards himself. Russell grabbed it, but let the man take it at Foreman's nod. Broadbent's brow furrowed:

'I dunno…' he ran his finger down the listed times: 'Yeah! Look 'ere! What they've done is bugger up these times! The old bird at the station – they've got 'er down as *five*-seventeen to *five*-forty-six – that should'a been *six*-seventeen to *six*-forty-six! Tha's what they've done! The rest still fits, but they've got'em down all wrong!'

'How do you suggest that could have happened, then?'

Broadbent looked up scornfully:

''ow the 'ell should I know? Like I said, it's not *my* job! These records're down to 'ooever's on the desk at the time.' He paused: ''ang on though, Ally was on that day – she's a useless little tart, all tits and no fuckin' brain, she's always buggerin' things up. I bet *she's* the one what cocked this up, too!'

'This Ally – she's the girl on the radio desk?'

'Yeah!' his voice was scornful: 'Useless little bitch! Blond-'aired bloody little tart, always doin' 'er make-up 'n paintin' 'er fingernails. She sen' me to a fare at Fourteen, Midland Road, once – you know where tha'tis, don'cher?

Russell looked at his superior, puzzled.

'It's this fuckin' cop-shop, tha's where it is! Should'a bin '*undred*'n fourteen!'

'Can we substantiate your story, Mr Broadbent?'

'Fer Christ's sake! I tol' yer, go check these fuckin' records! Yeh c'n talk to Jack, in the caff, he'll tell you I was there, I'm sure. An' the old girl – 'er name's Mrs Marshall, she lives in one o' the old cottages on the green, number four. She'll tell yer what time it was I dropped 'er off!'

'All right, Mr Broadbent, I think that'll do for now. We will check with these people, see if they can support your version of events.'

Foreman turned to his deputy, leaning back in his chair and stretching himself at the same time; he nodded, and Russell spoke into the recorder:

'Interview terminated at 12.08pm.' He switched the machine off, and extracted the two tapes.

* * *

Back in the office upstairs, their suspect safely returned to his cell, Russell turned to his superior:

'Well, what did you make of him, sir?'

'I'm not sure, Russell. He seemed really shocked when he heard that the record didn't tally with his memory of things; he doesn't strike me as a born oscar-winner, either. And if he *is* lying, why throw us a story which we should be able to knock over quite easily?'

'I see what you mean, sir. Unless we caught him on the hop, and that tale of mixed-up times was all he could come up with on the spur of the moment?'

'Maybe. If he thought he'd got away with it, that no-one had spotted him up at the quarry, he could have been totally unprepared for us to pick him up. But even so, it's a pretty weak tale; unless it's true, of course!'

'I suppose so, sir. Shall I start following up his story?'

'Yes – you take the café and Supercabs; I'll go and see the old lady in Little Thornwood – after lunch, that is!'

Chapter Fifteen

After a quick lunch from the police canteen, Russell drove down the road to Supercabs office. The girl who greeted him this time had to be the one Broadbent had described – a buxom, well-made-up blond, almost certainly of the peroxide variety, in a dress more decorative than practical. He introduced himself, and asked to speak to the proprietor, Martin. In the back office, he told the owner of the suggestion that their records were incorrect, and asked if he could interview the girl briefly. Martin confirmed that the girl had indeed been on that afternoon; he made no comment, although exasperation showed in his expression. Offering the use of his office, he went out to take over the despatch desk himself, sending her in to join the Detective-Sergeant.

The blonde flounced into the office, making a great show of crossing her legs as she perched on the edge of the desk:

'What can I do for *you,* Sergeant?' The girl's attitude was coquettish from the start, making Russell feel somewhat uncomfortable.

'We are investigating the death of a little boy, at the old quarry; Miss Morgan, isn't it?'

'That's right, Sergeant – but please call me Ally' she sniggered, unphased by his attempt to add gravity to the interview: 'It's Alice really, but that sounds so *old-fashioned,* don't you think?' Russell declined to comment, but went on:

'Well, miss, I need to check the records from last Friday with you. Mr Martin gave us a copy yesterday, but we've been told they could be wrong – some of the times may be inaccurate. Is that possible?'

'Oh no, I shouldn't think so, Sergeant – what's your name, I can't keep calling you "Sergeant" all the time?' The confident, self-satisfied smile was back.

'Russell, miss, *Sergeant* Russell. If I can show you this sheet' he passed a copy over: 'We need to check these two here' indicating the disputed times.

'They look okay to me, *Sergeant Russell.'* She was clearly more interested in playing games with him than taking the problem seriously: 'What's supposed to be wrong with them?'

'Well, miss, the driver says they should read 18.17 and 18.46, not 17.17 and 17.46. He claims he picked up that particular fare from the station about quarter past *six,* you see.'

'Oh, does he?' She looked again; suddenly her attention focussed on the figures before her, and a frown furrowed her forehead. Then the smile left her face, and she put one hand to her mouth:

'Oh, God! I think he's right! I *hate* that stupid twenty-four hour clock thing we have to use, I'm *always* getting in a muddle with it! Why can't we use *proper* time?'

'Are you sure, miss?'

'Yes, he's right – I remember, 'cos I'm supposed to go home at six, but that night Tom Skerritt, who takes over, didn't turn up, so I had to carry on for a bit. Mr Martin took over here' she pointed to the next call, the 18.55 request for the car to go to Glebe Farm 'so I could get away. I think Tom got in later. I'd just taken *that* one' pointing to the disputed call from Little Thornwood 'when he told me I could go.' Russell heaved a sigh, restraining his impulse to berate the girl for her carelessness:

'Very well, thank you, miss. I'm afraid you've caused us quite a problem, to say nothing of nearly getting Mr Broadbent arrested. I trust you'll be a bit more careful in future?'

'Oh, I will, Sergeant.' She looked up at him, the tears in her eyes beginning to make her mascara run: 'I'm so sorry, I didn't mean to cause trouble, it's just, I get so confused….'

Russell, taking pity on the girl, patted her on the shoulder:

'It's okay, miss; but please don't do it again?'

'Oh, I won't, Sergeant!'

'And you're quite certain we've got it right now?'

'Yes - quite certain. I… I'm ever so sorry….' Russell gave her an admonitory smile:

'It's all right - as long as we've got it sorted out.' He left her to recover her composure, and let himself out, telling Martin of the outcome as he passed through the outer office.

* * *

In the village of Little Thornwood, Foreman knocked on the door of number four, the Green. It was opened promptly by a diminutive, silver-haired lady in a smart dress, who looked up at the stocky detective enquiringly.

'Detective-Inspector Foreman, Ma'am. You must be Mrs Marshall?'

'*Miss* Marshall, Inspector! Won't you come in?' She waved him inside. Pointing him to a comfortable-looking, timber-framed cottage chair, she asked:

'Would you like a cup of tea, Inspector?'

'I really mustn't stop long, Miss Marshall, thank you.'

'Oh, don't be silly, Inspector! I've just boiled the kettle, it won't take a minute!' She bustled off into the kitchen, leaving the detective feeling more like an errant schoolboy waiting for the Headmistress than a senior police officer on an enquiry. She quickly returned, with a laden tea-tray, and set it down on the coffee-table between them.

'Sugar and milk, Inspector?' she asked, pouring tea into two fine bone-china cups.

'Yes, please – just the one sugar, if I may.'

The old lady handed him a cup with a smile: 'Now, to what do I owe a visit from so senior an officer, Inspector?'

'It's about the little boy who was killed last week, Miss Marshall.'

'Oh, dear, what a terrible business that was. I can't image how the poor child's family must be feeling!'

'They're very shaken and upset, of course; but they're managing, I think. It will be better for them when the Coroner can let them bury the boy's body, I expect.'

The little old lady shook her head sympathetically: 'How can *I* help you, Inspector?'

'You went to London for some shopping that Friday, I understand?'

'That's right; however did you know?'

'Your taxi-driver told us, Miss Marshall.'

'Oh, yes! Mr Broadbent; a bit uncouth sometimes, but he's not a bad man, I'm sure. He picked me up from the station that day. I'm afraid I sometimes get a bit carried away, and come home with too many packages to manage on the bus!'

'Why London, if you don't mind my asking? It's a long way to go for shopping?'

'Oh, Inspector, I used to work in the city. I was in the Civil Service, you know – nearly forty years, right from when I left university until I retired. I moved up here then for a bit of peace and quiet, but I still like to go back occasionally. I suppose I miss the bright lights!' She laughed.

'Did you retire early, Miss Marshall?'

'Now, Inspector, don't try to flatter me! I'm nearly sixty-seven, you know!' Foreman smiled: 'Can you tell me what time it was you got home that day?'

'Now let me see, it was about – oh – a quarter to seven. I'd got the 5.18 train from Euston, which gets in about ten past six – aren't these new trains we have now wonderful, they're so quick, aren't they? – so that would be about right, I think.'

'You're sure about that?'

'Oh, yes, Inspector. I had to be able to remember details and times and so on when I was working, you see.'

'All right, Miss Marshall; thank you very much, you've cleared up a difficulty for us very well. We're trying to trace anyone who was near the quarry around the time the Dorman boy was killed, you see, and there was a discrepancy about just when your cab went by there, after he left you here. But you've solved it for us very nicely.' He got up to go; she rose with him, and showed him to the door. 'Are you going to catch the man who killed that poor child, Inspector?'

'I sincerely hope so, Miss Marshall – we don't want anyone like that running around loose, do we?'

'No indeed – come and see me again if you need to, won't you?'

'I will - and thank you for the tea.'

* * *

Once again, back in the office, the two detectives conferred. Everything added up to confirm Broadbent's story; Russell had gone on to Jack's Café, not far from the taxi office, where Jack Hill, owner and chef, remembered the cab-driver coming in for his break, and placed the time at approximately that given by Broadbent, which along with Ally Morgan's shame-faced admission and Miss Marshall's statement, let the man neatly off the hook.

Foreman called down to the custody sergeant to authorise his release, and went down in person to show the man out, and apologise for the trouble he'd been put to.

Broadbent accepted his release with reasonably good grace, considering, even if his views on Alice Morgan were not repeatable - *Must be mellowing in me old age!* He couldn't resist having one jibe at the detective, though, as he stepped out through the street door:

'If you 'aven't got no-one else to pin it on, look for some poor sod what's already got a record, is that 'ow it works, Mr Foreman?' The D.I. held onto his equanimity, refusing to rise to the bait:

'Only when we're *really* desperate, Mr Broadbent.' He let the door swing shut behind the departing man.

Upstairs once more, he said to his Sergeant:

'Well, so much for our taxi-driver. Back to square one again, Russell.'

'Yes, I'm sorry about that, sir – I really thought he was our man for a bit.'

'Oh, don't worry – it looked that way at first, I agree. But right now, we don't have anywhere else to go with this case, do we?'

'I guess not, sir. We'll have to hope for some kind of lucky break, won't we?'

'That's right; but I might suggest to the Super that we go for one of these TV reconstructions, see if that will jog any memories.'

'It's got to be worth a try, sir.'

'Yes, well – they've got results before, for other forces. But I'm not sure it'll help, in this case - I think we've probably got all the witnesses we're going to get, so unless someone out there *knows* who killed the boy, and decides to come forward... Anyway, Russell, I've had enough for today, I'm off home. I'll see you in the morning.'

'Right you are, sir!'

Chapter Sixteen

For the next couple of weeks, D.I. Foreman's investigation into the murder of Philip Dorman made little progress, despite continuing efforts to push it forward in any direction which seemed to offer the hope of a solution. The lack of any real leads led to a feeling of frustration in the C.I.D. office; and of course other cases, some of them at least more readily solved, intruded upon the various officers' time.

It was on the Friday, two weeks after the detention and subsequent release of the taxi-driver, and three weeks after the boy's death, that Superintendent McFadden called the Detective-Inspector into his office:

'Come in, man, sit you down' the Scotsman indicated the chair facing his desk, and sat himself behind its imposing if out-dated bulk: 'How are you getting on in the Dorman case, Inspector?'

'Not much progress to report, I'm afraid, sir. We don't have anything solid to go on; there seems to be little I can do to push it forward.'

'I've had County HQ on to me, asking how it's going – it's quite a high profile case, lots of media interest, as you'll know. They say, do we want their help with it?' Before Foreman could reply, he went on:

'Now, don't jump the gun, man. Think about it – would their extra manpower and resources be of assistance?'

Foreman swallowed his initial annoyance at the implied slur

upon his ability to deal with the case; he hesitated before speaking:

'No, sir, I don't see how it would. It's not lack of men or funds that are holding us back, but simply that we've no decent leads. Whoever killed that kid was either very clever, or very lucky, or both. We haven't found the weapon, despite a fingertip search of the quarry and two days with the divers in the lake – the killer may have taken it with him, of course, but whatever happened to it, we haven't got it. And there's no-one with any kind of motive, unless we *are* dealing with a sex crime.'

'That has to be the case, don't you think?'

'It's the only thing that makes any kind of sense, I believe. But even then, we've no *proof,* except for the fact that the kid had no underpants on when we found him - and that could be explained in other ways.'

'There's no child-molester on record who's M.O. fits, I suppose?'

'No, sir, not that we know of. D.S. Russell's been onto Scotland Yard and the Central Records Office, without success – this is a case where that sex-offenders register that the Police Federation has been promoting would have been useful, I believe – if there was a national data-base of convicted paedophiles, it might have shown up a possible candidate. But if it was a sex attack on the boy, why are there no traces to prove it? No semen, on his body or his clothes, nothing at all to show whether he was molested in any way! Sergeant Russell suggested it might have been someone who's great thrill came from the act of killing, rather than any actual sexual activity; he could be right, I've heard about cases like that in the past. Not around here, mind, and not recently, otherwise we might have somewhere to start looking!'

He paused, and ran his hand tiredly through his iron-grey hair: 'And look at the facts, sir: No-one knew the two boys were going to the quarry that evening; and it was unusual for them to do so, according to the Moss kid. And even if someone *had* known,

Peter Moss himself had forgotten, until they got there, that he had to be home early because of their visitors, so they couldn't have expected to find Philip there on his own. So any kind of premeditation just isn't possible.'

'You're saying it was an opportunist attack?'

'It *had* to be.'

'Then who?'

'God knows! And he isn't telling, at least not yet. The only sensible hypothesis is that some pervert just happened to be passing, spotted the boy alone, and took advantage of the situation. Maybe the kid wandered down the lane to the roadside, and someone saw him there. Or our killer just went to the quarry on the off-chance of finding a kid he could grab – but that would tend to argue that it was someone local.'

'It could have been, surely?'

'It could, but I'd have thought we might have had some kind of tip-off, in that case. Let's face it, even the average criminal doesn't like child-killers. The other thing that still bothers me is that there was no sign of the boy being restrained in any way, as if he almost went along with whatever happened. He wasn't tied up, or drugged – forensics would have shown that up. I can only assume that he was held at knife-point right through, and didn't struggle in an attempt to avoid getting hurt.'

McFadden snorted: 'That's what we advise people to do, isn't it, if they're threatened – don't argue or struggle? Lot of good it did this poor wee beggar! Have you any loose ends at all?'

'No, sir. We've traced all the passing traffic on the old road, unless there's someone who hasn't come forward, who just happened to go by without anyone else seeing them. That fellow Broadbent, the taxi-driver, looked like a possible suspect, but his alibi stands up for the time we thought he could have been there; he was dropping off a Miss Marshall in Little Thornwood at the relevant time. And we've no other reason to think he could have done it.'

'Miss Alicia Marshall, with the cottage on the Green?'

'That's her.' The Superintendent's thin face split into a big grin:

'Aye, well, you can trust *her* testimony, I would think!'

'What do you mean, sir?'

'You know who she is, don't you, man?' Foreman shook his head:

'Retired Civil Servant, she told me.' McFadden burst out laughing:

'Aye, I guess you could call her that! We had a note from Special Branch, when she moved here from Hampstead, don't you remember?'

'No, sir, can't say I do. What would Special Branch have to do with an inoffensive little old lady like her?' McFadden laughed again:

'Your inoffensive little old lady, Inspector, spent the best part of forty years with MI6! She was one of our foremost spy-catchers, nine years as second-in-command of the whole damned department!'

Foreman looked as stunned as he felt, quickly going over his conversation with the spritely, refined old lady in the hope that he hadn't made too big a fool of himself. Then he grinned, and brought the discussion back to the subject in hand:

'The only sighting we have that hasn't been cleared up is the driver who passed a boy on a bike, cycling towards town, just inside the ring road. He can't give us any useful description; says the only reason he even remembered the kid is because he was pedalling hard up the slope, standing up on the pedals, and swaying about a bit so that he had to give him a wide berth. He says the boy was mid-teens, and dark-haired, but that's all he noticed. Can't even remember what he was wearing.'

'Do you think it's relevant?'

'No, I doubt it. Probably just a kid coming from Bevington or one of the other villages; doesn't want to come forward because he wasn't supposed to go into town, or something like that. I can't see a kid of that age being responsible for a callous stabbing like this, can you, sir? In the heat of a row, maybe, but Pat Swainson says the wound isn't consistent with that kind of spur-of-the-moment blow.'

'So where do we go from here, Inspector?'

'I wish I knew, sir. All we can hope is that someone, somewhere, will come forward with some fresh information that will give us the start we need. I've been talking to the BBC; they're preparing a reconstruction of events as we know them for the Crimewatch programme, to go out as soon as possible. That might jog a few memories.'

'Okay, Keith, I'll talk to County, tell 'em we're okay on our own. Let's hope the TV thing does the trick.'

'Thank you, sir. I'll keep you posted if anything comes up.' He got up, and returned to his own office.

* * *

While Foreman had been closeted with the Superintendent, Russell had had another visit from Caroline Dorman. In the Inspector's absence, he'd taken her to the D.I.'s office and got them each a cup of coffee before sitting down to talk to her. The inquest into Philip's death had been held the day previously, and resulted in a verdict from the Coroner of 'unlawful killing by person or persons unknown'. With the agreement of the police, he had released the boy's body for burial, which was why Caroline had called in to the station; after exchanging greetings, she went on:

'Philip's funeral will be next Wednesday, at three o'clock, at St Andrew's Church, Sergeant. Will you and Inspector Foreman be able to come?'

'Of course, Caroline, we wouldn't miss it!' She smiled:

'And no doubt you'll both be keeping a careful eye on the other mourners, too!'

'I'd hate to try to get anything past you, young lady! Yes, of course we will – it's not unknown for the killer to attend the funeral of his victim, so we'll be watching for anyone who maybe shouldn't be there, or looks out of place.' He held his smile for a moment, and then let his face take on a more serious expression:

'How are your family getting on now? I'm afraid we haven't had much to tell you lately.'

'Oh, not too bad, I think. Mummy's much better now; she still has the occasional quiet weep when she thinks we don't know, but she's coping quite well. Daddy is still in a bit of a mess, though, I'm afraid. He's getting better, but he and Pip did so many things together that it's difficult for him to get away from the memories. They've talked about moving house – I think maybe they should, it would make things easier.'

'What about your little brother, Andrew isn't it?' She sighed:

'He doesn't really understand, poor kid; he's only eight. He seems okay, but then all of a sudden he'll sort of forget, and ask where Philip is - and then he remembers that his big brother isn't there for him any more, and bursts out crying. That sets Daddy off as well, and we all have a sort of group cry for a while! We've tried to explain to him that Philip has gone on ahead to Heaven, that he'll be waiting for us to join him one day, but I'm not sure how much he's taken in.'

'I expect a lot of Philip's friends will come?'

'I hope so, it would do Mummy and Daddy good to think that they'll all miss him, too. And now that school has broken up, they should be able to. Dr Frankham has asked if he and some of the other teachers can come, so there should be quite a crowd there. It would tickle Pip – he'd come out with some silly quip about so many people coming to say goodbye to him. He was a cheeky, aggravating little beggar – but I do miss him so…' Tears welled up in her eyes; the Sergeant got up and came around the desk, and put a comforting hand on her shoulder.

After a few minutes, the teenager sniffed, and cleared her

throat: 'I'm sorry, Sergeant. If I can't control my feelings here, what sort of exhibition will I make of myself on Wednesday?'

'Don't worry, you'll be fine. And my name's David, drop the 'Sergeant', please!' She smiled tearfully up at him:

'Thank you - David. Can I ask, have you got a family?' He smiled happily at this thought:

'Almost – if you mean children! My wife's expecting our first at the moment. He's due in October, at least the hospital say it'll be a boy. If they're right, we're going to call him Daniel.' The girl's face cleared, and she smiled in genuine pleasure:

'Oh, that's wonderful! I'm so happy for you both – I hope everything goes well.'

'I'm sure it will; they're very good at the General.'

She sat in silence for a moment; Russell returned to his seat. Then she raised her bright eyes to his again:

'Do you think you will catch Philip's murderer, David?' He drew a deep breath, and let it out slowly:

'Honestly, Caroline, I don't know. We're stuck at the moment, with nothing to go on that might lead us to him. Inspector Foreman has been talking about getting the case on the TV, on one of the programmes where they show a reconstruction of events, you know? In the hope it might bring out some new information.'

'If there's anything I can do to help, tell me, please. I can't bear the thought that a man who could casually stab a little boy is walking around free! I'm sure my family would say the same.'

'Don't worry, we will.' He paused, and reached for a sheet of notepaper that lay on the desk. raising his eyes to the girl's again, he spoke hesitantly:

'Caroline - there's something I haven't told you…'

'Oh no! What?'

'No, no, nothing like that! We had one call, after your press conference…'

'Oh, that! Please don't remind me!' Russell grinned at her:

'You don't need be ashamed of that – I'd be willing to bet

that you had every man in the country between fifteen and ninety a little bit in love with you after that went out on the news! And it certainly awakened a few consciences, to judge from the calls we received. Anyway, there was this one call, from a woman who runs some big modelling agency in London, wanting to get in touch with you.'

'With *me?*'

'That's right. She called us rather than trying to trace you direct because, as she put it, of the delicacy of the situation you and your family are in. I spoke to her, and I promised I'd pass it on when I thought it would be right.'

'Pass what on, David?'

'Well, her agency is looking for a girl, for some photographs and the like, for a new advertising campaign for one of the big cosmetics firms. She did tell me the name, but I can't remember it now – my wife would know it, I'm sure! She wants someone new, a new face, as she put it, that isn't already known. Anyway, she wants to talk to you about it.'

'*Me?* Why?'

'Be honest with yourself, Caroline – you're a very pretty girl. And she obviously thinks you'd be suitable.'

'But me, modelling? Don't be silly!' Russell grinned at her:

'Here, take her phone number and address, think about it. It can't hurt to talk to her, surely? You can always say no.' The girl snorted derisively:

'All right, pass it over! But I don't promise to even call her.'

'That's up to you – I've done what I promised her, and given it to you.'

She stood up, and picked up her jacket:

'I'd better go and leave you to get on. We'll see you both on Wednesday?'

'I'm sure you will – I'll tell the Inspector. Goodbye for now; and give our regards to your parents, won't you?'

Chapter Seventeen

Just before three o'clock on Wednesday, July 31st, the two detectives drew up outside the gates of St Andrew's Churchyard, in Foreman's silver Volvo. A large number of cars were already parked there, including the matching black Mercedes-Benz hearse and limousine which had brought Philip's coffin and his family for the private church ceremony. Getting out of the estate car, Foreman went into the church to join the invited mourners, while Russell waited outside with the growing crowd of other friends and acquaintances, and representatives of the press. Among the gathering were a number of boys from Philip's form at Elwood Priors, all in their navy-blue uniforms as a mark of respect to their dead friend, along with several of the teachers; Dr Frankham was inside with the immediate family.

At the back of the crowd, where Russell didn't spot him straight away, stood Carl Evans, also wearing his school uniform. Seeing the Sergeant again at the school that day had been a real shock; the boy had thought the police were done with him. But he'd heard no more – it seemed that they'd accepted his story, that he was off the hook. Since then, his secret pride at having apparently hoodwinked a senior police officer and his whole team had given him a new, more outgoing view on life, apparent to his indifferent school-fellows in his sudden tendency to smile, something which had been a rare event before. He was still confused about his own sexuality, frequently finding himself subject to those exciting, frightening desires for further encounters with younger boys, but keeping himself sternly in check. He'd forced himself to come today, not wanting to see Philip's family in their grief, but feeling that it was his duty, to his form and to the school, to be there; and afraid that his absence would be noted, remarked upon.

* * *

At last, the formal part of the service over, the coffin emerged into the inappropriately glorious sunshine, and was borne to the waiting graveside, followed by John and Kate Dorman, their remaining two children, and other members of the family and close friends. Peter Moss, dry-eyed but looking very solemn, was accompanied by his father, a comforting hand on his shoulder.

Gathered at the graveside, the priest began the interment ceremony. The Dormans stood to one side; Philip's father in a smart black suit, his wife in a simple black dress. Caroline, too, wore a black dress, which in other circumstances would have made a very attractive picture, setting off her flowing blond hair and bright blue eyes; and little Andrew, looking bewildered as well as sad, in a plain white shirt and black shorts, with a simple black tie. Russell stepped forward to his superior's side.

As the priest picked up a handful of soil, and began to intone the inevitable, awful words: 'Dust to dust, ashes to ashes…' the eight-year-old broke free from his mother's restraining hands, and went up to the edge of the grave. Looking down solemnly at the gleaming oak box, he whispered:

'Goodbye, Philip – I'll see you in heaven one day, please wait for me.'

As is the way with a high, child's voice, his words carried clearly to everyone. There was a moment of total silence; even the priest's voice had faltered as the little boy's words cut across

123

his ritual intonation. Kate Dorman closed her eyes and bowed her head as her husband's arm tightened convulsively around her shoulders; Caroline, in control up until then, began to weep openly. Peter Moss turned and buried his face in his father's jacket, and several of the other boys from the school were fighting back their tears. Of the adults in the crowd, most found they had to avert their gaze or look away for a moment.

The priest picked up his thread, and continued the service of interment to its conclusion. When it was all over, many among the crowd wanted to speak to the family, offering words of condolence or support; Foreman waited until they began to disperse before approaching. Kate Dorman caught his eye:

'Inspector! Thank you for coming.' As she spoke, Foreman saw Caroline from the corner of his eye, taking Russell by the arm and steering him away.

'I'm glad to be here, Mrs Dorman. I only wish it wasn't necessary.' He turned to John Dorman:

'No man should ever have to bury his own son, sir. I can't tell you how sad I feel for your loss.' Dorman nodded; he sounded choked as he replied:

'Thank you, Inspector – I'm glad it's done, now.'

'Are you any nearer catching the man who killed Philip, Inspector?' Kate asked. He shook his head:

'Not really. It would be wrong to give you all false hopes; we don't have any solid leads at the moment. There's the hope that when the BBC do their reconstruction, we may get the tip we need; but right now, we're groping in the dark.' She reached out and put her hand on his upper arm:

'Please don't worry on our account – we want to see this brute behind bars, of course, but we do understand how difficult your job must be. We're grateful for the way you and Sergeant Russell have kept us informed all the time – you'll carry on doing so, won't you?'

'Of course, Mrs Dorman. And you can rest assured, we shan't

give up – the case will remain open until we've got the man who killed your boy.'

Andrew, standing front of his mother, piped up: 'I'm going to be a policeman when I grow up.' Foreman squatted down, his eyes level with the little boy's, as the child went on: 'I want to help stop bad men doing things like what happened to Philip.' The Inspector smiled at the boy:

'When you're old enough, when you leave school, if you want to be a policeman, you come and talk to me. I'll help you get started. And I promise you, Andrew, we're going to get the man who took your brother away from you, whatever it takes – all right?' The little boy nodded; Foreman stood up again.

Kate Dorman smiled at the policeman, and turned to walk with her husband and younger son to the waiting limousine. As she did so, she caught sight of Carl, standing alone near the grave, and spoke to her husband:

'You go ahead, John; I'll just be a moment.'

'Hello – Carl, isn't it?'

At the sound of the voice behind him, the teenager spun around, to be confronted with the mother of the boy he had killed.

'Thank you for coming today, Carl. Philip has told us a lot about you.' she smiled at the boy, who seemed to be tongue-tied.

'Th-that's okay, Mrs Dorman' he stammered: 'He was a good kid, we'll miss him.'

'Thank you. Philip always said how good you were to him and the others, keeping an eye on them without being too stern or strict. I'm grateful to you for looking after my boy.'

The sixteen-year-old felt a sudden surge of guilt and remorse swelling within him like the rising magma in a volcano, trying to burst free of its constraint. At that moment, he came so close to blurting it all out, to telling her of his guilt and throwing himself upon her mercy. But he took a grip on himself, telling himself that that wouldn't undo what he'd done, that to spend the rest of his life in prison would serve no purpose at all. Philip was dead;

destroying his own future would be nothing but a futile gesture - he just looked at the black-haired lady, in her plain black dress, as she smiled at him and turned to go. As she walked away, he saw Dr Frankham approaching:

'It was good of you to come today, Evans. And to wear the uniform. But we've come to expect such consideration and thoughtfulness from you, haven't we? Well done, my boy. I'll see you in September.'

'Yes, sir. Thank you, sir.'

* * *

As Caroline took Russell's arm and led him away from her family and the D.I., she smiled up at him out of tear-reddened eyes. Neither felt it necessary to speak at first, but when they were out of earshot, she asked:

'So how is your search for Philip's murderer going, David?'

'Not as well as we'd like. As I told you the other day, we just seem to have so little to go on; but it seems the BBC are going to do a reconstruction for the Crimewatch programme, so maybe that'll kick-start things again for us.'

'I hope so. Mummy and Daddy are putting a brave face on things, but it would make so much difference for them to know that Pip's killer was safely locked up.' she hesitated: 'Is another little boy going to have to die to give you the break you need, David?' Her words were soft and without recrimination, but sorrowful, almost hopeless.

'Oh, Dear God, I hope not, Caroline. It would be dishonest not to admit that that could be just what it *might* take, though. But I can promise you, we'll never let go until we *have* got him, however long it takes.'

Their strolling had brought them to a bench by the side of the church; they sat side by side in silence for a brief period. Caroline looked up into the Sergeant's eyes:

'There's something I haven't said to anyone, David. But I need to say it – will you listen for me?'

'Of course' he replied, puzzled.

'When Philip was killed – I'd already finished my term at college. But I stayed on in Bristol, with my friends. One of them was having a party, that Saturday, to celebrate her engagement. Now, I see how selfish I was. What if I'd come straight home, David? Philip might still be alive, don't you see?'

Russell saw the tears welling up in her eyes, and felt a wave of sympathy and affection for the beautiful girl beside him, in her desperate grief. She went on:

'If I'd been home, perhaps he and Peter wouldn't have gone to the quarry that day, he might have wanted to stay home with me, or go shopping instead. If I hadn't been so selfish, he might not have died!'

Russell slipped his arm around the girl's shoulders, and shushed her as she began to weep: 'Don't be so silly, Caroline. None of this is your fault, you couldn't have prevented it. You know what young boys are like, they go their own way, do their own things, whatever the rest of us think or want. Even if you'd been at home, Philip would have still wanted to be with his friend. It was a glorious day, remember – he wouldn't have wanted to stay indoors, they'd have gone for the fresh air and sunshine, older sisters notwithstanding!'

He held the girl's slim shoulders until they stopped trembling, and she dabbed her eyes with his handkerchief. She handed it back with a rueful smile:

'You're right, I suppose. He was always the independent sort. But I needed someone to say it, to convince me I wasn't just making excuses, letting myself off the hook. Thank you, David.'

Silence fell, until she turned to him again:

'About the note you gave me, the other day?'

'The agency thing, you mean?'

'Yes. I haven't called them, at least not yet. Do you think –

I mean, I'm not sure whether I should call them…'

'How do you mean?'

'Well, I suppose, they took the trouble to try to contact me, so they must want to talk to me; but it seems – I don't know, wrong, somehow. I mean, suppose something were to come of it – it would feel as if I was profiting from Philip's death, and I couldn't *do* that.' Russell thought for a moment before replying;

'I'm not so sure, Caroline. As you say, the woman did seem at some pains to reach you; and to her credit, she rang us to see what we thought rather than trying to get to you direct, which she could easily have done. I would say that you really do owe it to her to talk to her – after all, you can still say no to whatever she wants, can't you?' He paused: 'And if something *does* come of it, perhaps you should think of it rather as a legacy from Philip. It wouldn't have happened without him, so maybe it can be something to remind you of him, in years to come?'

The girl looked at Russell, her blue eyes smiling:

'You always say the right thing, don't you? You should have been a counsellor, or a priest maybe, rather than a policeman! I'll talk to them – but no promises, mind. I've got a degree to finish, remember.' Her smile faded: 'I read somewhere that, when we die, we don't really go altogether, but live on in the memories of those who loved us. Maybe Philip is the lucky one – We'll all get old and wrinkly, but he'll always be twelve years old, playing in the sunshine…'

Silence held them again for a moment, Russell finding himself deeply affected at the picture her words conjured up in his mind. Then she got to her feet; he stood up with her:

'I must dash, Mummy and Daddy will be wondering where I've got to!' With that, she hurried away to join her family in the waiting limousine.

* * *

When the Dormans had left him, Foreman looked around for his Sergeant, and spied him talking to Caroline. As he waited for them to finish their conversation, he became aware that he was not the only one watching them – some distance away a man he recognised as a press photographer was also gazing in their direction. As Foreman watched him, he cautiously raised his camera and took several shots of the girl and the policeman sitting together on the bench, capturing the moment when Russell had put his arm around her shoulders. Quietly, the Inspector walked over, approaching the man from behind. He reached up to tap him on the shoulder; the man turned:

Foreman looked up into wide brown eyes, some distance above his own – compared to his five feet nine, the photographer stood at least six feet four or five. Very quietly, he said:

'If any of those pictures get published, I will see to it that your paper never gets near any police briefing in this county as long as I'm on the force. I think that family have had enough trouble for a while, don't you?'

The man bridled; but then he relaxed, and smiled:

'You're right, Inspector! And I can imagine the innuendo some of the writers might put on a shot of your Sergeant with his arm around a pretty girl! Here:' He quickly rewound the film, popped it out of the camera, and handed it to the officer:

'Take it! It's a new film, there's nothing else on there. Do what you like with it!'

'Thank you, young man – you've restored my faith in the integrity of the press. When I've got something good for you, I'll give you the tip, shall I?'

'Hey, that would be great! Thanks, Inspector.' He turned to leave, but then looked back:

'And would you tell the family… I know we must seem like a pack of wolves to them sometimes, but some of us at least are truly sorry for their loss?'

'I'll tell them, son. And thanks.'

The photographer glanced across at Caroline, still sitting with Russell on the bench:

'She's really beautiful, isn't she?'

'She is, son. Maybe one day she'll laugh again.'

The newspaperman walked away; Caroline hurried to join her parents. Russell strolled over to his superior, and was surprised to be handed a film cassette:

'What's this, sir?'

'Liberated from the wolf-pack, Russell. Get it developed, if you like.'

The two detectives turned and walked slowly in silence to their car, feet crunching softly on the gravel of the cemetery path.

PART TWO

CRAIG

THE DEMON AWAKES

NOVEMBER 1994

Chapter Eighteen

OXFORD..... OXFORD…........ OXFORD……........ OXFORD.
The nameplates attached to the platform lamp-standards flicked
by the carriage windows at an ever-decreasing pace, until at last
one came to rest opposite the door. Craig Johnson was already
on his feet, hold-all and duffle-bag in hand; he opened the door,
and stepped down into the chill November evening.

Just thirteen years old, Craig was on the small side for his
age, even wrapped up in his well-padded anorak. Of what they
like to call mixed descent, his complexion was a warm brown,
the colour of milk chocolate; big dark eyes looked out from a
face that his mother always described as cute, with high
cheekbones and a pert, up-turned nose, under a thick mop of
glossy, jet-black hair which fell in heavy waves to his shoulders
– he looked a lot like his mother, and, although she was getting
on now, over thirty, even, Craig still thought she was a real beauty!
Her grandfather had been a black American G.I., in England
during the Second World War.

Around him, a crowd of commuters were descending from
the train, and beginning to flow with the inexorability of the tide
towards the ticket-collector and the exit. Craig paused, hitching
his duffle-bag onto one shoulder – he looked at the people rushing
past, and felt a surge of envy for them. They all had somewhere
to go; all he had was somewhere to come from. But at least he
was out, away from the hell that his home had become since that

bastard had moved in; and this time, he wasn't going back!

He stood, collecting his thoughts. A twinge of loneliness assailed him, as he thought of his mother – by now, she'd be wondering where he was... But no! That was what had defeated him before! Twice, he'd reached the end of his tether, and left. And both times, after a night or two kipping in doorways in the West End, the feeling of aloneness had beaten him, and he'd gone crawling back home, to a tearful but heartfelt hug from his Mum, and another outpouring of scorn and ridicule from Stan. He couldn't take any more of it, he just couldn't!

When it had been just him and his Mum, they'd shared a happy if hard-up existence; even with the benefits she'd been entitled to, they'd had to scrimp and save, but their flat in the dingy back-streets off of Sussex Gardens had at least been a cheerful place. Then, three years ago, when he was ten, she'd met Stan. She loved Stan, Craig understood that; and he was usually okay to *her*. But he had this fixation that the way to get the best out of a kid was to ride him all the time, to ridicule him, make him feel small and useless at every opportunity. Not a day went by without Stan finding some way to get at the boy. Craig wasn't stupid – he did well at school, as a rule. But every school report got Stan going – he'd pick on the boy's faults, and belittle his merits, until a report that he'd been proud to show his Mum became a source of hatred and torment.

And this Friday morning, he'd let slip that they had a maths test after lunch. Okay, so maths wasn't his strong subject, he struggled with the complexities of algebra and trigonometry! Stan had grabbed the opportunity to make fun of him again, telling him how useless he was, how he'd never amount to anything as long as he had a hole up his backside. Craig had lost his temper, and told his step-father to shut up and leave him alone – only the fact that Stan was already late for work had saved him from a beating there and then, and his parting words had been 'Just you wait 'til I get home – I'll deal with you then!'

And Stan wouldn't forget. When he got in from work, the first thing he'd do was give Craig what he called 'a good slapping for his cheek'. So he'd set off for school as usual, but then slipped back home after his mother had left for her job – she did a lunchtime stint in one of the local pubs – packed his holdall, stuffed his sleeping bag into the duffle-bag, taken all the money he'd got put aside, hidden in his room, and left.

Rather than head for the West End again, he'd gone to Paddington Station, with the thought of heading somewhere else; he knew from experience that there was no welcome awaiting him in the crowded, lonely avenues of W.1. Looking down the available destinations, he'd picked Oxford – it had a nice feel to it, somehow, and he had the impression that it would be a wealthy city, somewhere he might manage to make a new start for himself. And now, here he was...

What to do next? Where should he go? The City centre, probably – but he didn't even know where that was, which way from the Station! He'd have to ask someone. He looked around; the crowd was thinning now, just a few people waiting at the ticket barrier. He hitched up his duffle-bag again, and began to walk toward the exit.

As he headed towards the barrier, Craig became aware of someone walking alongside him...

Chapter Nineteen

The Porter smiled to himself as the young couple walked past him under the bright platform lights: Young love! Undergrads? Probably – they had that bright but slightly unkempt feel about them. The boy, no more than twenty, not especially tall or noticeable, dark haired and dark eyed, in his jeans and donkey-jacket; the girl, an inch or two the taller, hand in hand with him, her bag in the other hand, striking rather than really pretty with her soft grey-green eyes and mane of dark auburn hair, her slenderness concealed by the heavy coat she wore against the chill of the November evening. The kind who, in another twenty years time, you might call a handsome woman.

They passed the younger, half-caste boy as he stepped down from the train, and walked on to the next carriage, stopping by an already-open door. The girl turned to face her companion:

'Bye, Stevie – look after yourself. I'll be back on Sunday.' Her Black Country accent sounded out of place in the University City; the young man pulled her to him and kissed her briefly on the lips:

'Take care of yourself, Kerry. And give my love to your Mum – tell your Dad I hope he's soon up and about again. Call me, okay?'

'I will, my love.' She smiled, gazing into the boy's eyes for a moment. She kissed him back, quickly, and turned and stepped onto the train. Dropping her bag into a vacant seat, she returned to the closed door, waving to him as the train began to move, waving until he fell behind and disappeared into the crowd.

When he could no longer see the girl, Steven Evans turned away, towards the station exit. In the third year of his Civil Engineering degree, he'd dropped his first name when he'd moved to Oxford to take up his place at the University, preferring to be known by his second name in an almost subconscious attempt to leave his childhood and adolescence behind him; an attempt to become the normal young man he aspired to be, to turn his back on the strange and frightening cravings that sometimes still beset him.

It was four years and more since Philip Dorman had died. Carl had spent his last year at Elwood Priors focussing entirely upon his studies in a deliberate closing of his mind to what had happened, to the dreadful urges that had led to the other boy's death. But despite his single-minded concentration, despite the mental blinkers he so carefully maintained, the desire to be around younger boys sometimes became so powerful as to leave him feeling physically weak and psychologically drained. The television reconstruction had been a bad time for him, destroying once more his gradually-returning equilibrium, bringing back his fears of discovery, even if at the same time it had reawakened that burgeoning sense of his own cleverness in pulling the wool over everyone's eyes - but, despite the renewed interest in the case, there had been no result, no arrest, no solution.

He had deliberately kept away from all the younger boys; the Headmaster had agreed to relieve him of his form-prefect duties, thinking only that the trauma of the Dorman boy's murder had upset the sixth-former more than he wanted to admit. The result had been four top A-levels, and the ability to select any university he wanted to attend. The choice of Oxford had been almost automatic – he'd wanted to go there since he'd first gone to The Priors, and heard the Head speak of it in glowing terms; Frankham himself had studied there, gaining his PhD in Chemistry before turning to teaching. And the change of location had given him the opportunity to become Steve Evans, to leave Carl, the teenager of dubious and dangerous sexuality, behind him.

And, as Steve Evans, he'd quickly settled to the academic life, rooming in college until he'd been introduced to Kerry, just completing her degree in Archaeology, early in his second year. They'd soon fallen in love; or perhaps more accurately, she'd fallen in love with him. Evans wasn't really sure he even understood what the word meant, in this context – he'd loved his mother, of course, he knew what that meant, but this idea of love between man and woman? He was very fond of Kerry – she was great fun to be with, and they shared a number of interests, but did he really love her? Oh, they shared a regular sex life, of course, and sex with her was an exhilarating experience – he'd been a virgin until she'd got him alone at a party one night. And she was a good-looking girl, with her spectacular auburn hair and lovely eyes – and she had a superb body: But was he in love with her? He didn't know.

Even since they'd been living together, he'd occasionally caught himself looking, taking too much interest in a nice-looking young boy in the street or the supermarket. And Kerry liked to swim – they spent quite a lot of time, when the weather allowed, at the open-air swimming baths at Hinksey. He had often to force himself to focus on her, surprising her with his attentiveness, to keep his mind and his eyes from straying to the pre-teenage kids in their swimming-trunks. But, all in all, he'd been quite pleased with himself. Maybe the urges were still there at times, but he felt he had a grip on them, had himself well under control. And to observers, with his lovely girlfriend, he seemed like the epitome of happy, heterosexual student man.

But then, as he began to walk to the station exit, he saw the half-caste kid standing there, bags in hand. He'd seen the boy from the corner of his eye as they'd passed him earlier – now, as he walked up behind him, the kid swung his duffle-bag onto his shoulder, and started to walk in the same direction as himself. The youngster looked uncertain of where he was going, almost lost. No-one had come to meet him – was he expected in Oxford, did he in fact have somewhere to go? Or was he alone, and unexpected? That was a sleeping bag by the look of it, poking out of the duffle-bag over the kid's shoulder…

Not even thinking about what he was doing, he fell into step beside the boy, and glanced over at him: He was a remarkably good-looking kid – a cute, almost pretty, face, with a fine jaw, a pert, up-turned nose, and big dark eyes with lashes long enough to be the envy of any girl. And that heavy mop of black hair, tumbling in tousled waves to his shoulders… Eleven or twelve, maybe? Carl's conscience kicked him, hard: *Get away from here! Leave the kid alone! You've almost beaten this demon, don't let it back into your life now…* But the boy's closeness, his beauty, his vulnerability, was not going to be denied…

'Hello!' The boy looked around, surprised to be greeted; his reply was non-committal…

Chapter Twenty

'Hello!' A voice spoke, and Craig looked around; the youngish man, maybe around twenty, smiled at him out of dark brown eyes:

'Hello.' Craig's reply was non-committal.

'Are you okay? You look sort of lost.'

'Well – I'm new here. Can you tell me, which way do I go for the town centre?'

They reached the barrier; Craig handed over his ticket, and his companion gave the railwayman a platform ticket. In the lobby beyond, the man turned to Craig:

'Listen – I was about to grab a coffee. There's a little café just 'round the corner, why don't you join me, and I can direct you from there? It's nice and warm, too!'

Craig hesitated: He thought of all the admonishments from school, and his Mum, about not talking to strangers – but the thought of a warm café, and a mug of hot coffee, was very tempting; and after all, what could this guy get up to in a public place like that? And his manner seemed quiet, easy-going…

'Okay, why not? I'm not in a hurry.' The young man smiled, stuck his hand out, and shook Craig's:

'I'm Carl, Carl… Stevens. Pleased to meet you!' Craig was sharp enough to catch the slight hesitation in the man's introduction – was that his real name? Be careful! But it prompted him to be equally cautious with his own identity; as he began to reply, Craig cast about for a different surname. The image that flashed before his inner vision was that of the gorgeous blond girl on those advertising hoardings he'd seen from the train – she'd been on the telly lately, too, advertising those cosmetics – he didn't know *her* name, of course, but:

'My name's Craig Lauder – it's good to meet you.'

They walked around from the station to the café in a slightly awkward silence. Inside, the warm, steamy atmosphere was a welcome contrast from the chill of the street; the place looked bright and clean, but vaguely seedy, the kind of roadside café where you might expect to find lorry-drivers, or railwaymen on a mid-shift break.

Craig took a seat at the table his companion indicated, while Stevens went to the counter and came back with two mugs of hot, dark coffee and a Mars Bar apiece. He seated himself opposite the boy, tipped two spoonfuls of sugar into his coffee, and sat looking into Craig's eyes until the boy began to feel uncomfortable:

'So, Craig – what is it you're running away from?'

'What makes you think I'm running away?' He bridled defensively, but Stevens just smiled:

'Well, You're on your own, in a strange town, you don't know your way around, and no-one's come to meet you, so you're not running *to* anything, are you? And I get the feeling that you're not too sure just what you're doing here, or where you're going to go next. Seems to me that what's important is what you've left behind you. Tell me I'm wrong?'

Craig looked at the man for a moment – was he really that easy to see through? He shook his head, and for the first time returned Stevens' smile:

'No, you're right. I've... got problems at home – my stepfather. I just had to get away.'

'Why Oxford?'

'Dunno, really. It sounds like a good place; and they won't

think to look for me here, they'll think I've gone to the West End of London again.'

'You've done this before?'

'Yeah – once or twice. But this time, I'm not going back, ever!'

Carl sat back and looked at the boy for a minute or two; then he asked:

'How old are you, Craig?'

'Thirteen – last month.'

'Would you let me help you? I've just seen my girlfriend off for the weekend, her father's not well, she's gone home to see him. I've got a bed-settee thing in our lounge, I could put you up for a couple of nights on that, maybe give you a chance to begin to find you way around. You'll have to be gone before Kerry gets back, of course – she'll be home sometime on Sunday. It's warm and comfortable, and we've got food in the cupboard. Better than sleeping in the station or somewhere, in that!' he indicated Craig's sleeping bag, poking out of the duffle-bag.

'I don't know – I've only just met you, you could be... oh, you know!' He shrugged his shoulders; Stevens laughed:

'So could you! I don't throw out invitations to just anyone, but you strike me as a decent kid, and you need a bit of a boost right now, don't you? I promise not to bury you in the garden, if you promise not to pinch the family silver, okay?'

'Well, okay, if you're sure. It's kind of you to offer.'

'Come on then, drink up. The car's just down the street.'

They finished their coffees, and got up from the table. Stevens led the way from the café; a few yards along the street outside, he unlocked a nondescript maroon Ford Escort and got into the driver's seat. Reaching across, he unlocked the passenger door and pushed it open. Craig slung his bags into the back seat, and got in.

They drove around the town centre onto the Abingdon Road, and headed out of town, until Stevens swung right into one of the many back-streets and pulled up outside a large house, which had apparently been converted into one-floor flats for students. He unlocked the front door, and they went into the ground-floor flat. Inside, he told Craig to dump his stuff in the living-room, and went through to the kitchen. Rummaging in the fridge, he called out:

'Pizza and chips be all right?'

'Yeah, fine!'

Craig sat and relaxed on the settee, while his host busied himself in the kitchen. He felt drained, exhausted; he'd been living on his nerves all day, ever since he'd decided to get out, and now that that was done, a feeling of anticlimax had set in. The flat was warm, the settee comfortable, and he was almost dozing when Stevens called out that the food was ready, to come through to the kitchen and eat.

Over the meal, Carl told the boy that he was an under-graduate, studying for a degree in civil engineering; Kerry, his girlfriend, was doing post-graduate work in archaeology. Then, he coaxed the whole story from Craig, of how Stan had taken over what had been a happy home, and made it hell for the youngster, and how, after a couple of abortive attempts, this time he intended never to go back, to somehow make a new life for himself – if not here in Oxford, then he'd move on again, and try somewhere else. At the end of the meal, Stevens sat back and looked thoughtfully at the boy for a while. Then he said:

'Listen – I know someone who might be able to help you better than I can. The wife of a friend of mine runs a kind of hostel, for young people who've got nowhere else to go. I'll have a word with her tomorrow, and see if they can't take you in – if they can, they'll look after you, get you into a good school, all that sort of thing. It'll depend on whether they've got any room, of course, but I can ask, if you like?'

Craig looked up – it sounded too good to be true! That would be just the kind of break he needed, if it came off; but:

'Would they want to let my folks know where I am?'

'Not necessarily – I think they leave that to you. There's a phone, so you could maybe call your mother, just to let her know you're okay; you needn't tell her where you are, if you don't want to.'

Craig thought for a moment – could he really be that lucky, or was this guy leading him on, for some reason? But what on Earth could he gain from telling that kind of tale if it wasn't true?

'Yeah – okay, if you don't mind. Like you say, it would be great, if they can give me somewhere to live, even if it's only for a while.'

'That's settled, then – I'll talk to her tomorrow.' He glanced up at the clock on the wall:

'It's half past eight – you must be knackered! Why don't you go and have a good hot shower? I'll make some coffee – or hot chocolate, if you prefer? – when you've finished, and we'll relax and watch telly or something. Have you got some pyjamas?' Craig shook his head – he'd been anticipating sleeping outside, in the sleeping bag, in his clothes, he hadn't bothered to pack pyjamas. Carl laughed:

'Okay, don't worry! I don't usually wear any, but I've got a pair you can borrow. They'll be a bit big, but they're the old-fashioned sort with a string round the waist, so you'll be able to pull them tight. You might have to turn the legs up a bit, though!' He disappeared into the bedroom.

A few moments later, he reappeared holding a pair of green and white striped pyjama trousers, and held them out to Craig:

'There you go – I can't find the jacket anywhere, I'm afraid. Enjoy your shower - there's a clean bath-towel in there already – use that. Come back in here when you're done, and I'll make that chocolate!'

Craig took the proffered garment and went through into the bedroom. Closing the door, he stripped off, stepped into the bathroom and under the shower. Boy, it felt good! The hot water streaming down his body seemed to wash away with it all the tension and stress of the day; after ten minutes, he felt relaxed and cosy. Turning off the tap, he stepped out, dried himself thoroughly with the towel from the rail, and slipped into the pyjama trousers. He thought about finding a T-shirt to wear from among his own clothes – but he was quite warm, and too tired to bother.

In the living-room, Carl Evans sat back on the settee, his mind in a whirl. After four years of living a normal, straight life, even to the point of having a live-in girlfriend, the moment she'd gone away for the weekend, he'd picked up this kid on pure impulse! What was he going to do now? Common sense told him to keep his hands off the boy, get rid of him as soon as possible, and submerge again the feelings that he'd aroused, all unwittingly, in his host. But he was such a cute kid – just thirteen – and that gorgeous brown skin – and he'd be out of the bathroom in a minute, wearing nothing but pyjama trousers…

When Craig returned to the living-room, he found the man he knew as Carl Stevens lying back in the settee, his eyes closed. They opened as he heard the boy enter the room; he looked up and smiled:

'Feel better? Coffee or Chocolate?' Craig grinned:

'Much better! Coffee, please – two sugars?'

'Right! Sit down here, I'll be back in a mo.'

Craig sat on one end of the settee – the only other seating in the room was an office-type chair, beside a desk against the back wall which had a personal computer standing upon it. A few minutes passed, and Stevens returned, carrying two steaming mugs. He handed one to Craig, who took a sip, and grimaced. Carl laughed:

'Sorry, I should have warned you! Kerry is into saving the planet – the coffee we have is from one of those co-operative ventures, in Venezuela. It's a bit strong!'

Craig tried it again, and smiled:

'It's okay, really, not bad – just different to what I'm used to!' He didn't know that Stevens had slipped a good shot of Vodka into his mug, making the coffee a little strong to cover it up.

'There's nothing on the TV – how about some music?' asked Carl.

'Yeah, okay.'

'Do you like classical?'

'I don't know any, really.'

'Okay – try this, it's quite easy going. Bach, the Brandenburg Concertos.'

Selecting a tape cassette, he slipped it into the stereo, switched it on, and came to sit next to the boy on the settee. Neither spoke for a while – Craig found the Eighteenth-Century music surprisingly easy to listen to, especially in his relaxed state. He sipped at his coffee, and snuggled down comfortably in the settee, again coming close to dozing in the warm room.

Some time later, the tape finished, and silence fell. Craig stirred from his half-sleep, and realised that, sometime while the music was playing, Carl had slipped an arm around his bare shoulders. Feeling warm and cosy, he didn't trouble shrug it off, but settled himself again. He'd finished his coffee, and the Vodka had made him all the more relaxed, and dampened his inhibitions into the bargain – which was exactly what Carl had intended.

Somewhere deep in his mind, a feeling of alarm stirred as Craig felt the man's free hand on his chest, gently stroking his bare skin, tracing the lines of his rib-cage, touching his nipples, exploring his shoulders. But to move or protest would be too much effort; he was too comfortable, too sleepy, to bother. And anyway, it felt quite nice, really – like the warm, relaxing caress of his mother's touch, when he'd been small...

Eventually, realising that the youngster curled up by his side was all but asleep, Carl lifted the hand which had been laying softly over the boy's heart and slipped his other arm carefully from behind his head. He raised his head, and sat looking down at the boy, his gaze straying over the clear brown skin of his bare chest, then almost tentatively onto the front of his pyjama trousers, where the slit in the fabric lay slightly parted. *No!* He fought down the desire to slip a hand within, to touch…

Slowly, trying not to disturb the dozing youth, he got to his feet. He pulled the sleeping bag out of Craig's duffle-bag, and unrolled it. Lifting the boy's feet onto the settee, he reached underneath the front apron and carefully pulled out the extending part of the bed, and set it in position. Unzipping the sleeping bag, he placed it on the lower part of the bed, and gently lay Craig's feet into it, pulling it up around the boy as best he could. From the bedroom, he brought a spare pillow, and slipped it under his head; Craig stirred:

'Sleep well, Craig – I'll see you for breakfast.' The only response was a slurred 'G'night.'

In his own bedroom, he sat on the edge of the bed and leant forward, his head in his hands, elbows on his knees, and released a deep, shuddering sigh. It was all back with him - the same pulse-quickening excitement at the closeness of an attractive young boy, the tingle of exhilaration from the feel of his slenderness curled in the crook of his arm, the soft satin texture of bare skin under his fingers… And that same barely-resistible drive to somehow control the kid, to *own* him, take some kind of ultimate possession of him…

He drew a deep breath, forcing an artificial calmness over his mind, and went about making himself ready for sleep. But sleep took a while to come, as his thoughts ever and again returned of their own will to the brown boy sleeping in the next room.

Chapter Twenty-One

The next morning, Craig was awakened by Stevens' cheerful greeting:

'Morning, Craig! Breakfast time – how are you feeling today?'

He roused himself, feeling still half-asleep, and somehow thick-headed. He sat up in his sleeping bag, and shook his head to clear it, taking a moment to remember where he was. Looking up at his host, it all began to come back…

'Toast and marmalade be okay? We don't run to bacon or sausages, I'm afraid – we're just hard-up students, remember!'

'Yeah – that'll be fine, thanks.'

'Okay – I'll go and start cooking. You know where the bathroom is.'

Carl disappeared into the kitchen; Craig stretched himself, and climbed out of the sleeping bag. Carl looked up, and smiled through the open kitchen door at the half-naked boy; Craig smiled back, and bent to sort out a clean shirt from his holdall. He went through the bedroom, picking up his other clothes from where he'd dropped them the previous evening, and into the bathroom. He quickly washed his face and hands, and brushed his teeth; then, leaning on the wash-basin, he gazed at himself in the mirror, trying to sort out his memories of the day before.

The details of his flight from home, the train journey from Paddington, and meeting Stevens on the platform, all were fresh and bright. But later? He'd had a shower; he remembered the warm, cosy feeling afterwards. And then, in his borrowed pyjama trousers, relaxing, listening to that music, he'd started to feel more and more sleepy, dozy even. The memory of Stevens' arm around his shoulders, his hand on his chest... All that was kind of fuzzy, unclear – he knew it had happened, but it was almost as if he'd been an observer, not involved, as if it had been another boy, not him at all...

He shrugged his shoulders, and stepped back into the bedroom to get dressed – but he quickly looked to see that the door was closed before he removed his trousers. Dressed again in his jeans and a clean shirt, socks and trainers on his feet, he returned to the living-room. Carl called him through into the kitchen, telling him that the breakfast was ready.

Over their toast and coffee, Carl again broached the subject of Craig's future:

'Listen, Craig – I'm going to go and see the people I told you about later, to see if they can find a place for you in the hostel. If they can, I'll either drop you around there later, or sometime tomorrow. I'll be out most of the day – I've got to go into the college library, to do some work for my studies. But you should be okay, here...' He paused:

'I think, after what you told me last night, it might be best if you stay indoors today, out of sight. If your folks, or the police, are looking for you, they might have found out that you bought a ticket for the train – and if so, they'll know where you went. So, if you keep under cover for now, and then we'll get you to the hostel in my car, we should be able to get away without them spotting you – okay?'

Craig considered – he'd planned to go and begin to explore the city – but what Stevens said sounded like good sense, and if he could get into this hostel, he'd have plenty of time to look around, later. He nodded:

'Okay – sounds sensible.'

'Good lad! There's food in the kitchen – help yourself to some lunch, when you're ready. I'll be back late this afternoon, I expect – I'll pick us up a Chinese take-away, if that'll suit you?'

'Yeah, great! I love Chinese. Is it all right if I watch telly, or play some music?'

'Of course! Help yourself – there's some of Kerry's folk tapes there as well as my classical, if you prefer. Or the latest TV paper's around somewhere.'

'Okay, thanks. I'll be fine.'

They finished eating, and Craig got up to clear away their plates:

'I'll wash up, if you like?'

'That's decent of you, if you sure you don't mind?'

'No, it's okay – I wash up for Mum at home all the time.'

'Thanks, then. I'll get going – I'll see you around half-five or six, I expect. Enjoy yourself!' Carl picked up his coat – outside was another chill, grey day – and let himself out. Craig watched from the front room window as he backed the Escort off the paved apron which had at some time been laid where the front garden used to be, and drove off.

Left to his own devices, the thirteen-year-old folded away the bed-settee, and sat down to think for a while. What should he make of this guy Stevens? The offer of help, the accommodation in his flat for a night or two, and the possibility of the hostel place, were all wonderful, just the kind of fresh start he needed but could hardly have hoped to find. But, in hindsight, last night had left him feeling slightly uncomfortable at the memory of the man's unsought intimacy, even if, at the time, he had almost welcomed it in his state of both physical and emotional exhaustion. Was he gay? But he had a girlfriend – there was evidence of that in the flat, in the tidiness of the place, the feminine garments in the bedroom, the cosmetics in the bathroom, apart from the guy's own assertions. The thought of cosmetics brought a grin to Craig's face, as he remembered the gorgeous blond in those advertisements!

He could get out now, of course, get away from whatever the guy might have in mind. But it seemed like sense to hang on, find out if this hostel deal was on the level... Craig smiled to himself, and got up to look for the TV listing.

* * *

In the college library, Carl sat, pretending to work at the papers in front of him. What the hell was he going to do? On the one hand, he was furious with himself for giving in to the temptation of befriending the runaway that chance had put in his path, throwing away four years and more of fighting down his cravings. But then, the kid's body had felt so good under his hands – warm, smooth skin, and the slender beauty of youth... And to meet him like that, purely by chance; it was almost as if fate was telling him to stop play-acting, to give up the pretence of being 'normal' - to acknowledge his true desires, even if it meant throwing away his present life, and giving in to his real inclinations at the same time as keeping them a deep, dark secret.

But the immediate problem was, what to do with Craig? The answer already lay there, deep in his mind, but he was loth to accept it. The story of the hostel was a complete fabrication, of course – he'd come up with that to keep the boy on the hook, to make sure he'd stay put and not wander away before... before what? His options were, to tell him it hadn't worked out, and turn him loose, or... He shook his head, and tried to concentrate on the work in front of him.

* * *

It was just after six when Craig heard Stevens enter the flat. He came into the living-room, a take-away bag in his hand:

'Chicken Chow Mein, Sweet and Sour Pork, Fried Rice and Prawn Crackers. Okay?'

'Yeah, great!' Craig smiled. He'd spent the day with the television, and even played some more of Carl's music; he'd tried some more Bach, and quite enjoyed it – the Mahler had been a bit too heavy for him, but Holst's Planet Suite had turned out to be pleasingly familiar.

In the kitchen, Carl began to unpack the take-away while Craig got out the plates, with spoons and forks. Carl looked over, and laughed:

'You can't handle chop-sticks either, then? Kerry insists on using them, but I can't manage at all!'

They sat and ate, talking of inconsequentialities. Carl had poured them a glass of orange juice each, surreptitiously adding a good shot of Vodka to Craig's and watching as he drank it down. The meal over, he sat back and said:

'I saw Jean today, about the hostel – she says they've got a room you can have, but it won't be ready until tomorrow. Someone's just moved out, and she wants to give it a good cleaning, and air it out before you move in. So I said I'd take you round after lunch – how's that?'

'That sounds great! Thanks! What about cooking, and all that?'

'There's a shared kitchen – can you cook for yourself?'

'Yeah, sure! I've had to look after myself sometimes at home, when Mum's been working, or something.'

'That's okay, then. There's a bathroom on each floor; you'll be sharing that, with the two other boys on your floor – they have a kind of rota system, I think. And a washing machine, on the ground floor. The hostel looks after things like bedclothes, but you're expected to keep your own room clean, vacuuming the floor, and so on. If you keep it tidy, you'll be okay there for as long as you want.'

'Wow! It all sounds too good to be true! I thought I'd be dossing in doorways, but this is just brilliant! I'm glad I ran into you on the station!'

'So am I, Craig – it's good to be able to help someone out, and you seem like the kind of kid who deserves a break from life, after what you've been through.'

Carl got up from the table. Craig followed suit, and went to clear the things away, but his host stopped him:

'Leave them for now – we'll wash up everything in the morning, after breakfast. Go through and relax for a bit; I'll make some coffee.'

Craig went into the living-room, and sat down on the settee, switching on the television with the remote control. Carl followed a few minutes later, with two mugs of coffee – once again, Craig's had the added soporific of a good shot of Vodka. They sat watching a quiz programme for a while, drinking their coffee, until Carl suggested:

'I usually have a shower early on Saturdays, if I'm not going out – it's nice to sit around feeling all clean and fresh! Do you want to go first?' Craig looked at the clock – it was only seven-thirty. Did this mean a whole evening of Stevens cuddling up with him on the sofa, of the man's arm around him, his touch gentle but disturbing on his bare chest? Or – the possibility struck him – even in *other places?* He shrugged inwardly; if it got him the new start he needed - and by now, the vodka was beginning to have its effect, calming his fears, deadening his inhibitions…

'Yeah, okay, sounds like a good idea.'

'Go and help yourself – the towel's still on the rail.' Craig got up, and went into the bedroom.

Stripping off, he felt a vague sense of resigned trepidation; but then he told himself to think of settling into his room at the hostel, beginning a new life away from Stan – sheer joy! – and even ringing his Mum one day soon, to let her know he was okay. It would be good to hear her voice again… He had to admit to himself that he was already missing her, and some of his mates from school – especially Benny, they'd shared some good times, some great pranks, together in the two years they'd been in the same class. He'd call Benny, too, when he could. He'd understand, he knew all about Stan.

He showered, taking his time, then dried himself and dressed in the borrowed trousers again. When he returned to the living-room, he found that Carl had extended the bed, and laid his sleeping bag out ready for him. A fresh mug of coffee stood ready for him, as well.

'There you go – stretch out and relax! My turn now!' Stevens left him alone and went into the bedroom.

Craig stretched out on the bed, watching the television which was still playing in its corner. He drank the coffee slowly as it cooled, beginning to feel more and more relaxed, his unformed concerns about Stevens' intentions gradually dissipating as his third dose of Vodka that evening took hold. By the time Carl returned from the bathroom, wearing only a towel wrapped around his waist, he was feeling happily light-headed, even more sleepy and uncaring than he had the night before.

Carl lay down beside the boy on the bed, seeing in his half-closed eyes that the Vodka had done its work, relaxing him, and wiping away his inhibitions. He left the TV playing as he reached across to touch Craig's chest – *God, the kid's so pretty!* He revelled in the soft, satin texture of the boy's bare skin as he began to explore his young body…

Craig felt Stevens touch him again, just as he had the night before. But, once again, he felt too tired, too comfortable, to bother to protest. And again, the guy's touch was so soft and gentle, so caressing, his hands wandering all over his chest and shoulders. He felt the man undo the string at his waist, but he still couldn't be bothered to say anything, even when he felt the front of his trousers being laid open, leaving him exposed. He lay there, half-aware of Carl's gaze wandering over his nakedness, too tired, too comfortably dozy to care… Then he felt the bed bounce as the man got up, and left the room.

Chapter Twenty-One

Carl rolled off the bed, leaving the boy drowsy, almost comatose. He walked unsteadily through into the bedroom, went to the chest of drawers and delved into the drawer where he kept his socks and handkerchiefs, rummaging at the back until he found the carefully-secreted knife. Turning, he caught his reflection in the dressing-table mirror, and paused, looking at himself standing naked, his hair still plastered wetly to his scalp, the unsheathed knife in his hand. Gazing into the dark eyes that looked back at him from the mirror, he felt his carefully-constructed world of normality collapsing around his ears like the house of cards he knew it to be.

Even now, it wasn't too late! The kid was still alive – he could let him sleep, pack his bags and turn him out in the morning; make some excuse to cover the lies he'd told about the hostel, leave him to make his own way and go back to the cosy charade of life with Kerry. But, before the thought was fully formed, he knew it wouldn't happen that way, knew that it was too late – the demon was awake, and wouldn't be denied. In his mind's eye, the image of the boy in the other room took form – he'd probably be nearly asleep by now, lying there on the sofa-bed, so bare, so brown, so beautiful…

His eyes dropped to the knife, looking at the brightness of the razor-sharp steel, feeling its weight in his hand. He walked slowly through to the living-room, holding it to his side, concealed, in case Craig was awake and watching – but he lay still, breathing softly, deeply, as Carl had left him. Lowering himself gently to the bed so as not to disturb the kid, he sat looking down at him for a moment, at the drowsy child's slender brown body, lying bare from throat to crotch. With his free hand, Carl reached out to touch the boy. He let his fingers wander slowly, gently over the silken texture of the flawless milk-chocolate skin, tracing the lines of his ribs, caressing the peaks of his raised shoulders, the sweep of his collarbones...

Craig had felt the bed move as Stevens had returned, felt the gentle touch of fingers on his chest. By now, with the effects of alcohol on top of a tiringly inactive day, he was past caring about what was happening, too relaxed to worry even when the man's fingers strayed below his waist and into forbidden territory... But then, the quiet voice, the urging hands, suggesting that he turn over, offered a way to protect himself from that disturbing, arousing touch.

Lying face down, he felt Stevens easing his trousers further down his legs, hazily puzzled at what was going on... Suddenly, the man was lying on top of him, his weight holding him down – he tried to rise, to throw him off, as he realised with bemused horror just what he intended – but Stevens was too heavy, too strong...

* * *

When it was over, Craig lay still, his body wet with sweat, crying quietly into the pillow. Stevens had rolled off him, sat beside him on the edge of the bed; now, he reached for the knife he had laid within reach on the floor. His eyes wandered over the boy's sleek, strong back, selected the point that concealed the young heart within – he held the knife poised, the point almost touching the clear brown skin...

And then, a surging electric thrill raced through him as he

thrust it home. Craig stiffened momentarily, tensing as the blade drove through his heart, and then lay limp. Carl released his pent-up breath in a long, slow sigh, and eased himself back to sit upright, gazing almost in disbelief at the dead thirteen-year-old lying beside him as he came gradually down to the real world once more. Sorrow rose in his heart, a sadness that the boy had had to die to give him the release he needed – the kid had been so beautiful! He let go of the knife's hilt, smiling to himself - he'd aimed truly for the boy's heart, there was only the merest trace of blood where it protruded from between his shoulderblades.

He rose to his feet, the coldly rational part of his mind beginning to exert itself fully. In all the torment of the last twenty-four hours, he'd not allowed himself to think about the practicalities of disposing of the boy's body – to do so would have been to admit the certainty of his death. Looking down at the slim brown body, he realised that opening out the sleeping bag had been an inspired move – the kid lay neatly within a kind of ready-made shroud. Bending over, he braced one hand against the warmth of the boy's body, and firmly withdrew the knife, ready this time for the reluctance of the flesh to release the blade. He took it through to the bathroom, and rinsed it under the tap in the washbasin.

The knife once again concealed in its hiding place, he returned to the living-room. What to do with Craig's body? In a city built around the river, its waters provided the obvious solution – but this time, he wouldn't make the mistakes he had at the quarry. He knew, now, that the air in the boy's lungs would keep him afloat, so he would have to weight him down; he'd read somewhere that they had to do that with burials at sea, ballast the windings so that the body would sink. What could he use? Something to hand, that wouldn't be missed? The bricks! Outside the back door, a small stack of bricks, presumably left over from when they'd converted the house into flats, had tripped him so often – he'd always meant to move them, but hadn't got around to it.

He went through the kitchen, and stepped out of the back door. Frosty air against his skin reminded him that he was still naked – oh well, it wouldn't matter, even in the unlikely event that someone had seen him, undergrads were always regarded as vaguely eccentric! He bent down and picked up half a dozen of the bricks, and took them inside. In the living-room, he placed the bricks around Craig's feet and shins, folded the sleeping bag over, and zipped it up, making sure the kid was completely within the enfolding fabric. He got some stout string from the kitchen, and tied the top – he didn't want the boy's body floating out! Two plastic bin-liners pulled over the sleeping-bag from each end, just to make sure, and tied around. A few more bricks, forced into the holdall and filling the duffle-bag, and he was ready. He checked carefully around the flat to make sure that nothing remained to give away the boy's temporary presence, stuffing his discarded clothing into the duffle-bag on top of the bricks and drawing the top tightly closed.

Carl dressed quickly, in a dark top and black trousers, socks and trainers. Slipping on his heavy donkey-jacket, he took the keys and unlocked the car, lifting the tailgate and pushing flat the back seats. Outside the house, the front yard lay in deep shadow, the nearest street-lamp some distance away. He looked around to see that no-one was in sight, and then humped the heavy sleeping bag out of the door and into the car. Collecting the two bags, he threw them in, closed the tailgate and got into the driving seat. He looked at his watch – ten-thirty, nearly. It should be nice and quiet by now, where he planned to dump Craig into the river.

Starting the engine, he drove out into the Abingdon Road, and turned away from the city. At the traffic-lights, he turned left into Weirs Lane, and drove over Donnington Bridge. Across the bridge, he turned around in the entrance to the boatyard, and headed back across the river again. Just on the Abingdon Road side, a truncated entrance led off to his left, with just room to park a couple of cars. This time of night, the parking spaces were occupied, but he backed the Escort to the far end and stopped it where a footpath continued towards the weir stream of the river. Taking Craig's bags, he walked the few yards to where the path crossed directly above the weir itself on a concrete footbridge. He looked around – there were lights on in some of the back windows of the houses on Weirs Lane and Canning Crescent, but no-one in sight. Sure that there was no sign of life, he tossed them into the torrent pouring over the weir.

He returned to the car, and, after again checking that no-one was about, hauled the sleeping bag out. Raising it with some difficulty, he balanced the body on his shoulder in a kind of unskilful fireman's lift, and carried it to the footbridge. Another quick glance around, and it followed the bags over the iron parapet and into the turbulence below. Carl turned and leant upon the cold iron railing, looking down into the water foaming beneath his feet. The tension began to drain out of him – it was done; and there was no trace of body or bags on the swirling water below. The turbulence would soon have the fabric of the sleeping bag waterlogged, adding even further to its weight; there should be no chance of Craig being found for a good while, if ever!

Carl let out a quiet sigh of relief. Then, he stiffened – footsteps were approaching on the path, scraping softly on the concrete surface. Had he been seen after all? He froze, holding his breath – a shadowy, hooded figure, huddled in the depths of a dufflecoat, passed behind him with a muffled 'goodnight'. His terror subsiding, he managed a strangled response – he cursed himself for having forgotten that the path also led to a number of residential moorings on the lower part of the weir stream. God, that had been close – if he'd been a minute or so later...

Back in the car, driving home, he thought of Kerry. What the hell was he going to tell her? There was no point, now, trying to continue their life together; Carl knew that any pretence of a normal, straight relationship would be farcical. He had no choice but to accept what he was – the demon was awake, now, and all he could do would be to try to control its excesses, and stay out of jail whenever his cravings got the better of him. An almost smug smile played around his mouth - he'd done that once, four years ago, when he was no more than a kid himself; now made twice, unless he was much mistaken! And there was a kind of release, a freedom, in no longer having to be something he wasn't; and a thrill of anticipation, in wondering when, and where the next opportunity would arise, how the next young life would fall into his hands...

And Kerry? The only kind thing he could do was to find a way to ease her out of the hole she'd dug for herself by falling in love with him.

PART THREE

DANIEL

THE DEMON ABROAD

JULY - SEPTEMBER 2002

Chapter Twenty-Three

The town of Grancester had seen some changes in the course of twelve years. An important new industrial development, on what had once been the extensive railway freight yards, and two big housing schemes to the North of the old borough boundaries; even the up-market suburb of Alderley Park had seen considerable growth in its size and population.

With the increase in the size of the town, the local police establishment had been increased as well. Chief Superintendent Graham Paulson was now in overall charge; top dog in the C.I.D. office was Detective Superintendent Harry Wilson – both men who had been drafted in from the County HQ. Of the old team, many had retired: McFadden, Tremayne, Foreman. New men had taken their places, some local, some from outside; and new recruits had expanded the rank and file of the town's force. Latest of these to arrive at the station was a black-haired, blue-eyed young constable, fresh from the training school; his name was Andrew Dorman.

And they had a new station, too! The old Victorian building on Midland Road had grown too small for the expanded force; a new concrete and glass structure off the old Northampton Road, just within the line drawn by the bypass, was the new home of the town's constabulary.

It was here, in the third-floor offices of the Criminal Investigation Department, that the first tentative stirrings of a long-sought answer to an unresolved problem were to come to light.

* * *

Detective-Inspector David Russell had been back in Grancester for the best part of twelve months, after a couple of years at the County Police Headquarters following upon his promotion. One morning, a few weeks earlier, he had been sitting alone in his office; D.S. Tom Anders, his assistant, had just been moved to fill a vacancy, as an acting D.I., in Wellingborough. A knock came at the door:

'Come in!' A familiar face appeared around the edge:

'Good morning, sir.' Russell stood up, beckoned the man in:

'Doug Rimmer! How are you? Enjoying CID?' Rimmer smiled:

'Yes, sir, thank you. I'm fine - yourself? And your family?'

'Very good, thanks - sit down. What brings you here - are you back with us?'

'I am, sir. I've been up at Wootton Hall Park, like yourself, since I made D.S. last year; in Kettering before that, after I left here. Now, they've sent me home!'

'Pleased to be back?' Rimmer grinned cheerfully, this time:

'Yes - I've just come down from the Super's office. He told me to report to you!'

'You're taking over from Tom Anders? As my dogs-body?'

'That's about the strength of it, sir. Mr Wilson tells me I'll be expected to handle my own work as well, of course, but that I'm to act as your assistant whenever required. As long as it's all right with you, of course?'

'That's grand - I was wondering who they'd lumber me with!'

'I hope I'll fit the bill, sir?'

'I'm sure you will, Doug. We haven't worked together before, have we?'

'No, sir. I was involved with a few things, in Uniform, while you were with old Inspector Foreman as *his* assistant, years ago, but as I said, I've been elsewhere since I got my transfer to CID. Apparently Mr Wilson asked for me, thought I'd fit in okay back here; and it suited me, so here I am!'

'That's good - welcome back, Doug! I'm glad to have you on the team. You'll have to come round for dinner one night, meet Tracy and the kids, give us a chance for a chat, get to know each other a bit away from the chaos here.'

'I'd like that, sir - would it be all right to bring my wife?'

'Of course! I didn't know you were married?' Rimmer grinned again:

'Yes; nearly two years, now. Julie's a librarian, in Weston Favell library. No kids - not yet, anyway.'

'Good for you! Anyway; let me show you the cases we've got on our plate at the moment. More important, though - your first task as my assistant: Go and get us a coffee apiece. Mine's white, not too much milk, two sugars, okay?'

'Okay! Back in a jiffy.' Rimmer departed the office with cheerful smile on his face.

* * *

July the fifth – twelve years to the day after Philip Dorman had died at the hands of an unknown assailant in Bevington Quarry. Mid morning; Rimmer tapped on the door, and entered Russell's office:

'Sir?'

'Yes, Doug – sit down.' Russell waved his Sergeant to a seat. Rimmer began:

'You remember Sally Brennan? Used to be in Uniform here?'

'Yes, sure! Little brunette, nice girl.'

'You know she left to work in the Criminal Records Office, in London?'

'Yeah?'

'Well, she and I have always kept in touch; we get together at the weekends, sometimes, when she comes up to visit her folks in Northampton – she'll come over for dinner with Julie and me from time to time.'

'What is it, Doug? You didn't want to discuss your home life with me, did you?' Rimmer grinned:

'No, sir! It's just that I had a call from her yesterday, in the evening – she rings occasionally for a chat. She told me that C.R.O. had had a call from India, of all places, about someone we might know.'

'India? Where the curries come from?'

'That's right. It seems that the police there wanted to know if there was anything known about a guy called Steven Evans. Sal says there's nothing on their files, and that's what they've told the Indian officer who called; but this man apparently comes from Grancester, and she thinks she remembers an Evans being involved in some big case here, when she was on the local force.'

'But this Evans has got no convictions here in the U.K?'

'No.'

'What else do we know about this fellow?'

'Sal says he works for Kronburg's, the big German water-resources and Hydro-Electric specialists, quite a whizz-kid, apparently. He was with them in India for about four years; moved to a project in Norway in February.'

'What about before?'

'First class degree from Oxford, spent two years doing voluntary work for World of Water in South America after that, then went to Kronburg.'

'But he comes from Grancester?'

'So she says – born and raised here, left to go to Oxford after his schooling. The Indian force gave her a resume of his background to check on, to make sure they were talking about the right man.'

'So he'd have left here, what, ten years or more ago?'

'That'd be about right, I suppose.'

'So if he *was* investigated here, it must have been while he was still at school? Can't have been much, surely? Bit of schoolboy vandalism, maybe?'

'No, Sal's sure it was something pretty serious. But I can't think what – the name doesn't mean anything to me, I'm afraid.'

'Hmmm…'

Russell sat for several minutes, his hands idly fiddling with an expensive-looking fountain pen. He looked up eventually:

'Sally and I must be on the same wavelength. Evans… Evans – there's something about that name that's ringing very faint bells with me, too. God alone knows why! Perhaps it'll come to me, in time. If there's no record of a conviction, we're not going to find him unless we go through all the cases active around that time, and there must have been hundreds, so that's a non-starter. It can hardly be important enough to put that much effort into, can it?'

'Sal's coming up this weekend, sir – I could ask her to drop by and see you, perhaps the two of you together could puzzle it out?'

'Yeah, maybe. Ask her, will you? I expect I'll be in the office Saturday morning, as usual!'

Chapter Twenty-Four

Russell was in his office, as predicted, on the Saturday morning, when a knock came at the door. A uniformed Constable looked in, a grin on his face:

'Young lady to see you, sir!' He stepped back to usher in ex-WPC Sally Brennan, a petite, dark-haired woman in her mid-thirties.

'Come in, Sally! Sit down, it's good to see you.'

'Thank you, sir. It's nice to see you again – I've often thought I ought to drop in, but I've never got around to it, you know how it is.'

'Of course. And my name's David – you're not on the force here, now, so drop the ceremony, please! How do you like our new station?'

'Bit of an improvement, isn't it?' She laughed: 'The old place was so draughty, wasn't it? I can't believe they've turned it into a night-club, of all things!'

'Yes! Uniform branch spend nearly as much time there now as they used to, but now they're hauling the felons *out* of the place!'

'Are there many of the old team here still? Doug and I tend not to talk shop when I see them, so I'm a bit out of touch.'

'Well, McFadden's gone, retired – he and Bridie have got a little cottage somewhere in the Highlands, I gather. Jack Tremayne's retired too; he and his missus live in Northampton still - he pops in occasionally, just to see that we're all on our toes without him to keep us in order!'

'What about Inspector Foreman, your old boss?'

'That was sad – he lost his wife, about five years ago. She was a lovely lady, Annie – they always reckoned she was the only one he was afraid of, you know! He stayed on the force, perhaps because he didn't have anything else with her gone. He finally retired last year, they virtually had to push him out. And then he died in his sleep, during the winter. The doctor said there was nothing really wrong with him, it was just as if he'd given up bothering to live.'

'That's a shame! He was a grumpy old cuss, but then he'd come out with something that made you realise how much he really cared – about the job, about people. You especially, David – he always thought the world of you, you know. I overheard him call you the best assistant he'd ever had, more than once.'

'Yes, I know – not that he'd ever have told me himself, of course!' Russell picked up the pen from his desk, which he had a habit of fiddling with while he thought:

'He gave me this, when I was promoted. Told me that as an Inspector I should be using a proper fountain-pen! I only found out later what an expensive item this one is. Typical of him, wasn't it?' Russell sat back in his chair:

'And what about you, Sally? How are you doing?'

'Fine, thanks! The job at C.R.O. suits me, I must have been born to be a librarian, I think, like Doug's wife! Being on the front line, as a W.P.C. wasn't really for me, I couldn't keep from getting too involved with people.'

'That was a pity – you were good, Sally, especially at handling the public.'

'Yeah, well… Anyway, I'm happier now. I've got a nice little flat in Finsbury, and a regular fella – we're getting married next year.'

'Oh, that's great! Congratulations!' She grinned happily at him:

'Yeah, everything's going fine for me now. Anyhow – this guy Evans, that the Indian Police are interested in?'

'Yes – I expect Doug told you. The name rings bells with me, too. But I can't think why.'

'All I can remember is the name in the background of some big case, about ten years or so ago. Of course, it's probably not the same Evans, it's a common enough name.'

'Your man's father, perhaps? After all, your Evans can only have been what, seventeen or eighteen when he went to Oxford?'

'I suppose that's a possibility - I don't know anything of his early background other than that he came from here originally, according to the information we had from India.'

'You've no idea what the old case might have been?' She shook her head:

'No, sorry. I've really only got the vaguest memory, the impression that it was something quite important, out of the ordinary.'

'I can't seem to dredge the details up, either. Oh well, no point in worrying about it, I suppose - maybe it'll come back to one of us, sometime. Hey - can I offer you a drink? There's still a bottle of Keith Foreman's Scotch here somewhere!'

At this, the woman looked a little uncomfortable; then she smiled:

'No, thanks, David. I don't drink, these days. I had – a bit of a bad patch, before I left the force here. A relationship which went belly-up, in a big way. Oh, I got myself off the bottle before I wound up as one of AA's finest, but only just! The job at C.R.O. came along just when I needed to get away from here, gave me an easy way out. That was just when they were setting up the new data-base for the Sex Offender's Register, you remember? They needed the extra staff, and someone with computer skills and street experience fitted the bill nicely, thank you! Anyway, It's worked out fine for me, as I told you.'

'That would have been about six years ago?'

'Yes, just about – Parliament had just agreed to setting the Register up, then. Wasn't Inspector Foreman involved with that, somehow?'

'Yes, I remember him telling me he was on the Federation committee which was pushing for something of the sort, years before...' His voice trailed off:

'Now, why am I getting the feeling that that's got something to do with your Mr Evans? God, the human mind is a perverse piece of equipment! There's a connection there, but do you think I can spot it?'

'Doesn't add up to me, I'm afraid.' Sally replied. She glanced at her watch: 'Listen, I'll have to go – I promised to take my Mum shopping in Northampton today, and I'm late already.'

'Okay, Sally – it's been good to see you after all these years. I'll see if I can't find out why the name Evans seems to fit when you talk about the Sex Offenders Register – you see, it'll come to me at some totally inappropriate moment!'

'Let me know if it does! It has been nice to see you again, David – give my best wishes to your wife, and the little boy.'

'Daniel? He's not so little, eleven years old, now. And he's got a little sister, Sarah – she's three. I'll remember you to Tracy, as well.'

'Thanks, David. I'll see you again, I hope.'

'Yes – come by whenever you're in town, you'll be most welcome.' He stood up to see her out.

Chapter Twenty-Five

Russell slept well that Saturday night, and woke early on the Sunday morning – seven-fifteen by his bedside clock, when he turned over to see. He rolled onto his back, and lay quiet, enjoying that warm, cosy feeling that comes with awakening after a sound sleep.

Beside him, Tracy was still curled into her typical ball, snuggled up like a hibernating squirrel, breathing slow and deep. He smiled at the thought of her – after fourteen years of marriage, they were still very much in love, friends and lovers as well as man and wife. All right, she might not be the greatest beauty in the world; short, and becoming cuddly after two babies; but he couldn't imagine life without her, now, without her ready smile, the warmth of her brown eyes, the feel of her thick, curly hair in his hand, the simple togetherness of the two of them. And still, after all that time, she could excite him almost to a frenzy. Last night, for example; making love with her was as wonderful now as it had ever been...

The rest of the house was quiet, as he lay contemplating how very lucky he was: A job he still enthused about, a wife he loved, and two marvellous children. The kids! What a pair they were. Little Sarah, just three – tiny, dark-haired, brown-eyed, the image of her mother except for that determined line to her jaw, reflecting the streak of obstinacy which was the clearest of legacies from her father. She'd be curled up in a ball, too – just like her mother! - tangled in the sheets, the occasional hand or foot sticking out where you'd never expect it. There had been times when it had taken him some little while to disentangle his daughter in the morning. She was wonderful – cute, and bright, and affectionate – what would he do without her?

And Danny: He wasn't his Dad's little boy any more, as he'd said to Sally Brennan. Eleven, nearly twelve – God, how time could fly! But Russell was so proud of his son; Daniel, he preferred to be called now: '*Danny* makes me sound like a little kid!' was his usual protest. Only his mother could still get away with it! And Daniel was so much like him – tall and slim, sandy-haired, hazel-eyed, he could almost have been his father at the same age, if it hadn't been for the softer, rounder features he'd inherited from Tracy. The thought of his eager, elfin face with its inevitable quiff and cheeky grin made Russell smile to himself. And as if to emphasise the boy's growing maturity, he'd be starting at his new school in September – Russell felt another swell of pride as he thought of his son's getting a place at Elwood Priors, on merit rather than because his father could afford it; even if they could, now, thanks to Tracy's old Uncle Roger!

Russell loved every moment he spent with the boy; and Daniel still seemed to like to be with his father, even if he was beginning to exert his independence more and more as time went by. Russell's one real hobby outside of his work was building and sailing radio-controlled model yachts, and he would often take Daniel along on a Sunday morning; the youngster was quite a dab hand with the controller, he seemed to have an almost instinctive knack of being able to get himself out of trouble when a sudden gust threw the boat off-course, or threatened to capsize it.

There were several lakes they used, where his club meetings were held – sometimes, that was the lake in the old quarry, although now it was better known as Bevington Country Park. The local authorities had closed it, after Philip Dorman had been killed there – a number of years had passed before they'd opened it as an official public park, having first made the landscape a lot safer, laying out a pattern of pathways and building a visitor centre and other facilities.

Philip Dorman – that had been a tragic case. The waste of a young life, for no apparent reason. It suddenly struck Russell how like his own son the Dorman boy had been – he too had been tall and slender, and blond-haired, but his eyes had been grey, his face more aquiline of feature. And, like him and Daniel, Philip and his father had been very close, too. He could still remember the haunted look in the man's eyes, especially at the kid's funeral. And Caroline, Philip's older sister – what a beauty she was! He'd seen her picture so often in the years that had followed, in magazines, on posters, on the television. He was pleased that she'd had the courage to follow up that contact, and carve out a successful career for herself, even if she'd given it all up again later. Wherever was she now? They'd kept in contact for some time, but then, as it had become apparent that they weren't going to catch Philip's killer, short of some kind of miracle, he'd lost touch with her, only maintaining the necessary communication with the parents.

If only they could have got the bastard that had killed that poor kid! It had rankled with Keith Foreman until he retired, Russell knew; probably up to the day he'd died, if the truth be told. And it still touched a raw nerve with Russell himself, to think the boy's murderer was on the loose somewhere, even now. They'd never even really established a motive, for certain – Foreman had always had doubts about the assumption that it had been sexual, and there had been no real evidence…

Bingo! Suddenly wide awake, Russell sat bolt upright in bed, disturbing his sleeping wife who rolled over and mumbled something incoherent at him. That was where he remembered Foreman talking about the Sex Offenders Register! They'd been talking about the motive for the boy's killing, and Foreman had said how it might have helped to point a finger in the right direction. But where did the name of Evans fit into that case? Did it at all, or was his memory playing tricks? *Think, David!*

The Evans that Sally had been talking about would have been, what, about seventeen then. Philip had been twelve when he died, so not one of his contemporaries – there *had* been an older boy, hadn't there? Someone they'd interviewed, an older kid from Philip's school: Evans, Evans – yes, that felt *right*. Could it have been the same man the Indian police were interested in? Steven Evans, Sally had said his name was. The only thing to do would be to pull the file and take a look, see if the name was the same. He lay there, thinking hard - and the more he thought about it, the more Russell felt that he was right; but he still couldn't remember a Christian name. After all, it was twelve years ago, for Heaven's sake! And Evans wasn't exactly an uncommon name – the chances of it being the same person must be pretty small. Still, he'd check on Monday – or get Doug Rimmer to, anyway!

Tracy was wide awake, now. Russell eased himself out of bed, and stood looking down at his wife, thinking again how lucky he was. She smiled up at him; he smiled back:

'Cup of tea in bed?'

'Mmm, that would be lovely, Davey. You *do* know how to treat a girl, even if you don't let on very often!'

'Oh? Who washed up last night?'

'Go and make that tea!' He grinned, and padded downstairs in his pyjamas.

Over breakfast, a little later, Russell found himself looking at his son as he munched on his toast and marmalade. After his earlier musings, it struck him how John Dorman must have felt when he'd lost his boy – how would *he* cope, if Daniel was to die in such awful circumstances? He wouldn't, was the simple answer. Could he go on living, if his boy was dead? Even with Tracy and Sarah beside him? Please God, it would never be a situation he'd have to face!

The boy saw his father looking at him, and grinned:

'You all right, Dad?'

'Yeah, fine! I was just wondering, are you coming sailing with me this morning?'

'Yeah! Where are we going?'

'It's up at the quarry, today.'

'That's good – it's great up there! Can Jacko come, too? Only he was going to come round in a while…'

'Of course! Do you want to call him, tell him we'll pick him up in the car?'

'Thanks, Dad!' Daniel leapt up from the table and dashed to the telephone.

Russell felt vaguely disappointed that the other boy was going to join them – he liked his Sunday mornings with his son, on their own. But still, young Jack was a good kid; and he didn't often come sailing with them. And he was going to have to get used to his son spending less and less time with his old Dad. After all, only another year, and he'd almost be a teenager. The impending sorrow of parenthood suddenly struck him, tightening his throat so that he nearly choked on his tea.

As it happened, Tracy and Sarah decided to join them as well. It was a nice day, warm even if rather overcast, with a gentle breeze ideal for their sailing. Tracy sat in the sun, Sarah playing around her on the grass, while Russell and the two boys took turns sailing his latest masterpiece back and forth across the lake. After a while, he left them to it, and joined his wife.

Sitting there in companionable silence, his thoughts returned unbidden to Philip Dorman. It had been just by here, all those years ago, that the boy had died and been thrown into the lake: What *had* happened that day? How had the twelve-year-old, so like his own son, met his death? Maybe one day, he'd know – but it seemed a forlorn hope, after all this time…

Chapter Twenty-Six

On the Monday morning, Russell poked his head around the door of the C.I.D. office:

'Doug? Come in, will you?' Rimmer followed his superior into the D.I.'s office, perched on the corner of his desk as Russell took the chair behind it, saying: 'This Evans character, that Sally was on about – I've an idea he might have been involved in the Philip Dorman murder. You remember the case?'

'Do I?' Rimmer grimaced: 'It was me that fished the kid's body out of the lake, up at the old quarry!'

'Oh, right. Anyway, when you've got a moment, do you want to dig out the file and check? I'm sure we interviewed an older boy from Philip's school for some reason, and I'm pretty sure his name was Evans. But I can't remember his first name. Be worth finding out, just on the off-chance.'

'Bit of a long shot, though, isn't it sir? There must have been quite a few kids even in a small town like this with that surname.'

'Yes, I know! But still, this must be the reason Sally thought the name was familiar, I'd imagine. There's probably no connection at all with the man the Indian force wants to know about. Don't make an issue of it, I know we're up to our necks with the car-thefts as well as the arson attack on Matson's factory. To say nothing of this damned doorstep thief the press want to call the Cottage Burglar. Just take a look when you get a moment, all right?'

'Yes, sir. No problem.'

They went on to discuss the intricacies of the investigation into the car-ringing gang which they were closing in upon, and the planned operation which was intended to net the ring-leaders as well as the mechanics and thieves themselves. It took a while to work out the details; Russell's natural caution made him go carefully over every phase of the operation, partly because neither was used to the other's working habits as yet. The raids were set for the Wednesday Morning, at 6.00am, and planned to hit the garages and homes of the perpetrators at the same time.

* * *

In the event, everything went off smoothly. With the raids successfully concluded, and the accumulated evidence being sifted and studied in the incident room, Rimmer at last had a moment to give some thought to his superior's request to check the Dorman file. It was late the same day, when he finally collected it from the station's record department; in Russell's office, he opened it, and leafed through until he found what he was looking for:

'You were right, sir! Evans was the name of a sixteen-year-old you and D.I. Foreman spoke to about the Dorman boy. It seems he was a prefect at the school who was responsible for Philip's class. But his name was Carl, not Steven.'

'Well, there you go! Can't be right all the time, can we?'

Rimmer grinned: 'He was the right age, though. It would tie in with the history of Sally's target if it *was* him, wouldn't it?'

'Yes, I suppose so – did Sally tell you why the Indian force were interested in their Evans?'

'No – I'm not sure she even knew herself. If it was just a formal request for information, they might well have given no reason.'

'Hm. Oh well, I don't suppose it matters, there's probably no actual connection. But you might ask her, next time you see her, if only for interest's sake.'

'Okay. I'll ask her, when the opportunity arises.'

* * *

Four weeks passed; it was early August before Doug Rimmer and his wife entertained Sally Brennan to dinner again. Over the meal, he remembered Russell's query, and raised the question:

'Sal – sorry to talk business for a moment, but I should tell you, we found the Evans you remembered from an old case here. He was a kid of sixteen, interviewed as a peripheral witness in the murder of Philip Dorman.'

'Oh, God, yes! I remember the case. That was awful, wasn't it? I sat with the mother while you and the others were searching for the boy. I'll never forget the look in the father's eyes when he came home, after they'd found his body.'

'Don't tell me! I was the one who pulled him out of the lake.'

'We never got the killer, did we?' Rimmer shook his head.

'The lad Evans was sixteen at the time, so he'd fit in with what you told us about your enquiry – but his name was Carl, not Steven.'

'Could have changed his name, perhaps?'

'Maybe! It's still not really likely that it's the same guy though, is it?' He paused, then asked:

'Do you know what the Indian police had against this Evans fellow?'

'No, no idea. It was just a request to know if he had any form in the U.K. – the Indian Inspector who sent the question didn't say why, or what he'd been up to out there. Is it important?'

'Probably not. Let me know, though, if you can, will you? Dave Russell was wondering.'

'Yes - it's sort of intriguing, isn't it? I'll see if I can find out, when I get an odd minute or two.'

The conversation returned to more mundane matters for the rest of the evening.

* * *

Neither Inspector nor Sergeant gave the matter much thought until, one day in late August, Russell's office telephone rang:

'D.I. Russell.'

'Call for you, sir. Lady name of Miss Brennan.'

'Put her through, will you?'

'Okay, sir.' A click sounded on the line:

'Sally? How are you?'

'Hello, David. I'm fine – how about you?'

'Very well, thanks – over-worked as usual, of course!'

'David – are you about this weekend? I'd like to talk to you.'

'Yes, I'll be about – but I'm hoping to have a quiet time! Why don't you come out to the house, Saturday afternoon?'

'That would be nice – are you sure your wife won't mind?'

'Tracy? - No! She'll be pleased to see you again.'

'And I'm dying to meet your little girl! And Danny – he was only a little kid last time I saw him.'

'That's settled, then. You know where we live now, in Bevington?'

'Yes – Doug's told me.'

'That's fine then - see you Saturday.'

'David – would you mind if I asked Doug to join us, too? I think he should hear what I've got to tell you, and it'll save me going through it twice.'

'Oh? What's this all about, Sally?'

'I'll tell you Saturday, David. See you then.'

Chapter Twenty-Seven

Russell was relaxing after their usual light lunch on the Saturday when the door-bell rang. Daniel went to answer it, and came back into the living-room with Sally Brennan; Russell got to his feet:

'Hello, Sally. Good to see you again – you've met Daniel?'

'Yes! Quite the young man nowadays.' She smiled at the boy, who grinned back.

'And you remember Tracy?' Russell's wife stood up; the two women clasped hands:

'Of course! It's lovely to see you again.'

'And you, Sally – how's the world treating you in the big city?'

'Grand! I've got a super job at C.R.O., and a lovely fiancé.'

'Good for you!'

'David tells me you've got a little girl as well, now?'

'Yes! Sarah – she's up in her room at the moment, playing with her friend from next door. I'll introduce you later.'

'Please! I'm dying to meet her.'

Russell intervened in the women's chatter: 'Come through to my study, Sally – we can talk shop there without me getting my ear chewed! Is Doug coming?'

'Yes – he said he'd meet me here.'

'Dad? Is it all right if I go to see Jacko? I promised I'd cycle over there today.' Daniel asked, before his father disappeared from the room.

'Of course, Danny… Daniel. Just be careful, won't you?'

'I always *am*, Dad!'

'Go on, then!' The boy slipped out to the front door as Russell led Sally into the study. She indicated the departing youngster with a smile: 'He's so much like you, isn't he? You must be really proud of him.'

'Oh, I am! This query of yours about the Evans character has got me thinking about the Dorman case - looking at Daniel, I can understand better now why John Dorman went to pieces so badly when Philip was killed. I can't imagine what it would be like if I lost my boy like that.'

The study door opened to admit Tracy, who ushered Doug Rimmer into the room; he turned to her with a smile: 'Thanks, Mrs Russell – I'm sorry to disturb your Saturday afternoon like this.'

'Oh, don't worry, Doug. And I've told you before - my name's Tracy, please!' She left them together, pulling the door closed. Russell took his chair at the old leather-topped desk; Sally Brennan sat in the only other chair, while Rimmer perched on the edge of the desk. Russell looked speculatively at his out-of-town guest:

'Okay, Sally – what is it that brings you to see me in such secrecy?'

'Oh, not secrecy, David! I didn't want to disturb you in the office, and I wanted to be able to talk to you without any kind of formality, you understand?'

'What's it all about?'

She hesitated, as if unsure quite how to approach her subject. Then she began:

'It's about this Evans fellow. I know you found that there had been a lad by that name who was interviewed about the Dorman boy's murder, and that was, I'm sure, why I remembered the name from that time. Now, at first, I thought, like you, that the chances were that the man in India was a different Evans altogether, even though he would be about the right age.' She paused: 'Can I ask, was Carl Evans in any way a suspect in the murder? Was there anything to actually connect him with the boy's death?'

Russell glanced at Rimmer, a puzzled expression on his face, and shook his head: 'No, not at all, as I remember. He was older, of course – a prefect at the school, who was responsible for Philip's class. We only spoke to him in case he knew anything that might help, about the boys, or their movements that day.'

'Okay, thanks.' Sally paused again, collecting her thoughts. Then she went on: 'After Doug told me what you'd remembered, I thought I'd find out what I could, partly for my own interest, and because Doug said you'd like to know about the Indian connection. I sent a query to the Inspector out there – he was reluctant to tell me at first, I gather they've no evidence, or even any real suspicion, that Evans has done anything – it's all rather vague supposition, more an unresolved question-mark than anything stronger. But in the end he came through. David, their case has to do with a number of missing kids. Street children, from the towns all around the region, who haven't been seen for a while. All boys, and no-one seems to know where they are, or what's happened to them. Now, is that just coincidence, or what?'

'I *see* – it might make some kind of sense, but only if it *is* the same fellow. *And* if it was him who killed Philip Dorman. But he was only sixteen, then, for goodness' sake!'

Sally sat quiet for a moment, her eyes downcast. Then she looked up, an expression of scared excitement in her eyes, and spoke quietly:

'It *is* the same man, David. I'm certain of it.'

'What! You're sure?'

'I also contacted R.B.Kronburg GmbH, or at least their British office, and asked for more of Evans' details. He's been with them for five years – six months training in England when he started, four years in India, and now in Norway, since earlier this year.

He's got a top-class Honours Degree from Oxford, and did two years in South America, Brazil, Venezuela, Columbia, places like that, for World of Water in between leaving university and joining them. We knew that already, of course; but what they told me was that as a boy, he was educated at Elwood Priors School, when he lived here in Grancester – and, guess what? His full name is Carl – Steven – Evans!' She paused between each word to emphasise her point.

Russell sat back in his chair, and looked at his junior officer. Rimmer looked slightly stunned:

'Well, what do you know? *Could* he have killed the Dorman kid?'

'I don't know, now. I'm sure we didn't really consider him as a suspect at the time. It makes you wonder, even if all this is rather speculative, doesn't it?'

'I guess so. But if the police in India aren't actually after him, and there's no real suspicion regarding the Dorman case, it all sounds like a strange coincidence, doesn't it?'

'Yes, you're right – we can hardly make a big issue of it on the strength of what we think *might* be a connection, on such tenuous evidence. I'll tell you what, I'll take the time when I can to go over the Dorman file, remind myself of just what we had, see if there is any chance that Evans could be the killer. If that looks possible, we'll talk to the Indian force and see if it can be tied in with their problem.'

'What about Norway? If there is anything in it, there could be kids at risk there, now.'

'Oh, God! We can hardly say anything to the police there, or even Kronburg's, when all we've got is the faintest of suspicions, can we? If it looks like Sally's fears might be right, we'll tell them when we've got something stronger to back it up.'

'Yes, you're right, sir.'

Russell turned back to Sally Brennan:

'Have you got any contacts for us, Sal?'

'Yes, David. The Inspector in India is a guy called Bhudran; he's the officer in charge in a small town by the name of Andrabad, in a central province called Madhya Pradesh. I've written down his telephone and fax numbers for you – here.' She handed over a sheet of notepaper:

'I haven't got a contact in Norway, of course, but the man at Kronburg's U.K. office is a George Tucker – he was very helpful when I called him. His number's on there too. Their big project in Norway, where Evans is working now, is up in the mountains near a small town called Ahlsberg, up-country from Bergen. I'd expect Tucker would put you in touch with their people there, if it becomes necessary, and I suppose you could contact the local police as well.'

'Right – thanks, Sally. You've done a great job of following this through! We can't give it a lot of priority, unless it starts to look like a solid case, you understand? But we will try to check it out as soon as we can. We've had a tip-off that Roseberry's pushers are going to try to get drugs into the local night-clubs, and that's taking priority at the moment, I'm afraid. Ironic, isn't it? Main target is Sweeney's, in the old Midland Road Station!'

'Yes – I wonder what McFadden would think of his old station being a night-club! Does he know, do you think?'

'I doubt it – we haven't heard from him since he went back to his beloved Scotland. Jack Tremayne gets quite hot under the collar if you even mention it.'

'I can imagine!'

Chapter Twenty-Eight

Monday Morning. Entering his office, Russell looked down at his desk – or rather, the space he knew his desk to occupy. He could barely see any of it, under the mass of files and paperwork covering its top surface. Groaning inwardly, he took his seat behind it.

The plain-clothes division in the town always seemed to be running flat-out, just to keep up with the work-load. For every investigation they concluded, two more would arise to need his attention; for every piece of paper filed safely away, two more would appear on his desk. The modern atmosphere of accountability in the force seemed to breed pieces of paper with the fecundity of a well-fed rabbit warren. As he shuffled the confusion of documents into some semblance of a recognisable order, preparatory to dealing with at least the most urgent of them, he came across the Dorman file, still in his office after Rimmer's perusal of it, and put it to one side, to go through it when he could.

* * *

On the Thursday, he finally gave up trying to make time to read it in the office. Thursday evening was Tracy's regular night out – a half-respectable water-colour painter, she liked to go to a local art group when she could, even if his duties often meant that she had to stay home with the children. So tonight, at home, once Sarah was in bed, he could try to read the file – Daniel would probably be with young Jack, out in the garden, or away somewhere on their bikes, if this sunshine kept up through the day.

By the evening, though, a steady drizzle had turned the brightness of the morning to a colourless grey. After their meal, with Sarah safely tucked up, and Tracy away to her art group, Jack, who'd joined them for dinner, and Daniel disappeared up to his room to play computer games. The occasional cry of triumph or groan of disaster would echo down the stairs to the lounge, where Russell sat in an easy chair with the file at his elbow.

Reading through the papers, gradually, the details of the case began to come back to him. He felt himself almost like an archaeologist, slowly, painstakingly unearthing an extinct creature, extrapolating its form and nature from the dry evidence; with the fossilised bones of the documents in his hand, his memory began to fill in the detail, the feelings, the personalities: Kate Dorman, so strong on the surface, keeping the depth of her grief hidden until it overwhelmed her; John Dorman, almost destroyed by the loss of his beloved boy; Caroline, who'd virtually held the family together through their tragedy; and little Andrew, bereft and bewildered, whose innocent goodbye to his brother had turned solemnity to tragedy at the graveside. Russell smiled as he thought of the quiet, capable young Constable who'd so recently joined the Grancester establishment.

And some of the other characters he'd interviewed: Harvey Williams, the ex-military financier with the flashy Jaguar, the bristling moustache and the hearty but concerned manner; the flirtatious blond in the taxi office, who'd been so distressed when she realised the near-consequences of her mistake; Broadbent, the driver, unpleasant, crude, but none-the-less innocent, at least of this crime. And the boys and masters of Elwood Priors.

And Evans; Carl Evans, what of him? The first interview, at his home on the Saturday after Philip's death: He'd been upset, of course – he'd put two and two together from their initial questions and the radio newsflash quite quickly; too quickly? Maybe not, after all, he was intelligent, four top A-levels and a first class degree... He'd claimed to be at home all that evening; no real alibi, but then, no reason to doubt his word, either, and no reason to think he had any desire to kill the kid. Until now, maybe?

The second interview – why had he questioned the boy again? That's right, there'd been a suggestion of an older lad near the quarry, cycling into town – lousy description, of both the boy and the bike, from that sales rep. driving home after his day on the road But enough that he'd felt it prudent to double-check Evans' story... The boy had told the same tale as before, and in a manner such as to support the truth of it – and Russell remembered the Headmaster confirming that he was generally to be trusted. But there had been something about that interview, hadn't there?

Reading on, through Foreman's notes of their conclusions at that time, he remembered: Carl Evans had looked disturbed, even frightened, when he found a detective waiting for him in the Head's study. Just the stress of the events, as Foreman had thought – or guilt?

He went through the rest of the file, to find that it added nothing new to his knowledge of the case. Leaning back in the easy chair, Russell felt uneasy in his spirit. He had nothing, not really, to base even a suspicion upon: A hint of guilt, perhaps, in the sixteen-year-old's manner; a vague sighting which could as well have been any other dark-haired teenage boy – and yet... What about the Indian connection? But they had no evidence either, nothing, from what Sally had told them, except the coincidence of the man's presence in an area where a number of young boys had gone missing.

And Evans *could* have killed Philip Dorman. His alibi was unsupported; he *could* have cycled from Warrenton to the quarry, met the kid, perhaps assaulted him before stabbing him, dumped the body, and still been home before his mother. And if it *was* him, that might explain why Philip hadn't tried to get away – he knew Evans, and probably trusted him, to judge from the Headmaster's assessment. But it was still all just supposition!

Russell's uneasiness persisted. It wasn't in his nature to jump to conclusions; he liked to have a solid foundation for his thoughts, to keep all the options open until the evidence took him to a firm decision. But this time, if he was honest with himself, deep in his heart, he *knew* he was right, even if there was nothing to support his belief that he could point to with any certainty. Intuition, Ha! He laughed quietly at himself, remembering Frank Simmons, the old Desk Sergeant, long since retired, and his infamous intuition – I must be getting as old and daft as he was, Russell thought. And yet, Simmons had been a good copper; and his intuition had been proved right too often to be so lightly dismissed.

How could he progress? Find out more of the Indian investigation, for a start – did they have anything definite to connect Evans to the disappearances? They must have something, surely, to have asked about any previous convictions. What was the Indian officer's name? He'd left Sally's note on his desk. Anyway, no point in trying to contact him now, with the time difference, the guy would probably be in bed; he'd fax him in the morning. No, Dammit, he'd telephone! He felt an urgency about the matter which he couldn't justify on the basis of the evidence – but somehow, he knew he had to move on it, without too much delay.

* * *

The next morning, once more urgent matters were in hand, Russell picked up the telephone. Getting through to the officer he wanted to talk to proved to be a slow process – the line was okay, but

Bhudran was obviously a very busy man. It was at the third attempt that the Indian police operator was able to put him through. At last, a voice with the round, sing-song lilt of the educated Indian spoke in his ear:

'Bhudran.'

'Inspector? This is Detective-Inspector Russell of the Northamptonshire Police, calling from England.'

'Mr Russell? It's good to hear from such a distant colleague! How are things in England?'

'Not so bad, thank you, Inspector - we're having quite a good summer, for once!' Bhudran laughed:

'You mean it isn't raining at the moment?' Russell joined in his laughter:

'Not right now, no!'

'That's good! What can I do for you, Mr Russell?'

'You recently contacted our C.R.O. about a man called Steven Evans, in connection with the disappearance of some children in your area?'

'Oh yes, that is right. What do you want to know?'

'Can you tell me a little more about your suspicions? It may possibly tie in with an old investigation here in England.'

'Well, Mr Russell: We don't have any evidence, I'm afraid, or we would have been trying to have him arrested in Norway and sent back, you understand? Let me explain to you what has been happening here: We have a problem with children who live on the streets of our towns, Mr Russell – orphans, for the most part. They live by begging, or stealing, although a few do whatever jobs they can get. They are a nuisance, but no-one really tries to solve the problem. But I have been trying to keep an eye on the ones here in Andrabad, help them a little, perhaps, and keep them from stealing. I realised a little while ago that one or two of the boys I knew were not to be seen; and when I asked the other ones, they said that these boys had disappeared. They did not know what had happened to them, or where they were. One little girl told me she had seen one of the boys get into a car, with a man in it. She didn't see the number – and we really have only one sort of car here in India, Mr Russell! They only make them in two or three different colours, so it will be nearly impossible to identify it, I'm afraid.' Bhudran paused; Russell asked:

'Is there more, sir?'

'Oh, yes, Mr Russell! I contacted my colleagues in the other towns around here, and when they'd checked, they told me the same thing – in each town, there are two or three street children, all boys, who have disappeared; sometimes more, sometimes less. And several were seen to get into a car, a white Ambassador. Now, Mr Evans had a white Ambassador while he was living here – but as I say, that means very little; nearly all the cars here in India are Ambassadors, and white is the most popular colour - because it reflects the heat, you understand. We have found *his* car, and examined it, but there was nothing, nothing at all which would help us. But I am getting my cart before my horse, I'm afraid! The reason we wanted to look into Mr Evans and his affairs is because the neighbours where he lived had sometimes heard a child's voice coming from inside his house, although they knew he usually lived alone; and he had been seen once or twice to arrive at the house he rented with a little boy. We do not know if these boys were the ones that are missing, you understand? And we do not know that he has done anything improper with them, either. So we are not sure of anything – I had hoped to see if the British Police knew anything about Mr Evans, which might help us.'

'I see. Did you look at the house, Inspector?'

'We have; but there are new people there now, and we could find nothing.'

'You haven't found any of your missing boys, I take it?'

'No, Mr Russell – they have vanished into thin air! I would like to search for them, but they are... not considered to be important enough, by my superiors, you understand?' He paused:

'That sounds very inhumane, I know - but you have to understand that these children cause a real nuisance; and no-one is responsible for them, so no-one makes a fuss about them, about what happens to them. If a few disappear, there are those who would turn a blind eye, if you know what I mean?'

'Yes, indeed. What sort of ages were these missing boys?'

'All between about nine and twelve, as far as I can tell – many of these children do not know for sure how old they are themselves, you see. May I ask, what is it you are investigating that brings you to telephone me?' Russell sighed:

'I have an old case here, a boy who was murdered twelve years ago. He was twelve years old, and at the time, your Mr Evans was at school with him, although he was older, sixteen. They knew each other; but like you, I have no real reason to suspect Evans. He *could* have killed the other boy – but we have no real motive, and we never found the weapon.'

'How did your boy die, Mr Russell?'

'He was stabbed, Inspector. *Possibly* sexually assaulted, but there was no proof of that.'

'Very good. I will talk to my superiors again, see if they will let me try to find any of our boys. If I find anything, shall I call you?'

'Yes, please! I have a bad feeling about all this, I'm afraid.'

'I do too, Mr Russell. I'll call you if we find anything. Goodbye for now, then.'

'Goodbye, Inspector. And thank you.'

Russell sat back, leaning into the reclined position of his leather office chair, and swung his feet onto the edge of the desk. Thank goodness for the new furniture that had come with the new building, at least he could be comfortable at work now!

Well – what to make of that? Boys, all around the same age as Philip Dorman, going missing, a whole raft of them, by the sound of it! And Evans, in the vicinity, even seen with a young boy once or twice; and a kid's voice coming from his house.

Maybe this was beginning to add up. But: If he'd abducted and killed the boys in India, his motive must have been sexual, surely? That made sense in itself, but how did Philip fit in? Could a boy of just sixteen *already* be a paedophile? Or *was* it sexual - was the man rather a psychopath, who was killing for the sake of it? Either way, if Evans *hadn't* killed Philip, the whole thing became no more than a strange coincidence.

Chapter Twenty-Nine

Russell stuck his head around the door of the C.I.D. office:

'Doug? Shoot down to the canteen and get us some sandwiches, will you?' He paused: 'No, dammit, come on, let's get some lunch out. The Black Horse?'

'Okay sir, whatever you say!'

Rimmer put down the file he had been working on and followed his superior down to the car park:

'You drive, Doug.' Russell threw him his car keys.

'Sure thing, boss!' Rimmer grinned – Uncle Roger's legacy had stretched to a new Jeep Station Wagon as well. Big and strong, with a powerful six-cylinder engine, Rimmer had been itching for an opportunity to drive it. They left the car park, and drove to the pub in Bevington, five minutes down the road.

Over a drink while they waited for their sandwiches (Shandy for Rimmer, of course!) Russell brought his Sergeant up to date on the Indian officer's revelations:

'What do you make of this Evans business, Doug?' Rimmer considered for a moment:

'Well – It's getting to be too much of a coincidence, isn't it? But there's still no evidence, no solid connection.'

'That's how I feel. The only connection is his presence in both cases. If we knew what had happened to the kids in India it would help – for all we know, they could have been taken as a kind of slave labour force. I mean, they still use child labour in a lot of factories out there, don't they? Bhudran did say he'd try to get permission to start a proper search, so maybe we'll find out sooner or later. Or if we could link him with Philip Dorman's death in any positive way. He *could* have done it, but that doesn't mean he did. And why?'

'Sex? What other possibility is there? You and Foreman seem to have ruled out any kind of argument or grudge, and he didn't have anything on him to steal.'

'Yeah – but there was no evidence to support that; and it assumes that Evans was a paedophile. All right, *maybe* he is now, although we don't even know that for sure, but when he was sixteen? Is that possible?'

'I don't know, sir. Perhaps we should ask the company shrink?'

'Who?'

'You know, Doctor Huillier, the woman they called in for that psychological profiling for the rape case in Northampton, last March?'

'That's an idea, Doug – Do you want to call her, see if she can come over and talk to us sometime? Soon as possible?'

'Yeah, will do. Switchboard'll have her number, I expect.'

That afternoon, Rimmer duly called the psychologist, and arranged for her to visit the station the following Tuesday. Then other matters took precedence, and neither man thought much about Evans for a few days. Until the Tuesday, when things began to happen with a suddenness that almost caught them by surprise.

* * *

Doctor Huillier turned out to be a short, stocky woman in her late forties, greying, with heavily-rimmed spectacles, smartly dressed in a navy-blue suit. She sat in front of Russell's desk; Rimmer perched on its edge, as was becoming his frequent habit. After the usual exchange of greetings, Russell explained their problem:

'Doctor, we have a case, the murder of a little boy, which we suspect may have been sexually motivated. One of the principal suspects is an older boy of sixteen, but we're not sure we can attribute that kind of motive to someone so young, so we'd like your opinion?'

'What you're asking is, could a boy of sixteen be a paedophile, yes?' Her voice was attractively husky, with the barest vestige of a French accent.

'That's right.'

'Well – I'm not sure that question has ever been asked before, at least, not in so many words. I have never seen any research or discussion of the subject, so the honest answer is that I don't know for sure. However... let me try to extrapolate from what I *do* know: By that age, most teenagers are into dating and a series of short-term relationships, which are usually not fully sexual but stop short at kissing and cuddling and petting. So the *normal* child of that age is more or less confirmed in their sexuality, but perhaps not really settled into it in a mature manner. Equally, youngsters who are homosexual are often *aware* of the fact by that age, but are not usually actively pursuing their sexuality, perhaps more from a reluctance to admit it than for any other reason – and that can be masked by the fact that many teenagers, boys especially, experience a kind of temporary homosexual phase during adolescence, even if they grow up to be normally heterosexual. So: Is it possible that a boy of sixteen could already be showing paedophile tendencies? Theoretically, I suppose it has to be possible. But I would expect the tendency to deny any such feelings would be even stronger than in the conventionally homosexual teenager. Does that help?'

Even if the woman's conclusions seemed clear enough, the manner of her explanation had left Russell feeling mildly bewildered: 'Er - yes, I think it does, Doctor. But there's no evidence to support your view?'

'Not that I'm aware of. There *have* been cases of teenagers sexually assaulting younger children, but these have tended to be regarded as a kind of juvenile aberration rather than paedophilia as such. There was the baby-sitter and her boyfriend who regularly assaulted youngsters in their care a few years ago, for example. Perhaps these were instances of teenage paedophilia, which were not recognised as such at the time? I'll have to see if there was any follow-up, see if any of these kids turned into child-molesters in later life.'

'We can say that it *is* possible, if perhaps unlikely, for our sixteen-year-old to have assaulted and killed a kid of twelve, then?'

'Yes, I think so. I would think it most likely that any such act by a youth of that age would have been done on impulse rather than premeditated, an unintended giving-in to his subconscious desires. And remember that, especially during the confused sexual period of adolescence, the desire to cause pain or even death can have a sexual undertone in itself – the kind of thing which may come out as sado-masochism later.'

'Yes, of course! I remember talking about that with my old boss about this very case, years ago.'

'This is not a new case then, Inspector?'

'Oh, no. We're talking about the murder of Philip Dorman, just over twelve years ago.'

'Oh, I see. I remember hearing about it at the time. Tell me Inspector - do you know if this man has attacked other children, in later years?'

Russell glanced thoughtfully at his assistant as he replied: 'That's precisely why we're taking a new interest in the case, Doctor. If our suspicions are correct, he has been making a habit of abducting and murdering young boys for some time.'

'And he hasn't been *caught?*' She sounded incredulous.

Russell shook his head: 'He's been living in India for about four years; as you'll know, they have a problem with unwanted street children in many parts of that country. It seems he's been taking his pick of them, and it's only thanks to my opposite number in a town there, who's been trying to help some of these kids, that his depredations have been spotted. And even he has no proof that our man's responsible for their disappearance.'

'I see… And do we know where he was between the time of your first murder, and the beginning of these disappearances in India? There must have been a gap of what, seven or eight years?'

'He was at university, in Oxford, for four of them; and then in South America, largely Brazil, for two. With his last year at school here, and the odd interval, that covers the time in between.'

'Ah! Brazil - another country with a population of street children! I wonder if he was up to the same tricks there?'

The two detectives exchanged startled looks: 'Good God, you're right! I don't know if we could find out, though, if it wasn't noticed before.'

'Probably not, sir' Rimmer put in 'the authorities there are even less concerned about such kids than the Indian people. There've even been reports on the TV that the local police have been suspected of rounding them up and killing them themselves; so anyone grabbing the occasional one for his own purposes would probably have a blind eye turned, even if they did know about it.'

'Were any of these Indian boys raped, or otherwise sexually assaulted, Inspector?' Doctor Huillier asked: 'I assume there was no evidence of that with the Dorman boy, since you said you only suspected a sexual motive.'

'At this stage, we don't know. And you're quite right, there was no *evidence* of sexual assault in our case.'

'I see. How did these boys die, precisely?'

'Again, with the Indian kids, we won't know until they find the bodies. Philip Dorman was stabbed, once, in the chest.'

'Ah! You will see the obvious sexual connotation, in the use of a knife? I wonder if your suspect gets his great thrill from the act of killing, the thrust of his knife into their bodies - that might support my idea that his first murder, at least, was an act of impulse. I would guess that he found himself alone with the boy, sexually aroused, and with a knife to hand somehow. If there had been some sexual element in their encounter – although that could have been only in his mind? And he was overcome by the desire to *use* the knife, expressing his sexuality in that way.'

Russell sat back, a thoughtful look on his face: 'So, Doctor - You think his motives are sexual in an underlying way, even if he doesn't necessarily go in for any actual sexual activity with these kids? Sounds as if he's some kind of psychopath!'

'I'm leaning toward that conclusion, on the basis of what you tell me, yes.'

'And, if our suspicions are correct, this man is going to go on killing until someone stops him, would you agree?'

'Oh, certainly. If what we conjecture is right, this man is a predator, there is no other word for him. He will have developed a sense of invulnerability, I would surmise, if he has been getting away with this for so long - he will be feeling that he can go on taking his pleasure in this way without concern for the consequences, has probably even lost any sense that what he is doing is wrong, morally or legally. But the good thing is, he is likely to get careless, sooner or later. If he returns to a country where there is no community of uncounted children for him to prey upon, he will have to look to the normal population for his victims - and then, one slip, and he is likely to be caught.'

Russell ran a hand through his hair: 'The thing is, Doctor, we have no real evidence against this man at all. It's all just supposition, based on nothing more than the fact that he happens to be around where these things are happening. I can't *do* anything unless we can connect him positively with at least one kid's death - and even then, he's not in this country, so it would be up to the local police to deal with him. But that's our problem - you've been very helpful. Thank you for coming in to talk to us.' He stood up and shook her hand; she smiled sympathetically at him:

'I wish you luck, Inspector.'

Rimmer returned to the office after seeing the psychologist out of the building; Russell looked up at him, his eyes clouded with concern:

'If she's right, Doug…'

'It's frightening, isn't it? She makes him sound like our own version of Hannibal Lecter.'

'Yeah. Worse, even - how many kids has he killed already? I don't suppose we'll ever know.'

'No. Listen, boss, I was wondering - do you want me to check with Thames Valley, see if they've got any young boys missing in the Oxford area, from the time he was at University?'

'You'd better do that.' Russell looked up thoughtfully at his Sergeant: 'It's all starting to sound horribly feasible, isn't it, Doug? But there's still no damned evidence!'

'No, sir - but…' he broke off as the telephone rang; the Inspector picked up the receiver:

'D.I. Russell.'

'Mr Russell? Bhudran, in Andrabad, here. I have some news for you.'

'Oh? What have you got?' He put a hand over the mouthpiece, and motioned for Rimmer to pick up the other line. The Indian officer went on:

'We have found two bodies, Mr Russell. We are trying to identify them now, but I am sure they are two of our missing boys – they are rather decomposed, as you might imagine, but out pathologist is working on them. They were found out in the country, in shallow graves, in the middle of nowhere as you might say. I will let you know more as soon as I can.'

'Thank you, Inspector! We've been trying to confirm our suspicions about the old case here, and while we still have no real evidence, it is beginning to look like there might well be a connection, if your boys have been abducted and killed as we suspect. Keep me informed, won't you?'

'Oh, I will. It is late here now, I am going home to my wife, but I will try to call you tomorrow and tell you what we've found out. Goodnight, Mr Russell.'

'Goodbye, and thank you.'

Russell looked at his junior officer:

'Well!'

'Well, indeed, sir. Perhaps we *are* getting somewhere.'

Chapter Thirty

It seemed strange to be back home; back in Grancester, back in the same house. Even stranger, to be here without his mother fussing over him. Now that the strain of looking after her those last few weeks, the pressure of the arrangements that had had to be made following her death, and the final emotional climax of the cremation were over, he had time at last to relax, and feel the strangeness of it all.

He stood there in the kitchen, leaning on the edge of the sink, gazing out across the street. These old ex-council houses were all so near identical, he could have been looking into a gigantic mirror, set up in the middle of the roadway – he looked at the kitchen window directly opposite him, and, for a moment, almost expected to see his own reflection looking back. He smiled to himself, his mind ticking over on its own like a motor that someone had forgotten to switch off.

He'd known there was something wrong last Christmas – she'd seemed pale and drawn, although still her usual loving, bustling self. It had taken until the end of June for her to admit she was really ill, even if the doctors had diagnosed lung cancer back in February: At last, she'd called him and told him that it might be serious. Might be! Five weeks later, she was dead. Typical, he thought, smiling to himself; and, right to the end, she was the only one who still insisted on calling him Carl.

Steve Evans, as he was known to the rest of the world, had

been carving out a successful career for himself. Still was, really – he'd been assured that his job would be open with Kronburg's if he wanted to return to it later. But for now, he'd taken a post as a teaching assistant in the civil engineering department at the new University Faculty, on a one-year contract, accepting the job while his mother was still alive, unsure just how long he would be needed to look after her. He'd regretted leaving Kronburg's; but when he learnt of her illness, he'd felt he had no choice but to return to England and care for her, and that had meant quitting his job and leaving Norway. It had been a pity about little Ore, a shame to have had to kill him before he'd really wanted to...

He'd been with Kronburg GmbH, the German-based multinational, since he'd come back from his two years in South America; in fact, it had been someone he met out there who'd suggested he apply to them. Brazil had been fun; he'd been working as a volunteer with World of Water, the international charity which set out to provide clean drinking water and irrigation schemes in the third world, glad to get away from Oxford and its memories. He still felt guilty about Kerry, how he'd had to part from her – he'd tried to let her down gently, but there'd been a tearful scene... But he'd known he couldn't carry their relationship on any longer, not after Craig...

But Brazil *had* been fun! The country itself, especially in the hinterland, away from the major conurbations, was beautiful, and the work itself had been interesting, fulfilling; and the boys... He'd been able occasionally to use one of the trucks, sometimes on business, sometimes for his own pleasure; and you only had to drive slowly through any of the towns to have your choice of any number of deliciously brown kids. Every town had its share of street kids – they came in all ages, and both sexes, either orphans or runaways. And no-one to miss them, or even notice they'd disappeared, except maybe their grubby compadres - and who was going to listen to *them?*

He'd had lost count of how many he'd taken. It was so simple, with the inducement of a few coins, or just a ride in the truck, to select a suitable boy of ten or eleven and get him to jump in. The lack of a common language hadn't been a barrier – a big smile and a beckoning hand had sufficed. He'd always had a spot in mind, a place to take them, well away from any populated areas, before he picked them up. It had been quite easy to get them to undress; mostly of Indian or mixed descent, they apparently had no great inhibitions about stripping naked, any way. And then an hour or two, enjoying them - the feel of soft warm skin under his hands arousing him to the ultimate, double thrill of sex and killing. He'd brought his knife with him, of course.

And then India. After a six-month course of specialist training, back in England, they'd offered him the job in the Madhya Pradesh, consulting with government agencies about irrigation on the Deccan Plateau and in other areas. India was another country with a huge population of unaccounted-for children, street-children in the towns, much like Brazil. The Indian boys had been much harder to get naked – in the rivers, near water, they'd happily splash about completely nude, but anywhere else, oh no! It seemed to be something in their culture…

He had had to adopt a different tack. He'd rented a small house, on the outskirts of a nondescript town, soon after arriving in the country; when he'd tempted his chosen boy into the car he'd also acquired, usually with a handful of Rupees, he'd often take them back there, entering through the back yard to avoid prying eyes. Language had been a problem to begin with; but he'd always been good at picking things up, and soon had a foundation of some of the local dialects - and English was a common second language in India, a lot of the kids understood at least a little. Once indoors, of course…

He'd often keep a kid there for a while, especially if he had some time off – that way, he could take two or three days over enjoying their presence, the closeness of their lithe, healthy young bodies. He would allow his fascination with them to grow slowly, up to the final, greatest climax, thrusting the knife into their slim golden bodies, after... The Indian boys had always reminded Steve of Craig. Like him, they were mostly slim and beautiful, with big soulful eyes, although his had come from his African-American-English parentage.

But the boy who had always stood out in his mind was Philip – over twelve years ago, now, but he could still remember so clearly: The boy's tall, slim figure, his blond hair, his sparkling grey eyes; the soft, warm feel of his bare skin; and the incredible feeling when, for the first time, his knife had pierced a kid's heart...

Thinking of Philip reminded Steve of Ore. The Norwegian boy had been a lot like him, tall and blond, although his eyes had been blue. He'd met the lad a couple of weeks before his mother's fateful telephone call, and had been cultivating a friendship with him. He knew he was going to have to be a lot more careful in a civilised country like Norway, a boy like Ore was going to be missed; so he'd been trying to keep their friendship secret, without arousing the boy's suspicions. And he'd had to be sure, when the time came, that he wouldn't be found...

He'd have to go back to Scandinavia! Norway, Sweden, Denmark, all the peoples of the area had this wonderfully relaxed attitude to nudity – he'd been amazed at first to occasionally see people in their gardens, sunbathing naked, and their children playing happily without a stitch on. He'd even got Ore to play nude, in the back garden of the little house he'd rented in Helborg, that time he'd come to visit. It had been a shame to kill the boy so soon – he might have enjoyed days or even weeks more of seeing the kid regularly.

But then, he'd had no option, had he? Kronburg's had let him go straight away, under the circumstances, so that last day, before getting his flight home in the evening, he'd taken the boy up into the mountains in the hired car. He'd told Ore he had to leave, but the boy had been shocked at the suggestion of sex as a parting memory, tried to resist... At the last, the surge of pleasure as his knife thrust into the kid's slim, tanned back had been every bit as good as he'd anticipated. It was quite a remote area - they shouldn't find the grave, by the stream of snow-melt water, for a long time, if ever. And, of course, coming back to England had got him away from the investigation that must follow the boy's disappearance.

Yes, it was strange, to be here, alone in the house. But he was able to spend his days at the new college – in the grounds of his old school, would you believe it! He had a lot to do there, helping to source and install equipment in the new facility. Tomorrow would be the first day of term for the boys of Elwood Priors; maybe, come lunchtime, he'd take stroll along the hedge that was interposed between the two establishments of learning, take a look around in case there were any pretty boys to be seen...

Chapter Thirty-One

Early September – and back to school. Only this time around, it was back to a new school, so to speak.

Daniel was eleven, coming on twelve, and that meant going up from his old junior school to senior school, from the small community of Great Thornwood Village School, to the infinitely vaster campus of Elwood Priors. Not that The Priors was as vast as it had been when Philip Dorman started there, thirteen years before – a part of the extensive grounds had been leased by the trustees to the County University, for the construction of a new Engineering Faculty, which was to open that very Autumn.

Daniel had begun his schooling at one of the town schools in Grancester; but then, when he was eight, his parents had moved from the town itself out to Bevington village, and he had spent the last three years at Great Thornwood School. That had been a good year; his Dad had been promoted to Inspector, and old Uncle Roger had died. Not that Uncle Roger dying was good, of course, even if Daniel *had* hardly known him – but his bequest to Daniel's mother had more than paid for their move to the lovely old cottage in Bevington, just in time for his baby sister to arrive in the June. The only problem had been that Dad had had to travel to Northampton where he was stationed at the Police Headquarters for a year or two; but even that had changed now – he'd come back to the Grancester station, to replace old Mr Foreman when he'd finally retired.

He pedalled in through the gates of Elwood Priors that Wednesday morning, first day of term – Dad had bought him a new bike as a reward for getting into The Priors, one of only two boys from Great Thornwood to do so. And the other was his best mate, Jacko! The only thing was, Jacko's holiday had been mucked up by the tour company; they hadn't been able to go when they wanted, and, rather than lose out altogether, his parents had elected to take the dates they were offered, even if it meant he couldn't start at The Priors until next Monday. The School had understood, and given their agreement – but Daniel would have to start on his own, knowing no-one at all. But then, think of the fun he'd have showing Jacko the ropes when he finally joined him! He grinned to himself as he locked his bike, specially cleaned and polished for the occasion, into the rack.

In the entrance hall, he joined all the other new first-year boys, in their still-immaculate navy blue uniforms, waiting under the watchful eyes of two senior prefects. Before long, the Headmaster, Dr Frankham, entered through the towering oak doors at the far end of the hall, and called the boys to order. An imposing figure, tall and thin with a very academic-looking stoop, in his flowing black gown, he spoke to them briefly, introducing himself and telling them that they would join the rest of the pupils for assembly, and then go to their respective form rooms for further induction at the hands of their Form Masters. Each boy already knew which of the two first-year forms, 1A or 1B, they would be in; grading on ability or subject preferences didn't begin until the start of their second year.

After assembly, Daniel went with the other boys in 1A to their form room in the West Wing, built onto the old Manor House many years before. They spent what would normally have been the first two lessons with their Form Master, Mr Jawinski, the Head of Physics (and still known as Boris), getting to grips with their timetable and the plethora of School Rules and requirements. Jawinski proved to be a likeable man, enthusiastic about his subject and still, after fifteen years, keen to teach – he even had a sense of humour!

The short morning break arrived soon enough, and Daniel spent most of it in animated conversation with some of his new classmates; but he still wished that Jacko was with him. As they chatted, an older boy from the second-year sidled up to them:

'Hi! I'm Spooner – you must be first-years?' There was a general nodding of heads. The lad went on:

'Listen – I thought someone had better warn you, there's a couple of fourth-years planning to make things uncomfortable for some of you, the next day or two.'

There was a chorus of 'Who? Why? Which ones of us?' Spooner grinned:

'They don't care who – they'll just pick on someone at random, when they feel like it. The teachers don't tolerate any bullying here; it's only while you're new and don't know the system they can get away with it! If you have any trouble, report it! When Bulman and Jones get stomped on, they'll stop it, but they'll try it on until someone gets wise to them. Remember what I said!' He grinned, and walked away.

The youngsters looked at each other, and shrugged; better keep our heads down, was the general feeling. The bell rang; they collected their bags from the form room and departed for their first proper lesson in some trepidation – Chemistry with the Head!

At lunch, Daniel took his packed sandwiches and went to sit out in the grounds – it was a glorious, sunny early-autumn day. The old ruling that boys with packed lunches had to eat in the refectory had long been laid to rest. He strolled across the grass towards the spectacular glass-fronted buildings of the new Engineering Facility – only a low hedge with an occasional gap in it delineated the boundary between the ground leased to the University, and that still belonging to the School, with a few benches dotted along its length. Daniel stopped, looking over the hedge, admiring the glittering new building, wondering about the idea of studying engineering there one day, as he munched on his ham and cheese sandwich…

'Hey – you!' He turned – approaching him with an air of determination were two older boys, about fourteen. The first was heavily built, with a square face and dark, crew-cut hair, the second, trailing behind, skinnier and blond, with an unpleasant smile on his face. *Oh shit!* This just *had* to be Bulman and Jones! They came up to him, and stood in front of him with what they obviously felt were menacing grins on their faces:

'What you got for lunch, then?' *Best be polite, Daniel,* he thought:

'Sandwiches – cheese and ham.'

'That's shit! You don't want to eat that!' The crew-cut boy knocked the half-eaten sandwich out of his hand, and ground it into the grass with his heel:

'What else you got there?' The thin-faced boy asked.

'Some of my Mum's chocolate cake…'

'That'll do! Hand it over, I like chocolate cake!'

'Sod off! Get your own cake!' Anger got the better of common sense. The two older boys turned slowly to each other, their grins widening:

'Well, well! Cheek – and from an ickle first-year, too! We can't allow that, can we?'

'No, of course not – Frankenstein wouldn't like to hear him talking like that, would he?'

'Should we punish him, do you think?'

'I don't know – maybe. After all, we'd be saving the prefects a job, wouldn't we?'

'That's right, we would…' They turned their gleeful gaze back on Daniel.

'If there's any punishment coming around here, I think you two are in line for it, don't you?' A quiet voice spoke from over the hedge. None of the boys had seen the man approach along the University side of the boundary. They all looked up in surprise, Daniel looking over his shoulder at the shortish, dark-haired man who had come to his rescue. He spoke again:

'You two, get out of here! What's your name, lad?' he asked, switching his gaze to Daniel, and stepping through the gap in the hedge as Bulman and Jones sloped away, disgruntled:

'Russell – Daniel Russell, sir.'

'Oh, I'm not a 'sir', not one of yours, anyway! I work over here, in the Engineering College. I'm Steve Evans. Pleased to meet you, Daniel!' He put out his hand. Daniel took it, and they shook:

'Am I pleased to see you, Mr Evans! Thanks for… you know!' The man grinned at him:

'That's okay, glad I could help. I'll come with you, we should tell your teacher what happened – and my name's Steve, not Mr Evans, okay?'

They strolled back across the grass to the School, where Evans left the boy waiting in the hall to go in search of a Master. A few minutes later, the tall, cadaverous figure of Frankham himself came sweeping in in his billowing gown, with Evans in tow:

'Russell! You're all right, boy?' He turned to Evans, not waiting for an answer:

'Thank you for looking after Russell, Mr Evans, and for coming to tell me what's going on. We don't tolerate bullying here, I won't have it! Thank you again.'

'Any time, Headmaster!' Evans smiled, and bowed himself out. The Head turned to Daniel again:

'Come with me, Russell!' He led the way through an anteroom and into his impressive, oak-panelled office, and seated himself behind the massive desk.

'Now, Russell – you're the policeman's son, aren't you?'

'Yes, sir.' Daniel nodded.

'You heard what I said to Mr Evans – I will not tolerate bullying here, in any shape or form. I already know, from his description, the two boys involved – I've had trouble with them before. But, for the record, I need you to identify them – will you do that?'

'I don't know, sir…' Frankham smiled gently at the boy:

'I know it sounds like snitching, but you will only be confirming what I know already. And we have to stop those louts, before any more of your new classmates suffer, don't you think?'

'Yes, sir – okay, I'll pick them out for you.' Frankham's smile became a full-fledged grin, a rare sight on his thin face:

'We don't go in for identification parades like your father, I'm afraid! I'll have them brought in.'

He picked up the phone on his desk:

'Martha? Get hold of Mr Abelson, will you? Tell him I want Bulman and Jones in here – now!' He turned to Daniel again:

'Mr Abelson is my Deputy Headmaster. How are you settling in with us, Daniel?'

'Fine, I think, sir' Daniel was surprised and pleased by the Head's use of his first name – he hadn't expected the man to even know it without asking! 'It'll take me a while to find my way around, I expect, though.'

'This is rather a rabbit-warren of a place, isn't it? Still, you'll get used to it – I did!'

Daniel found himself warming to the Headmaster – here in private, he seemed friendly, and easy to talk to, quite different from his dominant presence in front of the school as a whole – encouraged, he asked:

'Have you been here long, sir?' Frankham smiled:

'Twenty – no, twenty-one years. Must seem like a lifetime to you, eh? I met your father once, in the course of his duties. Ten, twelve years ago? Something like that. One of our boys was killed, I'm afraid. Murdered. Great pity, very promising boy, very bright. They never caught the man, either. Terrible, to think he must be still out there somewhere.' A knock sounded at the door:

'Come!' Abelson, a short, rotund and balding figure with a

striking resemblance to Harry Secombe strode in, a very un-Harry-Secombe-like expression on his face; behind him, reluctantly, trailed Bulman and Jones. Frankham looked at Daniel, and raised his eyebrows. Taking his cue, the boy nodded.

'Thank you, Russell. Please wait outside.' The Headmaster was his usual brusque self again. Abelson led Daniel into the outer office:

'Wait here, Russell. You don't want to hear what's going to happen in there, believe me!' His grin made him look more like Harry Secombe than ever as he departed.

Daniel stood in the deserted ante-room to Frankham's office, trying not to listen to the voices from within. He couldn't make out any words, anyway, but the stern tones of the Head were interspersed with almost-inaudible mutterings from the two boys. At last, Frankham launched into a prolonged and obviously very emphatic lecture; Daniel resolved never to be the object of the Headmaster's displeasure, if he could possibly help it! And then the door opened. The two fourth-formers sloped out, their heads bowed – neither looked at Daniel as they passed him. Frankham beckoned the boy back into his domain:

'I've given those two the roasting of their lives, Russell. Not that they don't deserve it, they've given me trouble before, as I told you. If you hear of them going after any other of your compadres, you're to tell me, you understand? Just come here, and ask for me. Martha, my secretary, is usually in the outer office; she'll call me. Clear?'

'Yes, sir. And thank you, sir – they nearly spoiled my first day here.'

'Go on to your lessons, now, my boy. And thank *you!*'

Chapter Thirty-Two

That Wednesday morning, an early call had prevented Russell from seeing his son off for the first day at his new school. Russell and Rimmer were in one of the C.I.D. cars heading back from the latest exploit of the so-called cottage burglar when a call came through on the radio. The D.I. reached forward from the passenger seat and picked up the microphone:

'Delta 131; D.I. Russell.'

'Inspector – there's a phone call from India for you, do you want me to patch it through to the car?'

'Please.' He turned to Rimmer: 'It's Bhudran.' The Detective-Sergeant pulled the car over and stopped.

'Inspector Russell? Bhudran here. I have got the pathologist's report now.'

'Hello, Inspector – what have you got to tell us?'

'It is very interesting, Mr Russell. We cannot be sure of the identification, but the physical condition of the two bodies suggests that they could well be those of street children. They are rather undernourished and show signs of having a hard life. They both died from a single stab wound through the heart, although one was stabbed in the chest, and the other in the back. And there are signs that both had been subjected to sexual intercourse – in the back passage, you understand?'

'Well, what do you know? Our victim, twelve years ago, was stabbed once in the chest, just the same – straight through the heart. We didn't have any real evidence of sexual assault, except that he was found partly dressed.'

'Ah! It begins to sound as if we may have a common factor, does it not?'

'You can't actually link Evans with these children, can you?'

'Sadly, no, Mr Russell, at least not positively. We cannot prove that the boys he was seen with were any of the missing street children. But this must be more than a coincidence, I believe.'

'So do I, even if we can't directly link him with our murder either. I don't know how we are going to make any kind of case out of this, do you?'

'I cannot see how we can, at the present. I will keep searching, and if we find more of our missing boys we may find some useful clues. I will let you know, Mr Russell.'

'Thank you – I think I should contact the police in Norway, warn them of what we suspect. I'll be in touch, Inspector Bhudran.'

'Okay. Goodbye for now, then.'

The two detectives looked at each other for a moment. Then Russell said:

'Come on, Doug. Let's get back to the station. Where in Norway did Sally say this guy's working?'

'Somewhere up-country from Bergen, wasn't it – Ahlsberg, I think. The notes are on your desk, aren't they?'

'Yes, somewhere!'

* * *

In his office, Russell picked up the phone and asked the girl on the switchboard to try to get him the senior police officer in Ahlsberg. Rimmer, carrying two cups of coffee, joined him just as she rang back; Russell picked up the receiver:

'D.I.Russell.'

'Your call to Norway, sir. Chief of Police Kagstad on the line for you.'

'Thanks, Rachel.' There was a click on the line:

'Hello?' The voice had the light, fluid vowels of the Scandinavian.

'Chief Kagstad? Detective-Inspector Russell of the Northamptonshire Police in England here.'

'How can I help you, Inspector?'

'I understand that you have a new hydro-electric project being built near your town, by Kronburg GmbH?'

'That's quite right, we do. Why is that of interest to the English police?'

'Well, sir, we have reason to suspect that a man working on that project may be connected with a murder here in England, and also with a series of child abductions in India.'

'Oh? Tell me more, please.' The Norwegian suddenly sounded interested.

'This is all rather circumstantial, I'm afraid, sir. Twelve years ago, a young boy was killed here, stabbed. We never traced the killer. But recently, a number of boys of similar ages have gone missing in India – the local police there have just found two of their bodies. Both had been raped, and also stabbed; killed in a manner which suggests a possible link to our old case. And the common link, although we cannot directly tie him in to any of the deaths, seems to be a man by the name of Evans.'

'An Englishman, Inspector?'

'That's right, sir. His full name is Carl Steven Evans, but we believe he goes under the name of Steven now. He works for Kronburg's, and was transferred to your local project last February, according to their U.K. office.'

There was a silence at the other end of the line; then Kagstad spoke again:

'I see. Thank you, Inspector. We have a case here which may be connected also; a little boy called Ore Pedersen is missing from the town of Helborg, nearby here. How old were your victims?'

'The boy here was twelve – the ones in India seem to have been around the same age, or slightly younger.'

'I see. Ore is just eleven years old. It may be that we have a victim also, perhaps? I will talk to my officer who is dealing with his disappearance, and we will step up our search around the area for a body. What are we likely to be looking for, Inspector?'

'I'm not sure, sir. Our victim was thrown into a lake. The boys in India would seem to have been buried in shallow graves in the countryside.'

'Very good. We shall see what we can find, Inspector. I will talk to the man in charge at Kronburg also, see if he can tell me anything. Should I arrest this Evans?'

'We don't have enough evidence to ask you to do that, sir. I'll have to leave that to your judgement, depending upon what you may uncover. I wish you luck, sir!'

'Yes, Inspector, thank you. I will let you know how we progress. Thank you for the information. We will talk again soon.'

'Goodbye then, sir.' Russell hung up. Rimmer, who had been listening on the second line, whistled softly:

'Sounds like he's started already, doesn't it?' Russell picked up the fountain pen and began to toy with it. Without looking up, he said:

'Yes, Doug, it does.' He raised his eyes: 'Jesus! Why didn't I call him sooner? Maybe we could have saved that kid.'

'We don't know that he's dead, boss – or if Evans is responsible' Rimmer tried to console his superior.

'Oh, I suppose not – but it's too much to hope for, isn't it, that a boy of the right age goes missing just when and where we know the bastard has moved to, purely by chance? No, the kid's dead, Doug, I know he is.'

'We don't know how long he's been missing, though. Maybe Evans grabbed him before we began to put two and two together?'

'Possible. For the sake of my conscience, I hope so, Doug!

Come on, let's go and get some lunch. With Evans and our Cottage Burglar, I'm having a bad day!'

* * *

Over a sandwich in the canteen, the two turned to discussing the cottage robberies. That morning's raid had brought a new sense of urgency, since the thief had produced a hand-gun when the elderly man in the house had tried to resist. The thefts had begun some weeks before, the perpetrator targetting cottages in the local villages where he knew elderly people to live, forcing an entry after knocking at the door and stealing money and jewellery while the terrified owners looked on. When they had eaten, Rimmer set off in pursuit of information on the thefts, while Russell knocked on the C.I.D. chief's door:

'Come in! Oh, it's you, Russell, come in and take a seat.'

Harry Wilson looked not unlike his famous political namesake, and had become universally known in the division as The PM. Russell told his superior of the suspicions regarding Evans, and went through the entire trail so far, from Sally Brennan's first call to the conversation with Kagstad. When he'd finished, Wilson sat back and pursed his lips:

'So despite what seems like a pretty certain set of conclusions, we don't actually have any evidence against this man Evans?'

'Nothing that would stand up in a court, sir, no.'

'Hmm! Well, let's hope the Norwegians can nail him for us, eh? That seems like the best hope, doesn't it?'

'Yes, sir. It would be good if we could pin the Dorman case on him, though.'

'It would, wouldn't it? But I can't see how you're going to do that, can you?'

'No, sir, I can't. Either Kagstad or Bhudran might have a chance, if he's left any traces for them to find. But we haven't much hope, I'm afraid.'

'All right - well, keep me posted. Now, what about these cottage robberies? The press are getting too interested, with their silly nicknames, and now he's pulled a gun, I hear?'

'That's right, sir. First thing today, in Great Thornwood. Old gentleman tried to resist, and the man showed him a pistol. Could have been a replica, of course, but the old boy didn't want to find out the hard way – can't say I blame him.'

'No, of course. Are we any nearer to catching the villain, Russell?'

'Well, sir, we're certain he's from somewhere in the area. He always strikes in the early morning, and he seems to have knowledge of the locality and who lives where. But we've no clear suspect, and the fingerprints we've got are only smudged and partial, and we can't get a match as yet.'

'Okay, well, keep on it, Russell. And keep me informed – I'd like to be able to tell the press we're hot on his trail, if I can, and as soon as possible. Get them off our backs a bit.'

Chapter Thirty-Three

The following day, Daniel cycled in through the gates of The Priors in a mood of eager anticipation. Not only had the previous day left him feeling enthusiastic about the prospects at his new school, but today would see his first periods of maths and physics, the subjects he was most looking forward to. His eagerness stemmed, ironically perhaps, in part at least from the run-in with the school bullies, or more accurately from its aftermath, which had enormously boosted his confidence in the teachers, especially Dr Frankham. Locking his bike into the rack, he went to join his new classmates in their form-room, ready for assembly

He spent the morning break again talking with some of his new fellows – the boys were beginning to relax in each other's company a little, now. But at lunchtime, he again wandered off on his own. About two-thirds of the new boys were boarders, and so had to eat under the jurisdiction of the School's catering arrangements, which meant lunch in the refectory; and several of the day pupils had also elected for School dinners. Of those who had brought a packed lunch, some chose to eat with their classmates, others sat in the continuing sunshine, close to the old manor house itself.

Daniel again found himself drawn towards the new University buildings, across the grounds from the School itself. He sat on one of the benches next to the hedge, close to one of the gaps which allowed free access between School and College, and took out his sandwiches. Ham and tomato, today – he wasn't too keen on tomato, but what the heck; and it would keep his Mum happy if he ate it.

'Daniel! Mind if I join you?' The boy looked up; Steve Evans was standing the other side of the hedge. He swallowed a mouthful of sandwich, and nodded:

'Sure, if you like.' Evans came through the gap, and sat next to him:

'What happened yesterday, after I'd left?' Daniel grinned:

'The Head called those two into his office and gave them a real roasting! I was just outside, and it sounded like he was really laying into them – they wouldn't even look at me, when they came out!' Evans laughed:

'Yeah, I rather thought he'd stamp on them pretty hard – he didn't like bullies when I was here!'

'*You* were at The Priors?'

'Yeah! A long time ago, now – I left, oh, eleven years back. And now I'm teaching, myself, right next door!'

'Have you always been a teacher – before you came here to the College, I mean?'

'No! I'm only an assistant lecturer, anyway. I've been working in all kinds of places – I'm a civil engineer, really. You know what that is?' Daniel nodded:

'Sure! You build roads and bridges and things.'

'Close! I've worked in water supply, mostly, building dams and hydro-electric plants – and I spent two years in South America, mostly laying out an irrigation scheme in Brazil, when I first left college, as a volunteer. It was that experience, with my qualifications of course, that got me my job afterwards.'

'Wow! I'd like to do something like that, when I'm older. Is it difficult?'

'Not really, if you've got the right sort of mind. What subjects do you like best?'

'Oh, maths, and science – we had our first physics lesson this morning – that looks like fun!'

'Well, you're on the right track, then! Stick with those, get yourself a language or two as well, if you want to work abroad, like I've been doing. And grab any engineering training you can get, even if it's metalwork or that kind of thing – it'll all help.'

'Yeah, right…' Silence fell for a while, as man and boy demolished their respective lunches. Then Daniel asked: 'You live here, as well?'

'In the town, yes. None of us live in at the College, like some of your Masters. I've got a house, in Warrenton.'

'Yeah, I know it. We used to live in the town, but we moved to Bevington a few years ago – an old Uncle of my Mum's left her some money. Have you just moved here, then?'

'Oh, no! I was born and brought up here, in the same house. That's how I came to go to The Priors, I won a scholarship through my primary school. It was my mother's house then – she left it to me when she died.'

'When was that?'

'Last month.'

'Oh! I'm sorry!' Daniel felt embarrassed at having asked so tactless a question, but Evans just smiled at him:

'It's okay – she had cancer, it was a relief, for her as much as me, when she went. She'd been in a lot of pain, towards the end. I was in Norway when I heard, I left my job and came straight back to look after her, but she died within the month. It was lung cancer – she didn't know herself that she'd got it until earlier this year, and she didn't tell me until the end of June. She didn't suffer for long, thank God!'

Daniel kept quiet for a moment, respecting the man's sorrow. Then he asked:

'You've been to a lot of other countries?'

'Not that many – I was in India for several years, and Brazil, as I told you. I worked here in England for a few months between them; and I went to Norway after India. That was quite a shock, working on a hydro-electric scheme up in the mountains, in the snow and ice, after the heat and humidity of central India!'

'It sounds great, travelling the world like that! Will you go abroad again, do you think, or stay here now?'

'Oh, I expect I'll go off again, sometime. I took the teaching job here so that I can get everything in order after Mum died; I'd like to go back to my real work in a year or two. I don't know yet.'

Daniel was about to ask more questions, but the bell for the start of afternoon lessons rang in the distance.

'I've got to go – will you be here tomorrow?'

'I'll be in College – shall we meet for lunch again, if the weather's still nice?'

'Yeah! If you don't mind, that is?'

'I don't mind – it's nice to have someone to talk to. Especially a bright kid like you. See you then?'

'Yeah, sure! Bye!' Daniel grabbed his empty lunch-box and hurried back to the School.

The next day, Friday, they met again, at the same bench. After chatting casually for a while, and eating their lunches, Evans said:

'A lot has changed here, in the town I mean, since I left. There's a huge Industrial Estate, out beyond where I live – and all those new houses, up to the North of the town!'

'Yeah, they were just building them when we moved – Dad wondered about going there, but Mum wanted to live in the villages, so we bought the house in Bevington. It's an old cottage, really, or two of them, made into one. I'm glad we went there, it's a great place to live! I can cycle out into the country with Jacko – he's my best friend – and explore all over the place.'

'He goes to another school, does he?'

'No – he's coming here. But they're away until Monday. I'm looking forward to showing him around!'

'You'll have to introduce us, next week.'

'Sure!' Evans gave him a thoughtful look:

'You live in Bevington – is the old quarry still there, near the bypass?'

'Yeah! Only it's a country park, now. It was closed off for years, some kid died there, Dad said. But then they opened it up properly, just before we moved. There's a visitor centre place, with maps and things – and paths all around it, round the lake and through the trees. Dad says it's quite safe, now.'

'Do you go there much?'

'Oh, yeah! Jacko and I go there a lot. But we don't stick to the paths, of course – it's much more fun exploring through the woods. There's places in there where you can be right away from everyone else – no-one would even know you were there! That's much better – there's no fun in going where everyone else is, or just following the paths!'

'I wouldn't mind going there and having a look around sometime, to see how much it's changed.'

'Hey! Why don't I show you 'round? How about tomorrow, I've got nothing to do, with Jacko still away?'

'Are you sure? I mean, you must have better things to do. And wouldn't your folks object to you going off with a stranger?'

'You're not a stranger! But then, I suppose Dad might, hc's a bit funny like that. But they don't mind me going to the Park – I suppose; I wouldn't have to *tell* them you'll be meeting me there, would I?'

'As long as you're sure, Daniel. I don't want to get you into trouble?'

'Yeah, it'll be okay. It'll be fun – I'll show you some of our private places, too! If you don't mind scrambling through the trees a bit?'

'Okay – sounds good! I'll look forward to it.' Evans glanced at his watch:

'It must be nearly time – Yep! There's your bell – see you tomorrow, then? About two o'clock?'

'Okay – I'll cycle over and meet you there. Bye, Steve!'

Chapter Thirty-Four

Nothing further was heard from either Norway or India for the next couple of days, although Thames Valley Police came back with the information that they had no missing schoolboys still astray from the period of Evans' residence in Oxford. And Friday saw a surprising development in another case:

At 9.07am, the telephone rang in Grancester Police Station, and the operator answered:

'Northamptonshire Police, can I help you?'

'Hello, my dear. My name is Alicia Marshall – could I speak to the officer in charge of the Cottage Burglar investigation, please?'

'May I ask why you want to speak to him? D.I. Russell is very busy.'

'Tell him I have something for him which may help.'

'Is it information?'

'Oh, better than that, my dear!'

'I'll see if I can get him for you, Mrs Marshall.'

'It's Miss Marshall, dear; and thank you.'

The operator pushed a switch; the light on her panel responded:

'Russell.' In his office, the Detective-Inspector leant forward on his desk.

'There's a lady on the phone for you, sir, a Miss Marshall, about the Cottage Burglar.'

'Okay, put her through.' There was a click on the line, and then a firmly feminine voice spoke in his ear:

'Mr Russell? Alicia Marshall here, in Little Thornwood. I'd like you to come and see me, now if you will. And you'd better bring a couple of constables with you. I have a man here I think you're looking for.'

'What? Are you saying you've got our thief there now?'

'That's right, Inspector. I'd like you to come and take him away, please.'

'Where is he? Are you in any danger?'

'Oh no, he's quite safe, don't worry. I've locked him in the cellar.' Russell restrained the impulse to ask further questions:

'I'll be right there – please be careful, Miss Marshall.' He rang off, feeling totally bemused.

Collecting Rimmer from the C.I.D. office, the two officers took Russell's Jeep and drove, lights flashing, sirens blaring, to the village, a patrol car with two uniformed officers following. At Number Four, The Green, they were welcomed by the diminutive white-haired figure of Alicia Marshall:

'Inspector Russell? Please come in. And your colleagues, of course.' She led them into the neat, spotlcss living-room of the cottage:

'Please sit down. Would you like a cup of tea?'

'If you don't mind, Miss Marshall, we ought to collect your house-guest and take him back to the station straight away.'

'Oh, don't be in such a rush Inspector! He's not going anywhere, and the kettle's hot. Sit yourselves down, I'll only be a moment.' She bustled off into the kitchen. Russell and Rimmer looked at each other, wondering just what was going on and trying hard not to laugh at the absurdity of the situation. They all sat down as directed; Miss Marshall returned with a tea-tray, and set about serving them.

As he sipped his tea, Russell introduced his Sergeant, and then asked:

'How do you come to have our burglar in your cellar, Miss Marshall?'

'Oh, he tried to rob me this morning, Inspector. But I took exception to that idea, as you might imagine, and stopped him.'

'You... But he'd been carrying a gun!'

'Yes, it's on the sideboard, over there. You'd better take that with you, too.'

Russell looked at his Sergeant, who was finding it almost impossible to keep a straight face. He turned back to the little old lady, delicately sipping at her own cup:

'How did you manage to overcome our friend, Miss Marshall?'

'Oh, it wasn't difficult, Inspector. He thought I was terrified of him, and made the mistake of turning his back on me. If you know where to dig your knuckle in, it's quite easy to incapacitate someone. Mind you, it's lucky he's not a big man, if he'd been as tall as you, I doubt if I could have done it. I'm quite small myself, as you can see.'

'But the gun?'

'Oh well, if you twist a man's wrist the right way, it's no problem to disarm him. Especially if he's already in considerable pain. But he didn't want to co-operate, even then. I'm afraid I had to damage him a little.'

'You did *what?*'

'Oh, don't worry, I only shot him in the leg. I made him bandage it himself, and then put him in the cellar. These cottages aren't as old as people think, you see – they're only mid-Victorian, and they were built with a small coal-hole under the kitchens. I keep my wine down there, now. The trap-door's bolted, and it's very strong, so he won't get out until we let him. Come on, finish your tea, Inspector; have a biscuit, do. And you, Mr Rimmer, Constables.'

As the men complied meekly, she went on:

'I entertained your predecessor to tea once, Mr Russell. Mr

Foreman came to see me just about twelve years ago. It was about that poor little boy who was killed at the old quarry, where the park is now. You know, young Philip Dorman.'

'Yes, indeed. I was on the case with him, he was my old boss then. You helped to provide an alibi for someone we suspected, didn't you?'

'That's right, Inspector. That taxi-driver, Broadbent; I was in his cab when you thought he might have been killing the boy.' She laughed: 'You needn't look so surprised, Mr Russell! I have a near-photographic memory. It was very useful in my old job.'

'Of course!' he turned to Rimmer: 'Miss Marshall was in M.I.6 for many years.'

'Really?' The Sergeant sounded impressed as well as startled.

'That's right, Mr Rimmer – the tales I could tell you! But I'm not allowed to, of course; Official Secrets Act and all that, you understand.'

'We've been looking at the Dorman case again recently, Miss Marshall. We think we may have a new lead on who killed the boy.'

'After all this time? Oh, that would be good! I've often thought of that poor kiddie, and it seems so unjust for his killer to still be on the loose. I do hope you can catch him at last.'

'Well, it may be that he will be arrested and tried somewhere abroad – I'm afraid it sounds as if he's been making a habit of abducting and killing young boys while he's been working in foreign countries over the last few years.'

'Oh, that's terrible! I hope he gets locked up, and for a good long time, too.'

'We hope he will be, and soon.' Russell replaced his cup: 'And now, if you don't mind, we should relieve you of your captive and get him back to the cells.'

'Yes of course. Do come with me.' She got up from her chair, and led them through into the kitchen. Unbolting a trap-door against the wall by the back door, she lifted it and looked down:

'Are you ready to go with the Inspector, Mr Riley?'

She stepped back to allow the officers to enter the cellar. At the bottom of the steps, they found the perpetrator of the robberies, a short, stocky man in his thirties wearing a black sweatshirt and black trousers, one leg of his trousers had been cut open, and a bandage was tied around his thigh. Between them, they hauled him up none too ceremoniously, half-carried him through the cottage, and placed him in the back of the patrol car, which departed to take him into custody via the local hospital. Russell bade farewell to the old lady; as he turned to go, he looked back for a moment:

'Miss Marshall – if it's not too rude of me to ask, how old are you?' She smiled at him:

'Oh, I don't mind, Inspector! I'm seventy-nine.' She paused: 'perhaps it would be best if you tell the press that you happened to come and see me, and caught that man yourselves? It would look better, wouldn't it? And I really don't want those horrible reporters hanging around here, pestering me. We never did like the press in my office, as you'll understand!'

'If you're sure? I don't want to take the credit away from you.'

'No, please. It would be best, I'm sure.'

'Well, goodbye then, Miss Marshall. And thank you very much!'

'Goodbye, Inspector – goodbye, Mr Rimmer. I'll be talking to you soon, I expect.'

In the car, as they drove away, Russell glanced over at his Sergeant. Rimmer caught his eye, and dissolved into helpless laughter:

'I must be dreaming! She can't be real, surely?'

'I wouldn't want to get on the wrong side of her, would you?' Rimmer shook his head, tears of mirth streaming down his face.

Chapter Thirty-Five

That evening, after dinner, Russell was sat in the study with his son. They had an old tablecloth spread over the desk; both were working on model yachts.

Russell was beginning upon his latest project; Daniel had been given an old model by a club acquaintance of his father's, and was in the process of rebuilding it. The hull, of a miniature planked construction, was in poor repair, with a couple of damaged planks, and in need of completely revarnishing. Resting for a moment from his own work, Russell looked across at his son, and smiled with pride. The tousled blond head was bent over the job, the boy's slim fingers working delicately, but with a firm confidence as he carefully fitted a newly-shaped plank into the sleek shape of the boat.

Russell had enjoyed a lot of his son's company that week, with Jack Carter and his family away on holiday – although he felt rather selfish at the same time, as the boy was obviously missing his friend. The sailing this weekend was to be at a lake to the North of Milton Keynes; If he got the hull varnished, Daniel might just be ready in time...

The telephone rang, and Russell heard his wife answer it in the hall. A moment later, she tapped on the study door, and looked in:

'David – it's for you. Doug Rimmer, at the station.'

'This time of night? What's he doing there?'

'I don't know, love – come and talk to him!' He hurried through to the hall and picked up the receiver:

'Russell.'

'Sir? I was just doing my report about this morning – Kagstad's just rung, from Ahlsberg. They've found their missing boy's body, but that's not all – it seems Evans isn't there any more. He's presumed to be in England.'

'*What?* Can you come over here, Doug, and tell me all about it?'

'Of course, sir. On my way.'

Russell warned his wife that Rimmer was coming to see him; reluctant to disturb his son, when the knock came at the door, he led the Sergeant into the dining-room:

'What's happened, Doug?'

'Well, for a start, they've got the kid's body. Apparently, some hill-walkers found him. He'd been buried beside a stream up in the hills, but the melt-water had washed part of the bank away and exposed him. They've had some unusually warm weather lately, so there was more water coming down than usual. Initial examination suggests he's been stripped, raped and stabbed in the back, just like one of Bhudran's victims. At the moment, Kagstad can't tie Evans in positively, but he's pursuing witnesses and hoping to come up with something there.'

'What's this about him being back in England?'

'Yeah! Kagstad contacted Kronburg's, for Evans' local address, which was in a village called Helborg, by the way. They came back to him today, and said that the guy's no longer working for them. It would appear that his mother's seriously ill, and he has left them to come home and look after her.'

'So he's back *here?*'

'Assuming she still lives here, yes. Kronburg's still have this as his home address, apparently. Eighty-two, Newtown Road, Warrenton.'

'Can you check that out, Doug? I suppose the morning will

have to do, you won't be able to get far tonight. When did he leave Norway?'

'End of June, beginning of July. The Pedersen boy has been missing since around the same time, Kagstad tells me. Before we began to put two and two together, boss.'

'Hnh! That may salve my conscience, Doug, but it doesn't help that poor kid, or his family, does it? Quick thrill before he left the country? And how long before he tries something here, now he's back? We've got to stop him somehow, Doug!'

'Can we arrest him on what we know, boss?'

'I doubt it, Doug. We'll have to get files from India and Norway to back it up, anyway. I'll talk to Mr Wilson in the morning, see if we can't at least put a tail on him, see what he does and where he goes. Is he working, or just looking after the mother?'

'I don't know, yet. I'll find out by tomorrow, if I can.'

'Okay, Doug. There's not much more to be done tonight. I'll see you in the office, eight o'clock, all right?'

'Sure thing. See you then, sir. Say goodnight to Tracy and the kids for me.'

'I will. Night, Doug.' Russell saw the Sergeant to the door, and returned to the dining-room, where he sat and tried to think through the implications of Evans' return to Grancester.

* * *

In Warrenton, Steve Evans decided to treat himself to dinner out that night. Dressed in smart grey trousers and a sports jacket, he walked through the warm autumn evening up to Midland Road and thence to the town centre, where he went to Martelli's, the better of the two Italian restaurants. After a Bolognese starter and a filling Tagliatelle Carbonara, he sat back with a cup of coffee and a glass of brandy, contemplating the morrow.

Things were looking good, now. He still found it strange to

be here without his mother fussing around him, but they hadn't been very close in her later years, and he found himself only missing her with a sort of relaxed melancholy. His job at the new college was going to be a fascinating challenge – maybe he could study for his Master's Degree while he was there? And that gorgeous little boy!

What would tomorrow bring? He couldn't wait to meet the kid again! He sat, thinking of the boy's cute face, his lovely green-brown eyes, his thick mop of golden-blond hair. What was his body like? He'd looked nice and slim in his school uniform, the same navy blue he'd worn himself so many years ago. Daniel – even the name appealed to him, somehow. If the sun shone tomorrow, perhaps he could get the kid out of his shirt, see him bare to the waist, even touch him? The thought of soft warm skin under his hands began to excite him; the boy had said about a secret hidey-hole in the park's woodland – maybe, if the kid wanted to show him where it was, he might even get him completely undressed in its privacy… But he was getting himself too excited. He sat back, brandy glass in hand, and smiled to himself – let tomorrow bring what it would! It would be difficult to take his desires to their ultimate conclusion so soon – how would he dispose of the kid's body, if he killed him at the park? But if the spot was *that* private, would he *need* to…? And it seemed so long, since Ore…

Chapter Thirty-Six

The next morning, Russell telephoned Detective-Superintendent Wilson at home, and the head of C.I.D. drove in to the station to confer with the Inspector and his Sergeant in the D.I.'s office. Rimmer had already been busy; when Wilson entered he was just telling Russell that he'd confirmed Evans address, but that the mother had in fact died at the end of July, and that their suspect had taken a job at the new University Engineering Faculty:

'That's right next to Elwood Priors!'

'Yes – built on part of the School's land.'

'Bloody hell! He's got a supply of young boys on tap, then?'

'What's this all about, David?' Wilson enquired as he slumped into the chair facing Russell's desk. The Inspector brought Wilson up to date on the latest developments; when the D.I. had finished, Wilson considered for a moment:

'What do you want to do about him?'

'Ideally, I'd like to arrest the man on suspicion, sir. But I'm not at all sure we've got enough even to do that.'

'We haven't, have we? We can't tie him into the Dorman case – Bhudran in India has only a tenuous link to his missing kids – probably the best hope is that the Ahlsberg police will find some evidence which will pin their murder on him. In the mean time, we can hardly go harassing a member of the public on the grounds that he has a knack of being in the wrong place at the wrong time.'

'It's a bit more than that, surely, sir?' Rimmer put in.

'Hardly – look at it, Sergeant. Philip Dorman: All you've got is a sighting, which could as easily be any other boy of that age, near the scene, and Inspector Russell's impression that the Evans boy was overly concerned at being approached a second time for his story. And the fact that he doesn't have a solid alibi. No weapon, no motive. India: The man's been seen once or twice in company with youngsters, and kid's voices have been heard in his house; nothing to say that any of these children were among the ones missing off the streets, nothing to connect him with the bodies they've found. And Norway: Again, nothing to connect Evans with the boy's murder, at least so far. The only link throughout is the man's presence in each locality where kids have been attacked in what seems to be an identical manner. Without some kind of solid evidence to prove he killed at least one of these kids, you're nowhere. All right, I know it's stretching the bounds of coincidence to breaking point, but how can we lock him up on the strength of *that?*'

'What do you suggest, sir?' Russell asked. The Superintendent sighed:

'I don't know, David. Your fear is that he'll grab some kid here, I take it? The best we can do perhaps is to try to keep tabs on him for a few days, in the hope that Kagstad will be able to apply for extradition to Norway for the murder of their victim. It sounds as though he's taken a little time to settle in whenever he's moved before starting his killing spree; let's hope he does the same this time.'

'Yes, sir. But this time he's come home – maybe he won't need to settle in?'

'Just pray that he does, Inspector! We're very short of manpower – I'll see if Uniform can lend us a couple of constables over the weekend. Set up a daytime surveillance, keep track of him during his waking hours, and we'll hope that Kagstad comes through before we lose any kids. We'll discuss it again on Monday – all right, David?'

'All right, sir. Thank you.'

The C.I.D. Chief left them to it. Inspector and Sergeant were laying out the surveillance programme when he looked around the office door for a moment:

'I've spoken to Paulson – Uniform are going to call in two off-duty men and tell them to report to you, in plain clothes. All right?'

'That's fine, sir. Thanks.'

'Okay then. Good luck!'

* * *

An hour later, Russell was briefing the two men. One of them was Police Constable Andrew Dorman, the other Geoff Tate, an older man; Russell was less than happy at the younger man's presence, given their suspicions about Evans' responsibility for the murder of his older brother, but after reflection, he gave them their duties, only telling them to be aware of him approaching young boys. P.C. Dorman, in a summer shirt, jeans and trainers, was to go to Evans' house, and pick him up from there; the other officer would go home and rest, preparatory to taking over later in the day, for the evening cover. Rimmer was to begin the surveillence the following morning, with the two P.C.s taking later shifts again. When everyone was clear about what was to happen, the group dispersed.

Russell picked up the telephone, and got through to the Police Chief in Ahlsberg. He told Kagstad of the steps they were taking to keep a watch on Evans, and asked if there were any new developments at that end. The Norwegian informed him that their post-mortem had confirmed that the boy had died of single stab-wound in the back. There were other injuries, suggesting that he'd struggled whilst being held face-down on the ground. The most hopeful news was that the youngster's best friend had finally told the police that Ore had mentioned an Englishman he'd become friendly with, and that he'd even seen the man once. Kagstad was obtaining a current photograph of Evans, in the hope that the child would identify him; he promised to let Russell know straight away if he did, as that would at least give them grounds to pick Evans up for questioning. Russell put the phone down with a feeling of hope; perhaps they'd have the bastard behind bars in the next couple of days, after all! He thought for a moment, and then dialled another number.

The telephone rang in the lounge of 41, Keats Drive; Kate Dorman got up to answer it. The family had moved to another house, in one of the sidestreets of Alderley Park, soon after the funeral of their murdered son; the change of scene had helped to some extent, but her husband was still a depressed and colourless man, even after so long.

'Hello?'

'Mrs Dorman? It's D.I. Russell, Grancester Police.'

'Mr Russell, how are you? It's been a long time.'

'Yes - I'm sorry we've not been in contact for a while. I have some news for you: We have a new lead, which just might result in us finding out who killed your son twelve years ago.'

'Really? After all this time? Oh, that would be marvellous!'

Russell went on to tell her briefly of their line of enquiry, and his hope that Philip's murderer might at last stand trial, even if it was for another crime, and in another country.

* * *

In the study of Old Laundry Cottage, Bevington, Daniel Russell was again bent over his yacht. He was looking forward to Jacko coming home the next day – but at least, he'd had time this week to get the model repaired and nearly ready to sail. He ran his fingers over the newly-fitted planks in the hull – if he sanded the surface smooth, he could get a coat of varnish on before lunch. And then later, when he got back from meeting Steve Evans at the Park, it would be dry enough for him to rub it down and give it a second coat. So tomorrow, maybe he could take it with him when he went with his father, and sail his own yacht for the first time!

In his own way, Daniel was as proud of his father as the man was of his son. Still young enough to see police-work in the black-and-white perspective of good versus evil, the boy was pleased that his Dad was on the side of the righteous, and proud that he held a position of authority and respect. All right, some of the kids at his new school had been a bit sniffy when they learnt his father was a policeman, but even they'd gone quiet when Boris had let it slip, as if by accident, that Dad was a Detective-Inspector. Mr Rimmer had said to him, a few weeks before, that his father was probably the best detective in the county – the boy had treasured those words, and still remembered them, especially as the Sergeant had then made him promise not to tell his Dad. The high opinion of his father, and the sharing of a grown-up's secret had delighted the youngster. It would be great to show Dad the yacht when he'd finished it, but he'd have to make sure the job was done right, the final finish as good as he could make it!

He picked up a piece of sand-paper, and began to smooth down the edges of the glue that had squeezed out around the new planks. As he sanded, running his finger-tip over the surface from time to time to see how it was progressing, he thought of his planned rendezvous at the Park later. He liked going there, and meeting Steve gave it some point – it wouldn't be much fun on his own, without Jacko, but showing the man around, comparing the Park he knew with the abandoned quarry as Steve remembered it, would be interesting. And the guy seemed to be okay, easy to talk to, so it should be an enjoyable afternoon. Maybe he'd talk more about the foreign places he'd been to. Daniel had been to

France and Spain, and the Canary Islands, on holidays, but Steve had been to such exotic places: Brazil, India, Norway…

He ran his finger over the sleek shape of the model's hull. Yes, that was better! He reached for the tin of Yacht-Varnish, cracked it open, and began to stroke the clear liquid carefully onto the wood with a fine soft brush his father had left ready for him. It was marvellous how the dry, dust-whitened timber took on a warm golden glow with a covering of varnish. He frowned critically when he saw that the new planks were a slightly lighter shade than the original timber of the hull; but maybe they'd darken with the second coat, later.

He'd just finished when his mother's voice called from the kitchen, telling him to come in for lunch. Sealing up the tin of varnish, he dropped the brush into a pot of thinners and went through to wash his hands. In the kitchen, Sarah was already tucking into her lunch. Daniel took his seat, glancing up at the clock – yes, he'd be okay to eat and then get up to the Park in plenty of time.

* * *

As Daniel Russell sat down to his lunch, Steve Evans was just leaving 82, Newtown Road. He'd had a lazy morning – up about nine, coffee and toast for breakfast, then he'd done a little housework, trying to keep the place as tidy as his mother always had. Then he'd sat and listened to music for a while – Stravinsky's Rite of Spring. The forceful rhythms and climactic discords always put him in the mood for a new encounter; as he listened, he thought of young Daniel, of the eleven-year-old's lovely slender body which, hopefully, he'd soon be enjoying in the shade of the woods…

He went over their previous meetings in his mind – who could connect him with the boy? There was the incident of the bullies, of course. They'd seen him with Daniel, and so had Frankham –

although the headmaster hadn't appeared to recognise him. It had been eleven years, of course! But that had been one occasion – had anyone else seen them together, the last couple of days? Not that he knew of. And Daniel had said he wouldn't tell anyone they were going to meet at the quarry, because his father wouldn't like it! So if the boy went missing… The police would probably question him, as he'd been with the kid a few days before, but if they didn't know he'd struck up a friendship with him, and couldn't connect him with his disappearance, they couldn't accuse him of anything, could they? Even if they found his body, in the trees at the quarry. Evans smiled to himself – this was beginning to feel like Philip, all over again! Dodging the police investigation; and up at the old quarry, of all places!

Maybe this time, just to be safe, he'd have to lose the knife; in the lake, perhaps. It would be a shame – how many young lives had it ended? He felt he could probably remember every one, if he tried, but it would take a great effort to go through them all and count them up. How many times had he felt that surging thrill as he'd thrust its blade into a strong, tanned back, or a slim, brown chest?

The music finished. He switched off the CD player and went out to his car, planning to do a little shopping on his way to the quarry – or the Country Park, if that was what it was now. As he drove off, he didn't notice the nondescript grey Vauxhall Astra which fell in a little way behind. He'd bought a little Nissan on coming back to England; just an old banger, really, for his immediate needs. Perhaps, if the job went well at the college, he'd treat himself to something better. A second-hand Jaguar, maybe; he quite fancied one, and little boys usually liked flashy cars…

* * *

His lunch over, Daniel got up from the table:

'All right if I go out for a bit, Mum?'

'Where are you going, love?'

'Just up to the Park, on my bike.'

'On your own?'

'Yeah, well, Jacko won't be home 'til tomorrow. But I fancy getting out for a while, and it's a lovely afternoon, isn't it?'

'Okay, but you be careful, please? I know the Park's pretty safe, but if you go scrambling around on your own, and hurt yourself, they might not find you for ages – it's a big place, remember.'

'Yes, well…' Daniel always found it very difficult to be anything other than completely honest with his parents: 'I *am* meeting someone, actually.'

'Oh? Who? Anyone we know?'

'Well, no. His name's Steve Evans, I met him at school the other day.'

'Another new boy?'

'Well, no. He's a lecturer at the new Engineering College. But he's not all that old, not as old as you and Dad. He… saved me from some trouble with a couple of bullies, and we got talking. He's ever so interesting, he's been to India, and Brazil, working; and he's just come home from Norway, 'cause his Mum died. He comes from Grancester, but he hasn't been here much, not for years. He remembers the Park when it was the old quarry, but he hasn't seen it since; I said I'd show him 'round there.'

'Hmmm - all right, Danny, if you've promised. It sounds as if he's okay; but you be on your guard, right?' His mother hesitated, looking at her son and thinking how grown-up he looked in his new grey jeans and the fern-green shirt which picked up the colour of his eyes. She went on:

'You know why your father's so concerned about you not talking to strangers, don't you?'

'Not really – just 'cause it's the sensible thing to do, I suppose?'

'Not entirely, Danny. It's to do with the boy who was killed at the quarry, all those years ago.'

'He drowned, didn't he? In the lake?'

'No. Someone, they never found out who, met him up there, and attacked him, stabbed him with a knife. Your Dad was on the case, with old Inspector Foreman, and it made a deep impression on both of them. I know you'll think it's silly, but he's always been terrified of something like that happening to you.'

'Oh, Mum! Nothing's going to happen to *me!* And Steve's okay, perhaps I should invite him to come back for tea, later? Would you mind?'

'No, of course not. Why don't you do that, I'd like to meet him. Have you got your telephone with you?'

'Yes I have; I'll ask him about tea! See you later, Mum. Bye-bye, Sarah!' Waving to his little sister, the boy went out to get his bike, and pedalled away.

* * *

In his office, Daniel's father, ploughing his way through other, more routine matters, glanced at his watch – not too bad, with luck he'd be home by about three o'clock.

Chapter Thirty-Seven

Wheels sparkling in the sunshine, Daniel swung his bike into the entrance to the Country Park. He pedalled up the long dog-leg of the drive to the visitor centre – at the top, he jumped off and padlocked the bike into one of the racks at the end of the block housing the shop and restaurant.

To his right, at the back of the restaurant, was the car park; to his left, a gravelled area ran between the two buildings, down to the lakeside. The Visitor Centre and Ranger's office faced the Restaurant across the gravel. Looking around, he realised that he didn't know what kind of car Steve had, so he couldn't tell if the man had already arrived. He looked at his watch; a few minutes early. Oh well, he'd just hang around until he saw him. He began to stroll slowly across the gravel towards the lake.

* * *

Steve Evans turned his Nissan into the Park entrance. They'd changed this, for sure! The old, steep track up to the lake had gone – now, a tarmac-surfaced driveway turned to the right and eased the slope by following a longer, sweeping curve, coming back to the left in a dog-leg to arrive near the old open area by the waterside. At the top, he parked in the designated spaces behind the first building, looking around in mild amazement. Where he remembered a rough-surfaced wasteland, two long, low buildings now stood, timber-clad in a kind of clinker fashion, the rough-edged planks overlapping. The nearest appeared to be a small café, and a shop for souvenirs. He got out of the car, and locked it behind him.

Walking slowly, he made his way to the left until he faced down the gravelled space to the lake. The second building was obviously a kind of reception centre, with offices at the far end as well.

He could see no sign of Daniel – was the boy here yet? On the end of the second building, there was what looked like a map of the Park, and some notices, on a big display board; he'd take a look at that while he was waiting for the kid to show up, maybe try to get some idea of the way they'd laid the whole place out, perhaps even spot where Daniel's secret hideaway might be. He began to stroll in that direction, until he was interrupted by the sound of the boy's voice.

Daniel had glanced back, and caught sight of Evans as he headed for the map-board. He called out, and ran back to meet him:

'Hi, Steve!' Evans had stopped as the youngster approached:

'Hello, Daniel – good to see you again.' The boy's hazel eyes were sparkling with anticipation:

'Come on, let's go exploring!'

'Which way?'

'Follow me!'

The boy led him down the gravel towards the lake, and then around the far end of the restaurant building. From this point, paths fanned out into the Park, mostly with coloured waymarkers on little posts to give directions. Daniel turned right; his chosen path forked again after a few yards, and this time the boy went left, explaining to his companion that this way would take them into the wilder part of the scrub-land South of the water. As they walked, at first in silence, the image arose in Evans' mind from so many years before - scrambling over the scrub-covered rise and fall of this same ground, following Philip's lithe, agile lead, thrilling inwardly at the sight of his tanned, half-naked body…

* * *

Andrew Dorman parked the Astra in a bay opposite Evans' Nissan, and got out. In spite of the warm sunshine, he wore a light wind-cheater type jacket; his police radio was concealed in its inside pocket. Lifting it to his mouth, he called in to control:

'Delta 619: Subject is at Bevington Country Park, and out of his car. I'm following on foot. Over.'

'Roger, Delta 619. Out.'

The young constable, quite enjoying his first taste of plain-clothes work, hadn't dared keep too close to Evans' car as they approached the Park. He locked the Astra, and looked around for his target – damn! He'd lost sight of the man. He hurried towards the open area between the buildings, expecting to pick him up there – was that him, just disappearing around the far end of the restaurant? He ran down the gravelled space, attracting a few odd looks from people enjoying the Autumn sunshine. At the end, he was faced with the choice of paths that Daniel had so unerringly fathomed moments before – he hesitated, and then went straight on, walking as quickly as he dared whilst trying not to attract attention. The path straightened, so that he could see for some distance along it – no sign of the man: Oh God, what would the Inspector say if he lost him completely?

He retraced his steps, to try Daniel's right turn. This time, had he known it, he was on the right track, following the subsequent left turn away from the buildings – but he was too far behind, now, to pick up his quarry, as the boy hastened him along. Reluctantly, he returned to the open space by the car park, and took out his radio:

'Delta 619: I've lost Evans in the Park – I'll stay at the visitor centre and try to pick him up when he leaves.'

'Roger, 619. Inform us when you do.'

'Will do. 619 out.' He walked over to the restaurant and bought a can of Coca-Cola, and went to sit in the sun on a bench, feeling wretched, to wait for Evans to reappear.

* * *

In the depths of the Park, Daniel led his companion around the surfaced pathways. The two were almost equally enthusiastic, talking animatedly, comparing the abandoned quarry that Evans remembered with the Country Park that Daniel knew: The man, pointing out things and sights that he recalled from the time when Philip Dorman had shown him around his favourite playground; the boy, listening in amazement, pointing to the places he and his friend would go to play.

Following an almost random route, they found themselves retracing their steps for a while. There was a pause in the conversation – With a deliberate casualness, Evans began to talk about his time in Norway, and after a few sentences, mentioned equally casually how people there would often sunbathe nude. Daniel was astounded:

'You mean people, grown-ups even, go around with nothing on *at all?*'

'Oh yes – it's just regarded as normal, in most Scandinavian countries.' The boy looked up, wide-eyed; hesitantly, he asked:

'Did *you* try it?'

'Oh yes! In my garden. I had a little house, in one of the local villages, that I rented while I was there. I often used to go outside in the nude – I even used to cut the grass like it! You need to wear some old shoes, mind, or you end up with green feet!' They both laughed. Daniel asked, nervously:

'What… does it *feel* like, being outside, like that?'

'Oh, it's great! You feel so *free,* somehow. And it's really relaxing. You should try it.' The youngster gaped:

'You're not suggesting we take our clothes off *now,* are you?'

'Good God no! We'd get arrested! The law in this country doesn't allow as much freedom as it does in other places. We'd have to be somewhere private first.'

'Oh – right.' For the first time, Daniel felt a hint of doubt – was the man suggesting that they go somewhere on their own, and strip naked? Of course not, he was just making conversation! Before he could think of anything to say, Evans went on:

'But I'll tell you what – on a glorious day like this, I'm going to get as much sun as I can! Why don't you join me?' He quickly stripped off his shirt, and rolled it under his arm. The boy hesitated; but what harm could come from that? He followed suit – Evans reached out, taking his discarded shirt from him, saying he might as well carry both as one.

They strolled on in silence for a while. Evans sneaked the odd glance across at the boy – he'd been right, the kid had a truly superb young body! He just *had* to get him on his own, away from the crowds, deep in the woods… But at the same time, he felt annoyed with himself: Peeling off his shirt, he'd realised that he'd left the knife in his car – he'd have to make some excuse, go back for it, before they went off to find Daniel's secret hideaway. He'd daydreamed, speculated about this – now, once more in the boy's enticing presence, he knew he was going to succumb to the temptation. Risky, in such a public place – but the risk added a special edge to his thrill of anticipation:

'Daniel – I'm feeling a bit peckish – shall we go back to the restaurant, grab a sandwich or something?'

'I'm okay, thanks – I had lunch not long ago.'

'Oh, come on! I never heard of a boy who couldn't manage a packet of crisps and a Coke! I'm paying!' The boy smiled:

'Okay, then. Thanks.' The two walked slowly back to the Park's buildings. Evans idly chatted about the sights of Norway, trying to keep the boy's mind focussed there, ready for him to return to the idea of going nude later.

* * *

Andrew Dorman, still feeling thoroughly miserable at his failure to keep tabs on Evans, missed their return to the restaurant. By pure ill-fortune, he was looking the other way as the two slipped around the far end of the building, and in through the door. Daniel grabbed a free table inside – all the outdoor ones were occupied – while Evans went to the counter and bought himself a chicken sandwich, salt & vinegar crisps for Daniel, and two cans of Coke. Putting his purchases on the table, the man passed behind his young friend, slipping a hand on the boy's shoulder as he passed, experiencing a surge of desire at the feel of warm, bare skin – so soft, like fine silk! For his part, Daniel again felt a flutter of doubt – Steve's touch on his shoulder had been almost *too* gentle, too caressing, hinting at a familiarity the boy felt less than comfortable with. They ate slowly, in silence. His sandwich finished, Evans sat back, taking a swig of his drink:

'When you're ready, shall we go and explore the other side of the Park, in the woods? You were going to show me your secret hideout, weren't you?' Daniel looked up from his crisps, feeling a little less sure of himself; but after all, *he'd* suggested it, and he could hardly back out now, could he?

'Yeah, okay. But I need to go to the toilet first.'

'Right – I'll go and throw our shirts in my car, so we don't have to carry them 'round with us. See you in a minute?'

'Okay – the loos are behind the Visitor Centre – I'll meet you over there.' The boy got up and went out; Evans finished his can, and got to his feet.

Chapter Thirty-Eight

Daniel strolled across the gravel, and turned behind the opposite building, where two outside toilet blocks stood behind the Ranger's offices, in an enclosed area. The space behind the Visitor Centre and office was enclosed by the building on one side, and bounded by a thick hedge along the other, and across the far end, where the Gents toilet stood, faced from the near end by the Ladies. In the restaurant, prompted by his vague unease about his companion's attitude, he'd been tempted to slip his shirt on again; but Evans had slung it with his own over the back of his seat and leant back against it, so the boy felt uncomfortable at the idea of asking for it.

Daniel went into the Gent's and relieved his inner feelings; coming out again, zipping up his jeans, he saw two youths coming towards him, presumably also headed for the toilets. Then the telephone in his back jeans pocket began to ring...

* * *

Evans put the empty can on the table, and turned to leave the restaurant. In the car park, he threw their shirts into the back seat, and reached into the glovebox for the knife. He tucked it, in its sheath, into the back of his belt; then, nervous of the boy catching sight of it, picked up his light-weight linen jacket, and casually draped it over his shoulders. Locking the Nissan again, he remembered the map-board on the end of the other building - he strolled over, and stood in front of the map to study it.

As he looked at the map, two youths walked past behind him, and turned around the end of the building. Steve saw them from the corner of his eye, a lad of about sixteen, the other a year or two younger; he continued to study the map for a moment or two, and then turned to see what lay behind the offices. As he rounded the end of the building, past the Lady's toilet, he saw Daniel emerge from the Gent's. *I'll have that zip down again soon, young man!* The boy hadn't seen him yet; the two youths were walking towards the youngster, presumably heading for the loo. Then he saw Daniel pull the telephone from his pocket...

* * *

Looking around from his seat on the bench, Andrew Dorman spotted Evans as he emerged from the restaurant. He watched him go to the Nissan and reach inside, saw him stick something into the back of his belt, and then sling the beige jacket over his bare shoulders. As Evans strolled across to the map-board, he got up and wandered casually over to keep an eye on the man as he studied the display map of the Park, keeping a good distance between them so as not to be noticed, at the same time surreptitiously reporting in to the control-room. He saw the two youths pass behind the man, and then Evans turn and follow them. *Oh yes?* Andrew thought - he'd been warned to watch for any sign of Evans taking an interest in young boys, although these two were mid-teens, not what he'd think of as young kids.

From some thirty yards behind the man, he saw him round the end of the building, by the Lady's toilets. Taking a few more steps to the side, he could see beyond him into the open space between the two loo-blocks, where the two youths were making towards the Gent's. A younger boy emerged, doing up his trousers; then, he reached into his trouser pocket and took something out…

* * *

Russell looked at his watch as he pulled up outside the cottage – almost three o'clock. He got out, locking the Jeep where it stood on the roadside; Tracy would probably want to go shopping, later. Maybe, if she took Sarah with her, he and Daniel could put in some more work on the boy's yacht, try to get it ready for its maiden voyage the next morning – that would be good!

He let himself in, and went through to the kitchen. Bending over his daughter, he kissed her on the cheek as she reached up to him from her seat for a quick hug before returning to her pad and coloured pencils. Kissing his wife on her cheek, avoiding the soapsuds from the washing-up in the sink in front of her, he asked:

'Where's Daniel?' Tracy smiled at her husband:

'Oh, he's gone to the Park, on his bike.'

'All alone?'

'No, not quite, he was meeting someone there.'

'Oh, who's that?' His wife took her hands from the bowl, and leant on the edge of the sink, suds dripping from her fingers. She looked around:

'Well, I'm not entirely happy, to tell you the truth, love. He's arranged to meet a man there, a youngish fellow, I gather. Not as ancient as you and me, anyway, according to Danny! This fellow's a lecturer at the new Engineering college that backs onto The Priors, apparently. Danny met him on his first day; the guy saved him from harassment by a pair of bullies, and they got talking. He obviously likes him; the fellow's worked all over the world, by the sound of it, and he's been thrilling Danny with his stories. It seems he comes from around here, but has lost touch with the area – Danny promised to show him around the Park, because he only remembers it as the old derelict quarry.'

As he listened to his wife, a dreadful empty feeling began to grow in Russell's stomach. As she finished speaking, he asked tensely:

'What's this man's name, do you know?'

'Yes, love – Evans, Steve Evans.'

'Oh, Jesus Christ!' He spun around, ran into the hall, and grabbed the telephone from its rest. *Oh Dear God, please…* He dialled the direct number for the police control room.

'Control Room.'

'Russell – where's P.C. Dorman?'

'He just called in, sir. He's at Bevington Country Park, tailing your suspect.'

'Call him *now,* tell him…' He heard the control-room radio crackle to life in the background.

'Bear with me a moment, sir.' The operator responded to the call. Over the telephone line, Russell heard the voice on the radio:

'Delta 619: I've got two injured and a man on the run – I need back-up and an ambulance, fast!'

'Right away, 619.' The operator grabbed the telephone to speak to the Inspector, only to find he'd already rung off.

In Bevington, Russell shouted to his wife:

'I'm going to the Park – Has Daniel got his phone?'

'Yes, love, I just tried to call him, but he didn't answer – What's wrong?'

'Never mind now – just keep calling him, tell him to keep right away from Evans. I'll ring you from there.'

He scrambled into the Jeep, started the engine and spun it around in the village street. In the few minutes it took him to reach the Park, he kept praying: *Please God, not Daniel, not my boy…*

* * *

As he went to answer the phone, the two youths came up to Daniel. The younger one made a grab for the handset; despite his surprise, Daniel held on:

'Let go! What do you think you're doing?'

'Give me the phone, kid!'

'No! Why should I?'

'Because!' The older youth drew a knife from inside his shirt, and showed it to the boy before tucking it once more out of sight. Shocked at being threatened, Daniel let go; the two turned and ran.

Evans saw the altercation, without realising for a moment what was happening. Then the two youths were running towards him – they'd have to pass him to escape from the enclosed area between the two toilets. Seeing the phone in one boy's hand, guessing what had happened and thinking to further increase his kudos with Daniel, he moved to block their retreat.

After a moment's inaction, Daniel's fury at the sheer injustice of what had happened overcame his innate common-sense. He spotted Evans, moving to stop the pair, and set off at a run, after the youth who still held his phone; a fit kid, his long legs quickly had him on the thief's heels. He launched himself into what would have been very creditable tackle for a skilled rugby player, and took the teenager behind the knees. The youth, taken by surprise, fell to his left as his assailant wrapped his arms around his legs – he crashed full-tilt into the wall of the Lady's toilet, and flipped over onto his back, the phone flying from his hand into the air; he landed with a groan, to lay still on his side. Daniel picked himself up, and looked down at the thief on the ground – *Oh, God, have I killed him?*

Andrew Dorman saw the two youths speak to the boy, and then turn and run. He guessed they were up to no good – as Evans moved to block their escape, he ran forward to help. He saw Daniel tackle the younger robber from behind, just as the older one ran into Evans, barging him aside. The youth ran off; Evans went down, winded by the collision. Andrew went first to the boy, now standing, rather shaken, over his captive. The youth appeared to be out cold – he quickly hand-cuffed him to the toilet's drainpipe before turning to the man on the ground.

Daniel looked up as Dorman reached him, and was amazed to see him produce the hand-cuffs from a back pocket: *A policeman? Thank goodness!* He turned to Evans, who was kneeling on the ground, holding his stomach. Bending over him, he put his hand on Steve's shoulder:

'Steve? Are you okay?' The man didn't reply. The policeman came over to him, bent down and took him by the other shoulder:

'Sir? Are you hurt?' Evans raised his head, as if with great difficulty, but still said nothing.

'Oh, my God!' Looking down, the Constable saw that the hands clasped to the man's stomach and the top of his trousers were soaked with blood. He grabbed his radio, and made the call which coincided with Russell's telephone call to the control-room; then he slipped the man's jacket from his shoulders, rolling it and handing it to him with the instruction to use it to stem the bleeding.

Daniel had seen the blood, too. He knelt beside his new friend, tears of horror and shock streaming down his face, unable to speak. Through the roaring in his head, he heard the policeman speaking to him, asking if he was all right, and nodded jerkily. Evans felt the boy's arm slip around his shoulders, and raised his head; he smiled thinly, and whispered:

'I'm sorry, Daniel – so sorry.'

'Take it easy, Steve – you'll be all right, I know you will!' The man just shook his head as he slumped forward again.

* * *

Russell beat the emergency services to the scene by several minutes. Andrew Dorman saw him pull up, and signalled to him; he saw his son kneeling beside a man, slumped forward as if in pain, and ran over. Daniel looked up:

'Daddy!' He leapt to his feet, and threw his arms around his father's neck.

Russell held his son tightly to him – *Daddy? He hasn't called me that in years!*

'Danny? Are you all right?' The boy nodded:

'Yes, I'm okay. But it's Steve – he's hurt bad, I think. Help him, please?'

Russell looked at the young Constable:

'Ambulance is on its way, sir, and some back-up. I think one of the bastards knifed him as he ran off.' Russell nodded:

'Thank you, Dorman.' He took his son by the shoulders, and held him away to look into the boy's eyes:

'What happened, Daniel?' The youngster drew a deep breath:

'Two of them, Dad, they saw me go to answer my phone when it rang. One grabbed it, then the other showed me a knife. They ran off, but I got one of them. The other must have stabbed Steve. Will he be all right, Dad?'

'I hope so, Danny. The paramedics will be here any moment, they'll take care of him.' Daniel nodded; then he wriggled out of his father's arms, and went to kneel beside Evans again. The man still knelt, hunched over; he reached out one blood-soaked hand, and Russell felt a swell of pride in his son as the boy took it, unflinching, in both of his.

A minute or so later, the tableau broke up as first the paramedic ambulance and then a patrol car with two constables inside reached the scene. The ambulance-men quickly examined Evans, and then rushed him onto a stretcher and into their vehicle. They drove off, lights flashing, siren wailing. The two constables uncuffed the young thief, who was beginning to stir, groaning; he was obviously in some pain, so they took him also to the General Hospital for examination, with Russell's exhortation to keep a very close guard on him. More officers had begun to arrive, cordoning off the area with the help of the Park's duty Ranger.

When ambulance and police-car had both departed, Russell told Andrew Dorman to go back to the station and write his report as soon as a senior detective arrived to take over. Then, his arm around his son's shoulders, he guided the boy to the Jeep, and sat him in the passenger seat. Daniel's trousers and chest were stained with Evans' blood, as were his hands from where he'd held the injured man's. The D.I. rang home on his own mobile, to tell his wife their boy was safe, and warn her of his dishevelled state before they turned up on the doorstep – he didn't need Tracy going into a panic when she saw their son covered in blood! Before he drove away, he looked at the boy sitting beside him:

'Hey?' Tear-stained hazel eyes turned to meet his:

'Yes, Dad?' Daniel sounded choked, his voice husky with emotion.

'I know what's happened today has been really awful for you – but I want you to know that I'm very proud of the way you coped with it. And for stopping that kid from getting away, even if you did take a terrible risk doing it. I expect he'll tell us who his mate was, so we'll get the one who hurt Steve.'

'Thanks, Dad.' The boy managed a rather wan smile:

'Dad?'

'Yes?'

'I love you.' Russell could feel the tears behind his own eyes:

'I love you too, Dan.'

Chapter Thirty-Nine

Back in Bevington, Russell guided his still-shocked son into the cottage with a hand on his shoulder. Inside, little Sarah looked goggle-eyed at the state of her big brother – she began to ask questions, but was quickly shushed by her mother. Tracy took one look at her son, and took him from her husband, chivvying the boy up the stairs to his room; he began to tell her what had happened, but she shushed him too:

'Tell me later, Danny. Right now, you're going to have a good hot bath – and soak as long as you want. You can tell me all about it when you come down again.'

In his room, the boy allowed her to help him out of his clothes, something he hadn't permitted for a number of years. He sat on the edge of his bed, head in his hands, while she went to run his bath; then she returned, and chased him into the bathroom, reminding him to take as long as he liked.

Tracy Russell went downstairs again, where her husband also began to try to explain what had happened. She held up her hands:

'Davey, you and Danny can tell me all about it in a while, when he's clean and dry. Right now, I should imagine you've got things you need to do?' Russell smiled ruefully, and nodded:

'You're right, love. Later.' He went into the hall and picked up the telephone.

First, he called Rimmer at home, only to discover that the Sergeant had already been alerted by the control-room. He called him on his mobile, found that he was on his way to the Park, and asked the Sergeant to make sure the uniformed officers and a scenes of crime team had things in hand, and then go to the hospital and find out what had happened to Evans, and the youth Daniel had incapacitated. Then he called Superintendent Wilson, and told him what had taken place. He arranged to go and see his chief later in the evening, to discuss the situation.

Back in the kitchen, he sank gratefully into a chair as Tracy put a cup of tea in front of him. She put a hand on his shoulder, and asked quietly:

'So what made you freak out when I told you that man's name, David?' He looked up at her:

'Evans is the man we suspect killed Philip Dorman, twelve years ago. I can't prove it, but I'm as certain as I can be it was him. Danny was right, he's been working in foreign countries for years; it seems as if he's left a trail of dead kids wherever he's been, but no-one's caught him so far. So when you said Danny was going to meet him... I should have *told* you...'

'Hush, love. You'd no way of knowing that Danny had even met him, did you? How could you have guessed?'

'I know – but when I think how close he came to being the bastard's next victim...'

'Shhhh! He's safe upstairs in the bath. When he comes down, the two of you can tell me everything. Sarah – how would you like to go and play with Becky, next door, for a while?' The little girl, still bewildered by the strange events going on around her, looked up eagerly:

'Yes, please, Mummy!'

'Come on, then.' Tracy took her daughter by the hand, and they went to knock at the cottage next door.

After more than an hour in the bath, Daniel eventually came downstairs. Wearing only a green towel around his middle, he went and sat down in one of the deep floral-pattern armchairs in the living-room. His mother and father joined him; Russell drew the other armchair across to be close to his son, while Tracy sat curled up in the sofa. He began to talk to them, hesitantly at first, but then gaining courage – he told them the whole story, from Evans saving him from the school bullies, and the roasting that Frankham had given them, to cycling to the Park to meet the man that afternoon. He went on to describe what had happened there, dissolving into tears when he got to the point when he'd realised that Evans was badly hurt.

Russell took up the tale, for his wife's benefit, but without mentioning the suspicions about Evans' past, or the reasons for his sudden arrival on the scene. He was talking to Daniel, trying to relax the boy, when the phone rang; Tracy got up to answer it. Daniel was talking, quietly, about Evans; over his voice, Russell heard his wife's:

'Yes, Doug?'

'He's talking to Danny right now, I'd rather not disturb him – can he call you back?'

'Okay, I'll tell him. Thanks, Doug.' She put the phone down. Returning to the living-room, she told her husband:

'Can you call Doug on his mobile, when you're ready? He's got some news for you.' Russell nodded, still listening to his son.

Eventually, they left Daniel sitting quietly, watching the television. The boy was much relaxed, having talked out a lot of his trauma, but still very subdued. In the hall, with the door to the living-room closed, Russell called the Sergeant:

'What is it, Doug?'

'Evans died in the operating theatre, sir. They did all they could, but according to the surgeon he'd lost too much blood, and they couldn't get it into him quickly enough. He died about four o'clock.'

'Damnation! I wanted to talk to that bastard.' Rimmer's voice echoed his superior's grim tone as he replied:

'Well, at least he's saved us a lot of hard work, boss. And it seems kind of fitting for him to die like that, doesn't it?'

'I suppose you're right, Doug. It's rough justice, perhaps, for him to die on a knife when he'd taken so many lives the same way - but I'd have liked to see him faced in court with all the pain he's caused.' *And maybe it's unChristian, but I'm glad he didn't die easy!* Russell refrained from voicing his feelings.

'That's not all, boss – he had a knife on him. In a sheath tucked into the back of his trousers, under his coat. They found it when they stripped him for the theatre.'

'Did he now?' *Oh, Daniel, how close did you come?* 'That tells us a lot, doesn't it?'

'I guess so.'

'What about the kid Daniel stopped?'

'He's got a broken collar-bone, and suspected severe concussion. We can talk to him tomorrow, they say. I've got a uniformed P.C. on guard here.'

'Okay, thanks. I'm not going to tell Daniel about Evans until tomorrow, now – his mother's planning to give him half a sleeping pill tonight, make sure he has a good night's rest. I may see you later; I'm going to see Wilson in a while.'

'Okay boss. Say Hi to Daniel for me, will you? Tell him - I'm glad he's okay.'

'I will. Bye, Doug.'

* * *

The next day, after breakfast, Russell took his son into the study and sat him down. He closed the door, sat down himself, and broke the news of Evans' death. The boy took the news quite well – Russell suspected he'd been more than half prepared for it. He'd debated long and hard overnight about how much to tell the boy, and finally decided that he deserved the truth:

'Daniel – you're not a little boy any more, you're a sensible and intelligent young man. I want to tell you something, about Mr Evans; it's going to upset you, and maybe frighten you, but I want you to listen and try to understand.' He went on to explain in detail what the police knew, and what they suspected. The boy took it in, asking an occasional question.

When Russell had finished, Daniel sat in thought for a while. He didn't want to believe these awful things about the man he'd thought of as his friend; and yet... The way Steve has talked about going naked, as if he'd really intended for them to do it – and the way he'd touched his shoulder, in the restaurant, so caressingly... Maybe it *was* true – and if his Dad said so, it *must* be:

'I'd no idea, Dad – he seemed so nice, friendly, and helpful. I can't believe that someone like him could turn out to be... so evil!' Russell saw the shocked appeal in his son's eyes:

'One of the things you learn in my job is that people are rarely all bad or all good. Remember that he saved you from those bullies, at school; and he tried to help you, when those yobs pinched your phone, didn't he?' The boy nodded; then he said:

'Dad – after he'd been... you know... the only thing he said to me was, he was sorry – what do you think he meant?

'I'm not sure I know, Daniel; perhaps he was sorry you'd been upset by seeing what had happened?' The boy sat in thought, his head bowed. Then he looked up at his father, and asked:

'Do you think he might have been saying sorry for... all those other boys?'

'Almost like a confession, you mean? Maybe; he could have realised he was dying, and ...' Russell looked long and hard at his son: 'You'll be all right, Dan? I know it's all been a horrible experience for you. Do you want to have a day or two off school? I'm sure they won't mind.'

'No, Dad, I'm all right. Besides, Jacko's coming home today, I'll have to show him round on Monday.'

'Okay, if you're sure. I've got to go and see Mr and Mrs Dorman now, the parents of the boy who died at the quarry years

261

ago. I'll see you later – sorry we can't go sailing today!'

'That's all right, Dad, I'm hardly in the mood, anyway. I'll see you later.'

* * *

Russell rang the doorbell at number 41, Keats Drive, Alderley Park. Kate Dorman opened the door to him, and ushered him into the living-room. Andrew Dorman leapt up from an easy chair, but the D.I. waved him back to his seat:

'Relax, Andrew! You're not on duty now. I want to talk to your parents, and to you as Philip's brother, not as a policeman.' He took the seat proffered, and looked around at the family for a moment.

John Dorman, sitting on the settee next to his wife, still had a kind of faded look; his once-sandy hair was now a muddy grey, and, although the doctors assured him there was nothing physically wrong, he had the drawn, wasted appearance of a man in the early stages of a terminal cancer. His wife seemed much the same as she had twelve years before, although her black hair was now a distinguished steel-grey, making her blue eyes seem even more piercing. She was as smartly dressed as always, in a trim black skirt and pale blue blouse. And the quiet, self-sufficient young Constable, relaxing in a t-shirt and jeans, looking slightly uncomfortable in his superior officer's presence. Russell turned to the older couple:

'First, I should tell you how well Andrew acquitted himself yesterday. He was only seconded to me for plain-clothes duty because there were no longer-serving officers available. Nevertheless, when he found himself faced with a frightful situation, which he could not have anticipated, he reacted quickly and decisively, and did everything I would have expected from a much more experienced man. You have every reason to be very proud of him.' Andrew looked up in surprise:

'But I *lost* him, sir!'

'If I had a pound for every time *I* lost someone I was tailing, I'd be a rich man, Andrew! And you picked him up again, before any harm was done – your actions then were exemplary.'

'I just did what I thought was right, sir.' He spoke diffidently; Russell nodded, smiling:

'You did exactly right, Andrew. And as I'm sure you must have realised, the boy you ran to help was my son, Daniel. My wife and I owe you our heartfelt thanks for that – if you hadn't intervened, the other yob could well have turned his knife on our boy, too. It was a shame he got away, but you did the right thing by looking after the victim first. I shall make sure the Chief Superintendent knows what you did – and if I need uniform's help again, I intend to ask for your services.'

'Thank you, sir!' The young man was clearly pleased, as well as embarrassed. Russell addressed his parents again:

'Now, you'll remember I called to say we had a lead on Philip's killer? I've got quite a long story to tell you...'

When he had finished, they asked a few questions; throughout, Andrew had been looking increasingly annoyed and perplexed:

'Sir?'

'Yes, Andrew?'

'You sent me to tail this man, *knowing* that he murdered my brother?' Russell nodded slowly:

'I did. Please remember, I didn't ask for your services; you and Geoff were the only two men Chief Inspector Armstrong could spare me. I thought about telling you everything, but I decided against it. Answer me this, Andrew - if you'd known, would you have acted any differently?' The young man thought for a moment, then gave his superior a slightly embarrassed smile:

'No, sir, I don't believe I would. At least, I hope not.'

'And I'm certain you wouldn't, I trust your professionalism that far. I hope you can gain some comfort from the fact that you had a hand in bringing him to justice, even if it may not be the kind of justice we usually look for.'

'Yes, sir. And - off the record?' Russell nodded, guessing what he wanted to say: 'I'm glad he's dead. He didn't deserve to go on living, especially at the tax-payer's expense; but please don't tell the Chief Inspector I said that!' Russell laughed:

'I won't! And I won't disagree with you, either.'

Chapter Forty

Saturday afternoon, a week after the dramatic events at the Country Park, David Russell and his son again sat together in the study. Once again, the old cloth was covering the desk, and the two were working on model yachts – Russell's new project was taking shape, and his son was giving his boat a last coat of fresh varnish. Later, he'd fit the newly-charged batteries and try the radio controls, ready for its maiden voyage the next morning. And Dad had offered to take Jacko with them, too!

In police circles, the week had seen a lot of loose ends gathered together. Evans' knife had been despatched by secure courier to Norway, and the local forensic experts had established it as the weapon that had killed Ore Pedersen. With the youngster's best friend identifying a picture of Evans as the man he'd seen in Ore's company, and the indisputable confirmation of DNA evidence, the case against the man became conclusive. With that positive proof of his guilt in one case, Russell was convinced that his surmised connection with the deaths in India, and the murder of Philip Dorman, could be taken as correct. He'd contacted Bhudran in Andrabad, and Wilson had formulated and released a statement to the press.

The youth Daniel had so effectively brought down turned out to be a fourteen-year-old from the Warren, who was, in the current euphemism, 'known to the police'. At first, he'd been truculent and refused to answer any questions about his companion; but then Rimmer had told him he could face life imprisonment as an accessory to murder. The boy had broken down, and admitted that the knife-man had been his older brother; the police had quickly picked the older youth up, and both were now held in custody. As Rimmer told his superior later: 'I didn't know if we could have made the charge stick – but *he* wasn't to know that either, was he?' At first, the ground search at the Park had failed to turn up Daniel's telephone, a vital link in the evidence against the two; but then it had come to light, lying in the roof gutter of the Lady's toilet block where it had come to rest.

Daniel himself had quickly come to terms with what had happened; his friend's return from holiday, and the excitement of showing Jacko around Elwood Priors had done much to distract him from his shock and sadness. But Russell had been secretly pleased that his son seemed to want to be with him more than of late, sitting with him on the sofa of an evening, or coming into the study when he was reading or tinkering with a model's radio controls. So now they sat together, father and son, bending over their individual projects, the steady drizzle outside gradually giving way to a grey brightness as the clouds began to thin.

Tracy Russell had taken the Jeep, and her daughter, into town for the week's shopping. The doorbell rang:

'I'll go, Dad!' Daniel leapt up. He returned a moment later, his eyes wide:

'There's a lady to see, you, Dad – she wouldn't tell me her name.'

'Oh? Right, I'm coming.' The boy grinned:

'She's *ever* so pretty – what's it worth if I don't tell Mum?'

'Get out of here!' Daniel ducked as his father swung a playful fist at his head, and followed him into the hall. He stopped in amazement, gazing at the tall blond woman in her early thirties who confronted him:

'Caroline? Caroline Dorman?'

'Hello, David. It's Caroline Jefferson, now – but yes, it's me.

It's wonderful to see you again.' Russell stepped forward, hand outstretched, but the slender beauty pulled him into an embrace, kissing him on the cheek. Beside his father, Daniel stared goggle-eyed; as the two separated, he laughed:

'*Now* what's it worth if I don't tell Mum?' Russell laughed, slipped his arm around the boy's shoulders, and addressed his visitor:

'You've met Daniel, of course. Daniel, this is Caroline – the boy who was killed at the quarry was her little brother.'

'Oh! I'm ever so sorry.' The boy put out his hand, Caroline took it, and smiled at him:

'Thank you, Daniel. It was a long time ago now, but I still miss him, sometimes. I knew your father then. I remember him telling me you'd been born; you must be what, nearly twelve, now?'

'That's right – next month.' The boy's expression said that he was more than somewhat in awe of his father's beautiful visitor. Caroline turned to Russell again:

'Mummy has told me everything, about Philip and all the other boys. I'm just so glad that your Daniel is all right – it must have been a terrifying experience for him.' The boy smiled sheepishly as she went on: 'You wouldn't believe the change in my father, David. It's as if he's alive again – just knowing what actually happened to Philip seems to have given him the will to pick himself up again, after all this time. You know he sold out his partnership in the business, I suppose, not long after the funeral? He seems to have been living in limbo ever since, but now he's even talking about starting a new practice. At his age!' Russell smiled:

'I'm glad. But what about you, Caroline? You used to be all over the papers and the TV, but then you vanished.' She laughed:

'Yes, I know! I enjoyed the modelling, and it made me quite rich, I suppose, but I always felt that I was a kind of intruder, somehow. I made them let me finish my degree, you know – I can't get over how arrogant I was with them! But they let me; and then, when I met Jeff, I decided I'd had enough. He's a photographer; we're married, and living in a town called Northridge, in California. I've got my PhD, now; I work for a big chemical company just outside town.'

'Is he with you?' Russell asked.

'He's waiting in the car, outside.'

'Well, bring him in, for Heaven's sake! Tracy is out shopping, with Sarah, our daughter – you must wait and meet them. Daniel, go out and fetch the man who's in the car.'

'Okay, Dad.'

Two minutes later, the boy was back, with a tall, well-built man in a smart suit, with warm brown eyes and dark hair, which he wore quite long. He was carrying a little boy of about three years old, lying sleepily against his shoulder. If the eleven-year-old's eyes had been wide at the sight of Caroline, now they were fit to fall right out of his head:

'Dad! You should see their car! It's incredible – come here!' Jefferson grinned and stood aside to let Russell past. Daniel took his father's hand, and pointed down the path to where a spectacular vision of fifties flamboyance met his gaze. The car that stood outside their cottage was long and sleek, with extravagant tail-fins, ivory paint gleaming in the sun that was at last breaking through the clouds to make the chrome-work glisten, and bring a glitter to the sweeping golden spear along its side. Russell stepped back inside:

'What on earth is that car? I've never seen anything like it!' Jefferson grinned; Caroline laughed, and replied:

'Jeff loves his classic cars, I'm afraid! We keep that one in England so that we've got something nice to use when we come to visit my parents.' Her husband's soft New England accent took up the tale:

'It's a 'fifty-seven Plymouth Fury, one with the Hemi engine. They're quite rare, now, even in the States. As Carrie says, I love old cars – we've got a few more, back home.' Caroline interposed:

'Don't let him get started! He'll talk cars all day, if you let him! David, this is Brian Jefferson, my husband. Jeff, meet David Russell, the Detective-Sergeant who was on my brother's case years ago. Don't upset him, love – Mummy says he's an Inspector, now!'

'David! It's a pleasure to meet you – Carrie's told me so much about you. Call me Jeff, everyone does.' As Russell took the proffered hand, he said:

'It's good to meet you, Jeff.' He paused: 'Brian Jefferson? The fashion photographer?' He was surprised to see the man smile rather self-consciously:

'Yeah, I guess so. You've heard of me?'

'Of course! Who hasn't?' Jefferson grinned:

'It's usually the people I take pictures *of* who get recognised! That's the advantage of being behind the camera.' He looked down at Daniel: 'Your boy seems quite taken with my car; and I guess you and Carrie have a lot to talk about. How would it be if I took Daniel for a little drive; we'll be back in time to meet your wife, a little later?'

'Can I Dad? Please?' Russell laughed:

'Okay, go on then! But don't be a nuisance to Mr Jefferson, all right?'

'I won't Dad!' Jefferson handed the dozing child to his wife, and followed Daniel down the path to the gate:

'We won't be too long, I promise!' He called back over his shoulder.

When the two had left, Daniel eagerly asking more questions about the car, Caroline turned to Russell again:

'Look at me, David – I owe pretty well everything I've got to Philip, and to you. You were quite right – do you remember, in the church-yard after the funeral? I wasn't sure about this modelling business, and you told me I should think of it as Philip's legacy to me. That's just how I feel about it, now – sometimes I can almost feel him, up in Heaven, poking fun at me for trying to be famous! And without it, and without you persuading me to accept it like that, I wouldn't have a wonderful husband and family, and such a marvellous life. Jeff is terrific; I do love him so much, even if I sometimes have to go round the workshop to see which car has a pair of feet sticking out from under it! And now, with Daddy at last looking like he's going to get over Philip's death, I couldn't be happier!' Impulsively, she leant forward and kissed his cheek again: 'I had a terrible crush on you then, you know.'

'You did?' She grinned sheepishly:

'Oh, yes! I couldn't help it, even if I knew it was silly, especially when you told me about your wife, and the baby you were expecting. He's a lovely boy, David – you must be so proud of him?'

'I am! Tracy and I are very lucky, too, we've got two wonderful children – you'll meet little Sarah in a while; and Daniel is the best son I could wish for.'

'Mummy told me what happened last weekend – he seems to have got over it well?'

'He does, doesn't he? We forget just how resilient children can be, sometimes.'

'I'm pleased; and so happy that nothing happened to him, David.'

'And how about this little chap?' Smiling, Russell gestured at the child dozing on her shoulder: 'You haven't introduced us, yet.' She grinned:

'I haven't, have I?' Gently waking the little boy, she said:

'Pip – this is Uncle David. He's a very special friend of Mummy's.' The child looked at Russell; big, soft grey eyes under a thatch of blond hair. Russell found to his surprise that, somehow, his voice had stopped working, when Caroline said to him:

'David Russell – meet my son, Philip David Jefferson.'

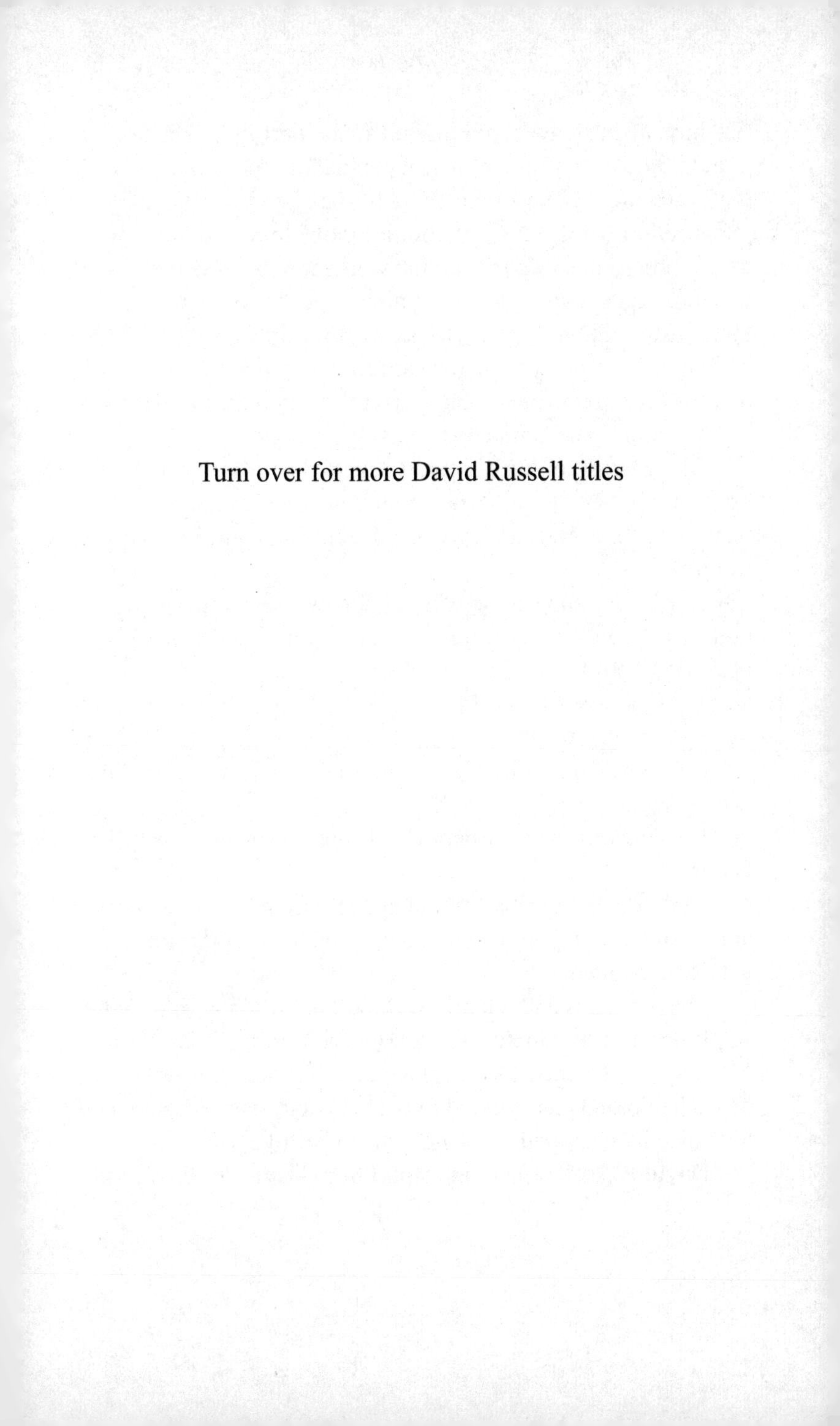

Turn over for more David Russell titles

(details on following pages)

If you have enjoyed *Cycle*, you will want to read the other David Russell novels, *Flashback, Strangers*, and *Winter's Tale*.

These titles may be ordered from any good bookshop.

Just ask for

Flashback by Geoffrey Lewis	ISBN 0-9545624-0-2
Strangers by Geoffrey Lewis	ISBN 0-9545624-1-0
Winter's Tale by Geoffrey Lewis	ISBN 0-9545624-2-9

published by SGM Publishing.

For a full up-to-date list of David Russell novels, please write to:

SGM Publishing
Cosgrove Wharf, Lock Lane, Cosgrove, Northants MK19 7JR

Tel: 07792 497116
info@sgmpublishing.co.uk

(see over)

The first David Russell novel
Published 2003

A ten-year-old girl is missing, on her way to visit a friend after school. Absconded or Abducted? D.I. David Russell is drafted in to begin the background investigation.

As it becomes clear the child has been taken, the events of that Friday evening are slowly unravelled, despite a lack of firm evidence. Red herrings are laid to rest; at last, suspicion begins to focus upon one man; and then another little girl disappears. Everyone thinks she has run away - but has she?

(see over)

The second David Russell novel
Published 2004

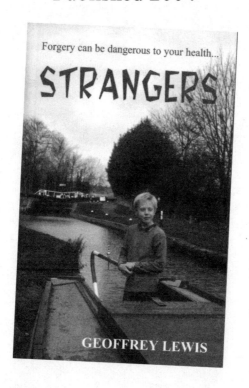

The Metropolitan Police have smashed a major counterfeiting gang - but the ringleaders have escaped. And Ron Walker has a problem: How do you protect your family when it is being threatened by a cold, soulless killer?

As the forgers try to re-establish themselves in the provinces, David Russell's investigation becomes a race against time, both to convict the men and to save Walker's grandson from the fate which is stalking him on the idyllic highway of the Grand Union Canal.

(see over)

The third David Russell novel
Published 2004

Murder, drugs, prostitution - and the love of a child...

WINTER'S TALE

GEOFFREY LEWIS

A young man is dead, shot down outside a nightclub. All the evidence points to his girlfriend - his murder the result of a lover's quarrel.

But D.I. David Russell is uncomfortable with this conclusion. As he delves into the man's background, and the circumstances surrounding his death, he is led into a shady world of drugs and prostitution, until the ripples of a seemingly-simple crime overlap with those of a covert international operation. But the answer, when it comes, is surprisingly close to home...

(see over)

OVER HERE

Annual trips to the Earls Court Motor Show in the late 1950s are perhaps what led car-mad schoolboy Steve Miles to fall in love with the sheer style of the products of the American motor industry.

As a teenager in the sixties, he would spend as much free time as he could wandering the streets of his home town of Oxford, on the lookout for such machines to photograph, and even take regular trips by train or coach to London. The end result was, by 1970, a collection of around ten thousand pictures, all of American cars, taken on the highways of England.

For many years, this incredible collection has lain untouched and unseen. But now, he has decided to unearth all those rare negatives, and to put together a selection of his pictures to be made available to the public; this book is the result. It is his intention to delve further into his enormous stack of negative files, and to produce additional volumes in the future, so that other enthusiasts can share in and enjoy these historic images.

For this first volume, Steve has selected pictures from the first batch of negatives of sufficient interest or rarity to justify inclusion, and put together a list of almost three hundred for this first book which have then been arranged in a suitable order.

The result is a collection of pictures taken on the streets of London between 1964 and 1970. The images are divided into different manufacturers and then arranged by year of manufacture: each is captioned, containing not only detail of the car and some background information, but often a note of where the picture was taken, and the occasional personal observation, which results in a relaxed, chatty style of presentation.

Some of the cars depicted are rare classics, others are quite mundane low-price models - but all were, at the time, in daily use. All, now, would be considered collectible. There are many gaps in this selection - but future volumes from his collection will go far towards infilling those gaps.

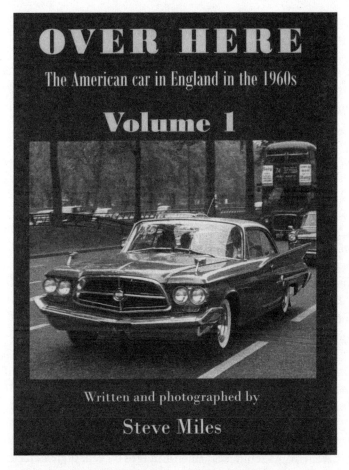

OVER HERE

The American car in England in the 1960s

Volume 1

Written and photographed by

Steve Miles

Published by SGM at the end of 2004, this exciting new title
may be ordered from any good bookshop.

Just ask for
Over Here by Steve Miles   ISBN 0-9545624-4-5
published by SGM Publishing.

Tel: 07792 497116
info@sgmpublishing.co.uk

(see over)

STARLIGHT

A new novel by Geoffrey Lewis

We didn't talk much, until Jake turned to me and said: 'I never said thank you, Harry.'

I glanced around, puzzled: 'What for?'

He smiled: 'For trying to stand up for me, yesterday!'

I shrugged: 'Oh - hey, no big deal, okay?'

He stopped walking, held out his hand: 'Okay. Friends, right?'

I though we'd already established that, but I took his hand: 'Right.'

We strolled on, until the bell recalled us to our lessons again.

* * *

Departing from the detective novels for which he is known, in *Starlight* Geoffrey Lewis tells a tale of schoolboy friendship set against the backdrop of the Oxford Canal in the days when the commercial trade was in decline; the canal itself threatened with closure. In a story where the mood ranges from heartwarming humour to unbearable poignancy, he conjures up the world of the 1950s; factual events and real characters flit past in the background as he leads the reader through the long heat-wave of the summer of 1955, as it was seen by an eleven-year-old boy living in a little North Oxfordshire village.

Views expressed by our proof-readers have been enthusiastic:

> *'The best thing he has written to date.'*
> *'I'm sending a bill for the box of tissues.'*

Starlight will be published later in 2005 - for more information, please check our website at www.sgmpublishing.co.uk or call 07792 497116. ISBN is 0-9545624-5-3. Cover price £6.99.